LOBO CANYON

H.K. Jensen

PublishAmerica
Baltimore

Hardcover 978-1-4560-3755-0
Softcover 978-1-4560-3756-7
PUBLISHED BY PUBLISHAMERICA, LLLP
www.publishamerica.com
Baltimore

Printed in the United States of America

✶ ✶ ✶ ✶ INTRODUCTION ✶ ✶ ✶ ✶

The unknown of the northern territories known as Canada was beckoning on the horizon, a strange new land mostly unexplored by white man, yet alive with mystery and intrigue.

Smokey Harrison was eager to face the unknown, and together with a new found friend, Kelly Tucker, they rode north of the border into a wilderness environment and unknown dangers with heads held high.

They rode as partners, sharing the good times and the bad, seeking their destiny, perhaps making their fortunes while doing so.

Though not for the lack of trying, they never found the illusive pot at the end of the rainbow, but a treasure far more valuable than gold. A wife and children of their own, even grandchildren too.

A wilderness posterity they could be proud of!

'... I killed this man, didn't I Smokey?
No Sage, it was me that killed him, you
just made sure that he was dead...'

* * * CHAPTER 1 * * *

From out of the gloom of an early morning haze rode a lone rider, highly pleased over the manner in which his young green-broke horse was settling in to life on the trail. Here, in the sand hills of a territory not yet organized into a State, several inches of hard-crusted snow covered the ground, making dangerous footing for Bandit's first time at this sort of thing.

Ten days had passed since Smokey Harrison had left home, and after breaking camp from a secluded brush-coulee where he had just spent the night, he had his hands full controlling his buck-jumping horse. Each morning it happened at the crack of dawn when he first stepped into the saddle, and though the horse was just having fun, Smokey sometimes had to hang on to the saddle horn with both hands to keep from bucking off.

The crunch of shod hooves breaking through ice-crusted snow spooked a snow bird family, who flew up in panic and fluttered off into the sage. A pair of saucy ravens who had been following the rider since daybreak, were taking turns uttering their raucous croaks; expressing their disapproval over his presence here in this inland sea of frost-covered sage and sand.

Talking to himself, the young cowboy voiced unrepeatable words before giving in and allowing a frisky Bandit to run. A good run is what the son-of-a-gun is in need of. It will take a country mile before he remembers that he is no longer a colt, and behave himself, he reckoned.

Leaving the hills and the snow behind, Smokey Harrison reined in Bandit for a much needed breather, caressing the neck of the only friend he had left in the world. An old cowboy uncle had helped him trap Bandit from the wild bunch that roamed the Rattlesnake Hills, twenty miles above the homestead of his parent's apple orchard. And with the self-made knowledge of his uncle, and much loving care from a young Smokey Harrison, a bond had been created between a three-year old colt and a boy.

Because of the spunk shown when breaking the young animal, he was given the name of Bandit. Although submitting to the saddle, the genes of his ancestry would always be with him, lurking right near the surface of an ingrained personality. Smokey was aware of this and treated him with respect, as all good friends should treat each other.

A trust grew strong between a horse and a boy, knowing that when the chips were down and the irons in the fire, one could depend on the other to be by his side.

Young Smokey Harrison had always been fond of animals, with the horse and the dog his favorite, in that order. As far back as he could remember there had been a dog in his life. The first was a faithful old collie named Skippy, and though he had a broken nose from a mishap with a rolling wagon wheel, Smokey loved him just the same. The boy and the dog became attached to each other, one protecting the other from any trouble that might venture their way.

And then it was time for his first pony. Even though the old mare was well along with age, a host of silver hairs mixed in with her coat of black; a young boy was smitten. To Smokey Harrison her name was none other than Smokey.

Much to the disappointment of his family, a rapidly maturing boy left home to fulfill a life long dream. Smokey was tiring of the ways of a hum-drum way of life at the small orchard where he was born and raised. A decision was made that would change his life forever—to ride away from the Big Bend country and become a cowboy.

He would cringe when his Mom had called him just a boy. He was nineteen years of age now, and in his way of thinking, was old enough to know what he wanted, and able to muster the grit and determination to face a new life in the making. He reckoned he was a mature man now, able to pay his own way and do his own thing!

Shaking away the memories, Smokey continued his quest, a lone rider seeking his destiny. Day after day he rode, pointing Bandit's nose into the north, seeking the territories of a new land called Canada. He had heard at a nearby trading post that it was a land full of wild Indians and outlaws, mounted police and whiskey smugglers. A wilderness land full of large grass covered hills and a vast expanse of prairie was the enticing part, all of which were just waiting for the arrival of the settler.

This was an exciting time for Smokey, yet a lonely one. No human life had he seen since riding away from his old home. One day he rode out of a virgin forest, and there spread out before his startled eyes lay a vast prairie of grass and sage. Looking long in the distance, he swore that he could see cattle, a vast herd of them by the looks of it; peacefully grazing along the far reaches of the skyline.

Bandit was equally interested, and with ears up at attention status, began to fidget and chomp at the bit. He too wished to find out what was across the sagebrush prairie.

"Could be buffalo, might even be elk," Smokey said, talking to his horse. "They both graze in herds, for safety I reckon. Sure hope it is longhorns though, we just might find ourselves a job ridin' the range for a big ranch!"

"Let's do it Bandit!" Smokey yelled, his voice rising by the minute, "Let's go and find ourselves a job!" There was no need for spurs to motivate the big gelding, who at the sound of Smokey's words burst into action, charging across the prairie like a race horse leaving the starting gate.

After a half mile run, Smokey reined in the horse for a breather. Bandit wasn't winded, but getting close to it. A half mile run at full speed was meant for a race horse on a track, yet it was Bandit's choice to do just that. He enjoyed a good run at least once a day, it was the way of the wild mustang genes that flowed strong in his blood, to be able to out run a pack of hungry wolves, even a cagey old stallion infringing on a harem of young virgin mares.

Closing in on the cattle, and they were longhorns, he spotted another rider coming his way. Reining in a still frisky Bandit, Smokey waited for the advancing rider. It appeared he too was excited to hear the sound of someone elses voice beside his own.

Excitement rippled through the lanky frame of a young Smokey Harrison. He was finally going to meet up with a real cowboy. The stranger rode a fine black horse, decked out in a well-used saddle. His range attire was just as Smokey had imagined it would be: chaps, boots and spurs, a loose bandana hung from his neck, and a big hat with a curled brim was fit snuggly over a mop of long neglected hair; and a six-gun fit snuggly on his hip.

"Howdy, stranger," he shouted, pulling in the big black until a long tail was dragging the ground. He was a pleasant looking fellow with a contagious smile spread across his whiskered face.

"Reckon you're the first person I've laid eyes on in a coon's age."

Smokey replied with a big howdy of his own making, and then walked over and shook the cowboy's gloved hand, who had now stepped down from the saddle—a friendly smile still on his face.

"Sure good to see you stranger—you're the first human I've seen in a lot of miles of riding. My name is Smokey Harrison, from way south of here in the Big Bend country.

"Most folks know me as just plain old Smokey."

"Sure my pleasure to meet you Smokey, mine is Kelly Tucker, and my friends know me as just plain ol' Kelly," after which they both laughed at the candor of their talk.

"What brings you way up in this north country," Kelly asked, "after living in that warm country down yonder?"

"I had my fill of picking and peddling apples," Smokey replied.

"I'm hunting a job on a ranch, a wrangling doggies like you're a doing."

"I'll tell you what, follow me over yonder to a camp I have tucked away in a brush coulee—we'll brew up a pot o' coffee and have us a medicine talk!"

Kelley Tucker's camp was a good one, protected on all sides from the weather. With a concealed spring as its source, a modest stream of water flowed from a dense thicket of willow brush, worth far more than an entire herd of longhorns. Located close by was a two-man tent, a rock-ringed fire pit complete with a turning spit, and a make-shift latrine located farther down the coulee.

Kelley soon had a coffee pot bubbling and a pair of antelope steaks sizzling in a well-seasoned fry pan. After a tasty wilderness meal, the two new-found friends sat around the fire chewing the fat, and getting acquainted with each other.

"I've got a good job here," Kelly said. "Except for one blasted thing."

Looking Smokey in the eye, he continued his talk. "The boss pays good wages, but from one month to the next he never gives me a day off. Says he doesn't want me riding down to a gold camp in the valley and getting drunk; and romancin' them gals that hang around an old sod-roofed dance hall.

"I love to dance, why I have ridden fifty miles and back just to attend an honest to goodness dance!"

Smokey was all ears listening to Kelly's talk. He liked what he was hearing, and asked him if he knew where he could find a job.

"I reckon the boss might hire you on—sure hope he does—wrangling these blasted longhorns night and day is getting to be more than I can handle alone.

Dark shadows of an approaching night were moving across the high country prairie, settling into the summer home of a herd of longhorn cattle. Here, in a hidden coulee, two young cowboys sat around a blazing camp fire, enjoying each others company and making plans for the future.

Long into the dark night they talked, the only light was from their fire and the glow from a star-studded sky. Both were comforted by listening to the sound of another voice besides their own. A bond was created that night, a bond that would last far into the future; riding as partners into whatever adventure destiny might see fit to deal them.

The next morning, Smokey rode down country to ranch headquarters, and there met with the owners of the border ranch. An elderly couple greeted him with much enthusiasm, inviting the young rider to come on in and set awhile. They introduced themselves as John and Matilda, nothing more or less.

After sitting Smokey down into a hard-back chair, Matilda brought the young cowboy a steaming cup of tea and a plate of honey-coated scones. "You poor hungry boy, you must be starving," she said.

"This will tide you over for now, but you must stay and have dinner with us," and with that said she hustled back to her kitchen.

John had settled into an old rocker, a smile on his whiskered face as he watched a slightly embarrassed cowboy. Smokey had never tasted tea before, he was raised on coffee back where he came from, and was a bit cautious as he tried a wee sip.

The scones he did like, and began devouring them with much gusto. And so there he sat, a full cup of tea in one hand, of which he knew he could never drink; and an empty saucer in the other, with nothing left but the crumbs.

John, whose smile had turned into a chuckle, had been watching it all. "…'tis a habit my wife brought with her from old England, this tea drinking is. I prefer coffee myself—and drink it with Kelly Tucker when he's around.

"He is much like you Smokey, says that tea wouldn't even make good medicine for a constipated horse.

Not wishing to insult a kind old lady, who had invited him into her home and was even going to prepare him a meal, Smokey girded his loins and downed the cup of tea. On the verge of throwing up, he was still shuddering as he watched old John double over with a contagious laughter.

"You are a brave one lad," he said, attempting to control himself. "I am impressed with the courage you have shown, drinking a cup of my wife's tea like you have done here today!"

It was then Matilda returned to see why her husband was laughing so. Noticing Smokey's empty cup, she said, "I am happy you have enjoyed my tea Smokey," and reached for his cup to refill it.

"There is plenty left in my tea pot—allow me to fill your cup again—by the time you drink this one, dinner will be ready to eat!"

11

A look of utter disbelief appeared on Smokey's face, causing old John to cut loose with another burst of uncontrolled laughter. With her teapot in hand, Matilda was all set to pour him another when the young cowboy put his hand over the empty cup, reason enough for her to step back and listen.

"No! No Ma-am, I don't reckon this cowboy could handle any more of your tea right now, a hot cup o' coffee would sure hit the spot though!" Matilda turned away from Smokey and returned to her kitchen, casting ominous glances at her husband who was completely out of control.

After a delicious meal prepared by a kindly woman, who never let a stranger pass by her door without offering them food and shelter, the men were ushered out to the porch to do their smoking.

Liking the looks of the young man sitting beside him, John offered Smokey a riding job at thirty dollars a month and keep. This surprised Smokey some, who was preparing to ask the old timer for that very same thing. Yet, he was thrilled to the core.

He was now a bono-fide cowboy with a job, who along with Kelly Tucker, would be riding the range taking care of John and Matilda's herd of two hundred head of longhorn cattle.

"You may start today by cleaning out the horse barn, which Kelly has not taken the time to do lately—then you can ride out to the cow camp and go to work riding for the J-M brand."

Rolling up his sleeves, Smokey went to work loading an old creaky wheel barrow with horse manure, then wheeling it out through the barn door and dumping it in a pile. All afternoon he worked, attempting to finish the smelly job before sunset. When the barn was in a presentable condition he was soaked with sweat, his boots and jeans were in bad shape as well, soiled with the unsavory stains of long neglected horse droppings.

It was near midnight before he arrived at the cow camp. To his surprise he found Kelley pulling the saddle from his bronc.

He had just returned from a few hours of riding night herd on old John's high-strung cattle that were prone to run at the slightest disturbance.

"Good to see you back, Smokey, did old John hire you on?"

"I reckon so," Smokey replied. "I had to drink a cup of tea, and shovel horse manure all afternoon though—an initiation of sorts, to satisfy Matilda and John that I was plumb serious about it all. Only then did he say I could ride up here and find you."

As tired as he was, Kelly still had enough energy left to erupt in a contagious burst of laughter. Tears were streaming down his cheeks before he finally found his voice again.

"They did the same thing to me, only I was ordered to dung out a hen house as well. As far as drinking Matilda's tea was concerned, I downed a cup the same as you did, and then had to vamoose outside and puke it all up."

The two young cowboys roared with laughter, happy to now be riding pards, comrades in the truest sense. After a cup of Kelly's coffee that was strong enough to dissolve a horseshoe nail, they crawled in their blankets and called it a day.

Kelly Tucker was sure thankful to have another rider at the camp to help him. A pack of timber wolves had recently invaded the ranch, causing all kinds of concern, including sleepless nights.

Old John figured a two man crew was sufficient for his needs, not realizing the work involved; and the sleepless nights. Kelly was overjoyed that Smokey would now be the means of taking a burden off his shoulders, perhaps he could now get a decent sleep that his over-worked body was so desperately in need of.

Right after the arrival of Smokey they alternated shifts. One would ride night hawk every other night, while the other slept. This gave their young bodies the chance to recuperate from the long grueling hours spent in the saddle.

The two riders were rarely together except in the early morning hours. The rotation plan seemed to be working out quite well unless an emergency arose.

The night of the wolf attack was like a living hell on earth. It was Smokey's turn at riding night hawk. The pack had chosen this night to move in close to the herd, their eerie howls causing unrest throughout the bedding grounds of a herd of animals that were born to run.

Many of them had bounced to their feet, the clicking of their massive horns could be heard clear back at the coulee camp, bellowing there rage at unseen shadows blending in with the darkened woods. Back at camp asleep in his blanket, Kelly was awakened by the ruckus, and knowing that trouble was brewing, threw his blanket aside and saddled his horse.

He discovered Smokey at the far side of the bedding grounds doing his best to keep a spooked bunch of renegades from running. If they broke away the entire herd would follow in a wild scramble into the forest. Bandit was staggering with fatigue, having given his all to keep the crazy ones from starting a stampede. Smokey too was nearing the end of his own endurance when Kelly Tucker showed up.

With the timely arrival of Kelly, the two cowboys were able to contain the unruly ones—saving a stampede they wouldn't have been able to stop.

One night before Kelly rode out on night hawk, he loitered awhile, the two cowboys sitting around a blazing fire. Though he hadn't told Smokey before, he reckoned he should tell him now. "I was ready to quit and ride away before you showed up. Several times I asked old John for more riders, several times he refused me. And now, with just the two of us, we're still run ragged.

"Why he wouldn't even bring in more horses—the amount of ridin' we're a doin' we need at least two more apiece—a *remuda* it's called down Wyoming way.

"We need a *remuda* and more cowboys to ride them, that is all there is to it!"

Smoky too was tiring of the twelve to fourteen hours of steady riding, and so was Bandit, who lately was showing the strain of it all. Several times as of late, both he and Kelly had worked together on night shift, attempting to keep the beef-hungry wolves from sneaking in and making off with new-born baby calves.

It was a tough situation to be in. If the cowboys were to fire their rifles at the meat hunters it would only incite a ruckus in the spooky herd. A terrified herd bouncing to their feet, horns a popping, tails in the air ready to run.

Smokey was plumb upset over the way Bandit had been abused, one horse had accomplished the work of three, and it had taken a toll on his beloved mustang. "I'll leave old John before I work Bandit into the ground again," he told his pard, and meant every word of it. "We've got two months wages coming, which should carry us over until we can find something better.

"Let's do it Kelly—let's quit and ride on!"

After fearing for the survival of their horses and themselves, two young cow punchers rode away from John and Matilda's J-M ranch. Though young in years, and the only cowboys on the payroll, they had given their all to wrangle two-hundred head of stampede-crazy longhorns from scattering to the far winds.

Old John didn't believe in hiring on more hands, resulting in the two horses Smokey and Kelly rode wasting away into utter exhaustion, and their own bodies as well. There had been just too many twenty four hour shifts for both the horses and their riders.

✱ ✱ ✱ CHAPTER 2 ✱ ✱ ✱

After a Saturday night of whooping it up at the nearest lumber town, two young cowboys were riding back to camp with heads hanging low, their pockets empty of jingle and both nursing a horrendous hang over. They were now employed by a large lumber syndicate of which there were many in the Pacific Northwest.

While working here they both began living the wild life, a life full of wine, women and song. They were full of it, the temptations more than they could handle—hanging out with unsavory characters, doing nothing more than riding down a path of chaos and utter destruction. After more of these escapades than he cared to remember, brushes with the law and such, and it was vigilante law, Smokey Harrison decided it was time for a change. "Time we were movin' on," he told his pard.

"...'fore we get ourselves in more trouble than we can handle. Think about it Kelly, we could get ourselves shot—even strung up to a branch of a tree—like that feller we seen hangin' back yonder!"

"Reckon you're right," Kelly Tucker replied. "We're partners remember, reckon ol' Kelly will ride with you where ever you want to go."

Kelly Tucker was Harrison's riding companion, and the best friend that he had at this time. They had partnered up while punching longhorns at the J-M up at old Johns border ranch. As neither had a brother of their own, they considered themselves as brothers, and treated each other as such.

Smokey Harrison desired nothing more than to make something of his life, to ride away from the wild side and start a new life; and to know that Kelly agreed to come with him was the best news to come his way in a long time.

One day, heartened by two months of hard-earned wages in their jeans, they saddled their broncs and headed east to the Rocky Mountains, if nothing else to see what was on the other side. Smokey owned little but his saddle horse and riggin', a Marlin .30.30 rifle, a Colt sixgun and saddlebags stuffed with his possibles, spare shirt, socks and such. Lashed behind the saddle was a blanket roll and a leather satchel stuffed full of oats for his horse. Kelly was equipped in much the same manner.

Eventually, the mighty Rockies blocking out the eastern sky, they rode out of a dense forest and found themselves right in the center of an extensive gold mining operation along a creek known as Wild Horse; including a boom town and all that goes with it. Reining in their broncs on a high rise of ground overlooking it all, Smokey spoke. "Why it's just like an ant hill down there.

"Must be several hundred people movin' around—back and forth they go, between the town and the creek, even back in the woods!

"I,ve never in my born days seen anything like this before."

"Nor has ol' Kelly," he too was in awe at what they were seeing.

Riding on into town, their intent had been to buy much needed supplies and then continue on their way. But such would not be the case. They both became afflicted with a severe case of gold fever,

The months passed by in which jobs were easy to come by. They mucked with pick and shovel along Wild Horse Creek for various employers, and eventually were able to stake a claim of their own. Much to their surprise they found a better than average lode, and began making a good profit.

Life in the gold fields is one hard grueling one day after another, seven days a week. The days were long, the nights even longer. Being young and full of it, the partners were soon investigating the night life in such an isolated place, and found it to be even more lively than the lumber towns, if that were possible.

They frequented the saloons, of which there several to choose from, seeking diversion from the long tedious days in the diggings. Their favorite turned out to be the Golden Dove, the only one that advertised dancing. Several of the dancing girls were from local mining families, and several more came from the stump homesteads scattered back in the woods. And then there were still more, the hardened kind who had been brought in from far away places.

Kelly Tucker loved to dance, not a night went by that he couldn't be found at the Golden Dove, dancing with a young farm girl from a stump farm back in the pine woods, who was working at the Dove to help her struggling parents feed a large family of growing children.

Her name was Laura, a shy girl with blond hair, and a pleasing personality when one got to know her. She was more than pretty, and a very good dancer. Kelly soon fell in love with Laura, as she did him. He even bought her a new dress and a pair of dancing shoes, as the ones she wore were well-used hand me downs from an older cousin. As Kelly soon found out, they were the only decent dress and shoes that Laura owned, she had no other choice.

And much to his chagrin, the new dress lured other male dancers swarming to Laura like bees to a field of clover. It got so bad that he was lucky to get a dance or two of his own.

After selling their claim on the upper reaches of the canyon, along with the dust they had already harvested from the same, the two partners had a sizeable stake in their pokes; which they divided evenly between them.

Come time to continue on their journey, Kelly was reluctant to leave, informing Smokey he wanted to spend one more night with Laura. "I'll meet you up there somewhere," he said, pointing up to the summit of a high pass.

"Have patience Smokey, wait for me!

"You know that I can track anything that moves, that horse you're a ridin' will be as easy to find as eating pancakes on a Sunday morning."

* * * *

Smokey and his horse were bone-weary when they topped out on the Continental Divide of the Rocky Mountains. It was nearing sundown on this high summit when the cowboy finally stepped down from Bandit's saddle. The pass was barren of any living thing except for several clumps of stunted alpine pine.

"I reckon we'll camp here tonight big guy," he said, knowing both he and his horse were plumb tuckered and in need of a much needed rest.

Pulling the saddle and gear from the horse, he led him to a seep of water pooling on the down side of a melting snow drift, finding enough to satisfy both the cowboy and the horse. Returning to the scrub pine, he kindled a modest fire and found the coffee pot in his saddle bags. As he worked his attention was centered on the mass of jumbled rock below

19

him, shaking his head in wonder that he had made it to the top of the treacherous shale slope.

Smokey Harrison, coffee cup in one hand, the other shoving a log on the fire, was getting worried, his eyes never leaving the nearby trail. His riding companion was long overdue for their rendezvous here at this lonely summit along the Continental Divide.

"Sure hope the son of a gun hasn't got himself into trouble," he muttered, his eyes never leaving the steep shale slope below.

"He reckoned he had to spend one more night with that gal of his," Smokey muttered once again, his eyes were still concentrated on the mass of shattered rock.

"The son-of-a-gun sure hated the thought of leaving her behind with that wild bunch at the Golden Dove!

"Sure don't blame him none either!"

Darkness was rapidly invading the high country, casting weird shadows across the dimming landscape, blotting out the forested valley below. Smokey was up pacing about, moving back and forth between a small camp sheltered in a cluster of alpine pine and the devil's own trail he had blazed up through the shale. After much endless pacing, he was stopped by the faint echo of a gunshot far down in the valley. He never stirred, his senses straining to hear, to see. There was nothing to hear, nothing to see, yet once he could have sworn he had seen a faint flicker of light.

That some one was down there, he was sure of. It must be Kelly, he reckoned, he must be signaling me that he's not far behind. "Reckon I should let him know where I am," he muttered, and picking up his Marlin fired a round into the night.

After a series of ricocheting echoes had settled down, he heard an answering shot and then knew for sure that Kelly was down there, and might need some help. It had now turned as black as Hades itself.

He kindled another fire near the edge of the downward slope, hoping that Kelly would be able to see it, knowing the light, feeble as it might be, would give his partner a chance to find him.

Smokey Harrison knew it would be impossible to start down until first light in the morning. After adding more fuel to the signal fire, he shot one more round into the night, then returned to camp and rolled up in his blanket, his jaded body badly in need of a few hours sleep.

* * * *

Kelly Tucker was in mixed spirits when he walked into the Golden Dove. It had grieved him to know his old pard had ridden away without him, yet for their plan to work, he must do his part here.

It was Laura that he was concerned about. He knew that if he rode away without her, the little gal that he had fallen for would be in more trouble than she could handle alone. He couldn't help but notice as of late, that more and more of the mining crowd were lining up to dance with her, she was obligated to her boss to dance with them, or lose her job.

Laura dreaded dancing with the miners, who were always soused to their eyebrows, reeking of unwashed clothing and bodies and rot-gut whiskey; and hugging her so tight that she could hardly catch her breath. And, their foul breath was getting to be more than she could stand!

The new dress that Kelly had given her was ruined, soiled and reeking of strong, rancid sweat, and all manner of other foul things that clung to these seekers of gold. So far she had evaded their advances, knowing that it would be only a matter of time before she was dragged up the stairs to a fate worse than death.

The young cowboy pushed through the bat wings, standing for a moment to get his bearings. He was angry, damned mad in fact over the way Laura was being treated here at the Dove, and this very night he planned to put a stop to it.

The crowd inside the old waterhole was sure enough a rowdy one, whooping it up and giving the girls a horrendous work out on the dance floor. Whiskey was flowing as freely as water under a bridge.

One old sourdough, drunk out of his mind, was seen waltzing with a broom stick as his partner, one hand holding up the stick, the other gripping an empty bottle of booze. The unfortunate fellow passed out on the floor, upsetting several dancing couples. In no time at all, a well-muscled bouncer elbowed his way through the crowd and drug the old sourdough out through the swinging doors, and there booted him head first into a mud hole on the trail that served as the gold town's main drag.

Kelly Tucker couldn't believe what was unfolding before his eyes. He feared for the safety of Laura, and try as he may he couldn't spot her. His steely eyes swept through the crowd, back and forth they roved attempting to find an innocent farm girl from the back woods that had won his heart.

And then from over by the stairway that led to the questionable upper story, he noticed a commotion taking place, and the scream of a terrified girl. He knew it was Laura screaming. He recognized her voice and knew in an instant that he was right. Shoving his way through the crowd, his voice was roaring in anger. "Stand aside you folks, ole Kelly's a comin' through!

"Make way—you hear?" His voice still out of control, startled several hard cases into doing nothing more than getting lost in the crowd; besides his six gun was out of the leather pointing straight at their gizzards.

Rage swirled around him like a wild fire in a dry forest. Elbowing the last of the crowd aside he discovered Laura stretched out in front of him. Face down, her dress hanging in wild disarray, being dragged up the stairway by one of her naked arms. Her captor was a swarthy looking gambler that hung around the Golden Dove, a house dealer of poker now and then. Laura was screaming her head off, fighting as best she could to get her arm free of his unyielding grip.

"Leave her be!" Kelly roared, starting up the stairs, the girl's kicking feet were just in front of him. His six gun was prepared to do battle, when he roared one more time, "Let go of her arm—now!!"

A swarthy, drunken face swung around to see who had the nerve to interfere with his devious plans. "The hell you say cowboy," he growled.

"Don't butt into something that is none of your business—she's mine—bought and paid for!" With that said, his free hand dipped into an inner pocket, swinging a hidden derringer towards the advancing cowboy.

Two shots rang out through the now silent crowd. A never to be forgotten drama had just been enacted before their very eyes. Laura was now free, wrapped in the arms of the cowboy sobbing her head off. Kelly was holding her close, his shooting hand still holding a smoking six gun.

The woman molester, and that is what he would be known as for the rest of his days, was howling with pain and fury. A bullet hole had appeared through the palm of his shooting hand, another through the wrist of the hand that had held Laura his prisoner.

The dance hall crowd remained silent, watching in awe as the cowboy removed his coat and wrapped it around a near naked Laura, and then a hearty cheer arose from all that was there, offering their support for the cowboy and his dance hall girl.

A hush returned to the Golden Dove, the crowded dancers making way for a well-dressed dandy, who was forcing his way through the crowd. There was no doubt in any ones mind that he was the big boss, and arriving at the scene he was vivid with anger.

"What's going on here!" he demanded, glaring at Kelly Tucker and Laura.

"Looks like you have shot the hell out of my poker dealer. And you Laura! It appears like you have been right in the middle of it all. One of these days you will go up those stairs, you just as well set your mind to it now as later.

"Go on, get! Get back on the dance floor and earn your keep!"

With that said he raised his hand to backhand her across the face, only to find his hand grabbed in a steely grip. Kelly Tucker was livid, forcing the man to drop to his knees, crunching finger bones until they were broken, listening with pleasure to screams of agony echoing around the room.

"She's not going anywhere with a cowardly woman molester like you. Laura is going with me, never to return!

"A hangman's noose should be cinched around both your grimy necks, fitting punishment for a pair of woman-molesting cowards like you pair!"

"No way!" screamed Laura's former boss. "I have a contract signed on the dotted line, she is mine for two more years."

"Have you paid her any wages?" the cowboy demanded, a grim look spreading across his face, "for the time she has been in your employ."

"No, he hasn't!" Laura sobbed. "Not a red cent, the old skinflint wouldn't even advance me enough to buy a decent dress."

Kelly was smiling when he spoke, "That makes your so called contract null and void, pilgrim. It isn't worth the paper it is written on."

Laura's dress that Kelly had given her, and that she was so proud of was a ragged mess from the mauling the poker dealer had forced upon her. One more time the cowboy warned him of what would still happen.

"You owe Laura a twenty dollar gold piece for her dress your big shot gambler ripped all to pieces, and something else, another twenty bucks for the dancing wages she's got coming.

"Dig in your poke, *hombre*! Do it right now, 'fore I rip this arm right out of its socket."

After receiving the gold pieces, and the big boss was only too willing to part with them, Kelly Tucker spoke again, "Make way you folks, I'm a takin' Laura back to her parent's home," and with that said, took his weeping girl's hand and led her out the swinging doors.

Two saddle horses were waiting at the hitch-rail in front of the Dove, one was Kelley's. The other was Laura's who would ride into the gold diggings and back home again every night, to keep her job at the old dance hall.

After helping Laura into the saddle, he stepped into his own, "We've got to get out of this place fast darlin', reckon there's some *hombres* who will be hot on our trail."

Putting spurs to their horses, they headed for a trail that would take them to Laura's home in the forest. Nearing the outer limits of the town a shot rang out, Kelley slumped low in the saddle, both hands gripped tight on the saddle horn to keep from falling. He had been shot in the back by an unseen coward. No doubt one of the hellions from back at the Dove had pulled the trigger.

Laura screamed into the dark night, rode up along side the cowboy and managed to leave her saddle and find a seat behind a sagging Kelly, her strong arms holding him in place and secure in his own saddle.

Laura's little dun mare sped down the trail for her home in the forest, leading Kelly's horse to a pine-pole corral in a stump-pocked clearing, and a log cabin that was the home of her mistress, Laura.

✶ ✶ ✶ CHAPTER 3 ✶ ✶ ✶

An awesome display of stars twinkled a mysterious glow down on a cowboy and his horse. Here in a modest camp high up on the summit of Kutenai Pass, Smokey Harrison was tossing in his blankets unable to find sleep. He had spent a nerve-wracking night, up and about at the slightest sound.

All it took was the snap of a twig, a shifting slab of shale on the big slide, or even the footstep of some mountain creature that made him this way. All of this was over shadowed by the absence of his partner Kelly Tucker, who should have met him here the previous day.

It was nearing first light when he sensed a change, his keen senses probing the waning darkness. A tingling in his toes racing up to the hair rising on the back of his neck was a warning that he could not ignore. Something or someone has entered the camp!

Kelly has tracked me down after all, his mind told him. The son-of-a-gun has kept his word like he said he would. Then another thought turned his blood cold—maybe it is someone else who is here!

With much caution he felt for his trusty Colt, and found it under the blanket within easy reach of his shooting hand. Tossing the blanket aside he arose, six-gun in hand, his eyes sweeping the camp site. Turning his head slightly, he checked the two fire sites and found nothing amiss with the first one.

But a change had occurred at the signal fire! Something or someone was hunkered down by the smoldering ashes, their back to him—as if gazing long down into the valley below.

He was smiling now, recognizing Kelly's long duster coat and black hat with the silver-adorned hat band that he was so proud of. "That you, Kelly?" he asked, and walked over to the ashes of the signal fire. "I reckoned you must have got yourself lost, and couldn't find me."

First light was fast returning to the high country, chasing away the dark shadows into the valley below. "Wake up, ol' pard," Smokey spoke again, his voice rising some. "We'll stir up the fire and brew us some coffee, then have us a medicine talk that we're both sure a needin'!"

The figure arose and turned to face him, "It's me, Mr. Harrison," came the girl's reply. "I'm Laura Tucker, not Kelly as you thought.

"I've come to tell you the bad news!"

Smokey Harrison was thunder struck by her talk, just couldn't believe what he was hearing. Here stood Kelly's dance hall girl, dressed in his clothes.

"Where is Kelly, what has happened to him?" a sense of urgency in his voice.

Ignoring his question, the girl continued her talk', "I'm sure a needin' some of that coffee you are talking about, I'm real tired and hungry too.

"…'bout done me in—took me all night to climb up through these dern rocks," and pointed down the dangerous shale slope.

Smokey could tell the girl was in bad shape, staggering some as he led her over to his bed of pine boughs, and after removing Kelly's hat he laid her down and pulled the blanket snug around her chin.

"Thank you" she muttered. "I'm so tired—so dad-burned tired!" And losing the battle to keep her eyes open, fell into a deep sleep.

"She's a downright pretty little gal." Smokey muttered, standing there beside the sleeping girl. "Ole Kelly's sure enough one lucky hombre!"

The young in years cowboy prepared a meager breakfast and was sitting on a rock beside the sleeping girl, nursing a cup of coffee when she became restless, moaning and muttering strange things that he was hard put to understand.

"...Kelly's bin shot!" And this he did understand. "... bushwhacked...shot in the back by a lowdown miserable coward...!"

"No!!" Smokey exclaimed. "This cannot be, ole Kelly would never allow anything like this to happen!"

The girl continued tossing and turning, moaning and muttering strange things in her sleep. Smokey stayed close by in case she needed him, his own mind in a confused state, not knowing if the words she had spoken were for real.

Smokey Harrison paced for hours it seemed, back and forth between the sleeping girl and the big rock slide that she had scrambled up in the dark of night. Then, much later, her eyes opened, she sat up and looked around in wonder, confused as to where she was and how she had got to this high pass in the clouds.

"Could I have a cup of that coffee, that smells so darn good," she asked, noticing Smoky sitting over by his horse. "Reckon I've been a burden to your plans, Mr. Harrison, staggerin' in off the big bunch of busted rocks like I did.

"Is that bacon I can smell in that pan over yonder? I'm starving—I haven't et anything to speak of for at least two days now."

Relieved to hear the girl speaking in a coherent manner, the cowboy went to his modest cooking fire and brought her a cup of coffee, which she eagerly accepted. He then brought over a pan of freshly fried bacon and a sourdough biscuit.

As he watched her devour the food, he realized how hungry she must have been, and that she had indeed been starving. Chattering as she ate, she began to tell him bits and pieces of what had happened since he had rode away from the gold diggings known as Wild Horse.

Smoky was having trouble keeping things straight in his mind. "Start at the first, Miss Laura, I reckon I'm getting confused some."

She had now finished eating her meal, and smiling at the big cowboy, thanked him for his kindness and sharing his food with her. She then began the story of what had happened.

She told of her job dancing with the drunken miners, and how she despised working at the Golden Dove, knowing that sooner than later she would be forced to go up the stairs with them—one at a time!

And then she spoke of Kelly saving her that night, and how he used his gun on the gambler. After which he manhandled her boss, mangling his shooting hand and forcing him to pay her for a new dress, hers having been ruined by this same dealer of cards.

"Kelly even forced him to pay me for the wages I had coming," she added, "The old crook would have never given me a dime if Kelly hadn't threatened him with the business end of a hang-man's noose."

"We then left the dance hall, our horses were waiting close by. We were riding away, heading for my home—a half-hours ride is all—when I heard a gun shot and saw Kelly slump low in the saddle.

Tears were flowing as she continued, "I knew then Kelly had been shot in the back as we were leaving the gold town, I helped him stay in the saddle until we reached my home.

"My Mom is an excellent nurse, and after we got him into bed she began her doctoring. The bullet had gone clean through his shoulder, all Mom had to do was clean the wounds and prepare one of her special herb poultices for each one."

Smokey Harrison was in awe listening to her story, and uttered a silent curse for not being there to back up his old pard. He was equally proud of how Laura had stood beside him, and assisted him to safety.

"We told our folks we loved each other," she continued with the story. "My Dad is a back woods preacher, and he agreed to marry us—Kelly in his sick bed—I was standing beside him."

Kelly's wife began to giggle, "You must not call me Miss Laura anymore, I am now Mrs. Tucker."

Then her countenance changed, she appeared troubled of how to present the rest of the story.

"As you must know, Kelly is a stubborn man!

"He insisted on getting out of his sick bed, to ride up in these mountains and find his old partner—you Mr. Harrison. He told us that he must keep a promise he had made to you, and was beholden to not break a promise!

"It took all three of us, my Mom and Dad and his new wife to keep him in the bed, and it wasn't an easy thing to do. I finally told him that I would ride up here and find you and not to worry none, as his Laura would tell you why he was unable to be here.

"He relaxed some after that, said he guessed I was right, besides the ruckus to keep him in bed had caused his bullet wounds to start bleeding again."

Later in the day, after several more hours of sleep, Laura was up and about and feeling much better. Smokey was relieved to see her this way and heaved a sigh, thankful that she had made it through her ordeal.

Her young body had received the care that it needed, she was her old cheerful self once again. She began to tell more of her story, and told Smokey that she and Kelly worked out a deal to buy the homestead from her parents.

"My Mom and Dad have been planning on moving down to a settlement along the Kutenai River anyway," she explained. "There is a good school there for the kids, and plenty of jobs to be had working in the lumber camps."

This was just fine with Laura as long as she could be by her husband's side.

Smokey Harrison was saddened to know that he might never see his old friend again. Yet, he was relieved that Kelly Tucker had discovered a welcome surprise at the end of the rainbow, more precious than a pot of gold.

Come time for Laura to return to her new husband, Smokey offered to escort her back down the western shale slope to where she had left the horse. And it was Kelly's bronc that would be chomping at the bit to head back for home.

"No, Mr. Harrison," she answered. "I can make it on my own. Having climbed up in the dark—I can surely make it back down in the daytime!"

"Tell you what, Mrs. Tucker," and they both began to laugh at his candor, "if you will call me Smokey, why then I will call you Laura.

"And something else, I will escort you half-way down the slide." A compromise had been struck, one that they both agreed on.

Wearing the moccasins that he kept in his saddlebags, for just such occasions, they started down, Smokey in the lead with his long gun in hand, Laura following close behind, the pockets of her husband's duster that she wore stuffed full of biscuits and jerky.

Nearing the half-way mark, or so Laura was led to believe, they stopped for a breather. Smokey knew what he was doing, having scaled the slide in the daylight. In fact they were only several hundred yards from where Laura had left her horse. Laura had been kept so busy answering Smokey's questions that she hadn't noticed.

Smokey's keen eyes were constantly on the move scanning the slide and the nearby forest below. Suddenly, he hushed her chattering and gestured off across the slide, pointing to a bear and three cubs. The old sow was busy overturning slabs of rock, seeking the hiding place of the whistlers of alpine country, whistling marmots they were known as. The cubs were sitting on their rumps, watching with interest their Mom digging them out a meal.

"She's a grizzly all right, plumb cranky at times," Smokey whispered. "'specially so when feeding a batch of cubs!

"Your hoss can't be too far from here," he continued to whisper. "I reckon we should Injun on down and get you on your way."

"Oh, Smokey," she protested. "You have fooled me, leading me to believe we were still up on the slide.

"See that group of fir trees, just down yonder, that's where I left Kelly's horse—sure hope he's all right."

Stooping low, much like Indians sneaking up on an enemy, they made their way down into the fir trees. The horse sensed them coming, and neighed a loud welcome that echoed long into the silent forest.

The horse had been tethered in high, lush grass, which was now cropped down to the bare ground, but was in dire need of a drink of water. Laura felt guilty for leaving him so long without water, and promptly led him over to a small seepage from a well concealed spring. The horse was able to quench his thirst, and after Laura gave Smokey a warm hug, she climbed up in the saddle ready to ride.

Smokey handed her his rifle, and said, "I want you to hand me the gun when I climb this tree.

"That old she grizzly is coming this way, lickety split." They both could now hear the sound of something huge crashing through the brush. "I sure hate to kill her, with the cubs and all, but I have got to defend myself if necessary."

After receiving the rifle from an alarmed Laura, Smokey roared, "Get outta here fast! Ride little lady—put your spurs to that bronc—and ride. Ride!!"

Laura was only too willing to do as she was told, and soon vanished in the vastness of the forest. Though faint it was, Smokey's keen hearing picked up a mournful sound drifting his way on a mischievous mountain breeze

"...by, by Mr, Harrison—thank you for saving my life...!"

* * * *

The old sow charged into the small clearing with a challenging roar, huffing and snuffling, outraged at the human scent that was disturbing her so. Her nose was pointed into the breeze, sniffing long into the direction of Laura's hurried departure. Then, not satisfied at all, the grizzly turned her attention to the clearing.

The cubs were tagging along behind their Mom, both now sitting on their rumps watching her outraged performance, both sniffing the breeze, learning the ways of the wild ones.

The grizzly Mom had now turned her attention to the fir tree, and sensing the scent of a human presence high above her, reared up on her hind legs, her front clawed-paws scraping the bark into dangling strips that reached to the ground. Listening to another roar gush out of her slobbering mouth, Smokey reckoned she was reaching high to grab one of his legs and pull him down.

The fir tree was swaying back and forth from the action of the grizzly, who was now attempting to shake the human from his perch. Smokey, fearing for his life, fired a shot straight down at the bear, the bullet clipping a notch in one of her ears leaving it dangling low and bloody.

Dropping down on to all four feet, the sow began swinging her massive head back and forth, still roaring blood-curdling roars, still staring up at the two-legged one. "Go on, git!!" Smoky roared back at her. "Vamoose outta here—you force me to shoot again, I'll kill you for sure!"

After swinging around to check on her cubs, the bear turned her head once again towards the tree, roaring her feral rage at Smokey Harrison. Only then, with her cubs tagging close behind her did she vanish into the dense forest.

The cowboy, shaken up a bit from a close call from an outraged Mom, fired two rounds into the air after the departing grizzly family.

The echoes from the gun shots were loud and clear, rebounding from the forest floor up into the cloud-shrouded summit on the Pass; and back again.

Accompanied by the gloom of an early morning fog moving down from the high places, an eerie silence settled over the forest. Now back with both feet on the ground, Smoky reckoned it was time to be heading back up to the summit and be on his way.

"Time I was riding away from these mountains—hope I can find that prairie country I am looking for," he muttered, as he replaced the spent cartridges back into his 30.30.

"I reckon Kelly and Laura will be fine now. My old friend has found himself a mighty fine little wife, and the start of a horse ranch that he has always wanted.

"He is sure one lucky hombre, and Laura one lucky little gal!"

Some time later Smoky reached the summit of the pass, a strenuous climb, but a good one. He looked back down with awe, still amazed at the grit and determination of a young girl, who had climbed up through the shattered rubble in the dark of night to deliver him a message from her gunshot husband—Kelly Tucker.

And the confrontation with the grizzly bear! It will be an adventure that I will tell to my grandchildren, he reckoned. Sure hope I am lucky enough to have any to tell my story to.

After one last look around his modest campsite on the wind-ravaged pass, making sure it was left as he found it, Smokey appeared satisfied. The summit appeared as if no one had camped here for the last two nights and three days, and that is the way it should be; leave a campsite as you found it! This was only one of the hundreds of such unwritten rules of conduct firmly embedded in with his knowledge of the wilderness!

* * * *

A dense morning fog was lifting from the high country along the Continental Divide. The rugged nature of the Rockies was mind-boggling to a lone rider, sitting in the saddle ready to ride down through a maze of fractured rock, leaving Kutenai Pass behind him.

Far across a wide, desolate valley reared the summit of Tornado Mountain, a landmark that would come in handy as a guide on his journey across the mountains. Smoky Harrison reckoned it was time to continue on his journey, riding with caution while seeking his destiny and a new life that must be out there somewhere.

Looking one last time at the campsite, knowing that he would never see it again, Smokey could never forget the grit and determination of Laura Tucker, a cheerful, optimistic young lady who had risked her life in bringing him a message from his old pard Kelly Tucker; and they had only been married several short hours.

He would never forget her chatter, and the pleasant giggles that were so much a part of her personality.

Shaking the memories out of his over-active mind, Smokey Harrison reined Bandit, his appaloosa gelding, down into a maze of shattered boulders that littered the lee side of the Pass. This was the beginning of a journey into the vast unknown for the young cowboy, seeking a new life, a life of his own choosing, not that of the wild and wooly times that were behind him.

As it had been on the western slope, he found no well traveled trail, just a faint trace here and there, enough evidence to know that he wasn't the first to pass this way.

The *kutenai* tribes knew of the Pass, using the route on their annual trek to the eastern prairie on the hunt for buffalo. Once on the prairie, it became a nerve-wracking time for this semi-docile people to avoid the dreaded Blackfoot, a decades-old enemy, who if the occasion arose, would attack and slaughter them in a bloodthirsty manner.

After their pack ponies were loaded down with the rich, nourishing meat, taking the hides as well, these mountain-bred people headed back into the west, their destination the *kutenai* Pass, and their winter camps scattered far and wide in the secluded valleys on the far side.

The ride to the bottom was long and hazardous, with many stops made to settle the nerves of both the horse and the rider. Nearing the bottom, all hell broke loose. Bandit, sensing an end to the hellish slide, and eager to return to firm footing, became a handful for his rider to hold to a reasonable pace.

Fearing a wreck, Smokey vaulted from the saddle, both reins in hand attempting to slow him down. "Whoa!" he shouted. "Take it easy big guy—we're nearly at the bottom—calm down 'fore you hurt yourself!"

The horse gave one last lunge on to firm ground, which sent Smokey sprawling down into the fractured rocks and scree. The shoulder of his buck-jumping horse had struck him a mighty blow, and as he lay in the cluttered mess, attempting to regain his breath an agonizing pain surged through his body. Gritting his teeth, he attempted to move and cried out in pain, then settled back his mind now a blank void; Smokey's senses had left him, he was unconscious, shock had taken over his body.

Bandit was not far away, standing quiet, bridal reins dangling to the ground, puzzled as to why Smokey had not come to get him. The horse favored one front leg, the tip of the hoof was raised up off the ground, the fetlock was rapidly swelling—injured by the reckless manner in which he had scrambled off the dreaded rock slide.

After what seemed like an eternity of waiting, the horse limped over to a freshet of spring water seeping out from under the slide. Here Bandit was able to quench his thirst, after which he began to feed on the tender plants that flourished there.

Timberline of the forest came up to the base of the slide, and it was here the horse was enjoying eating a well-deserved meal. Suddenly, Bandit stopped chewing the grass that was still in his mouth. With ears on the alert, he raised his head, staring with much interest far back into the forest.

His animal instinct told him that something was out there, not knowing if it walked on two legs or four. Bandit became restless, without Smokey's friendly hands and mind-soothing voice here to settle his nerves, he was at a loss of what to do.

Preparing himself to vamoose from this place if necessary, the horse stood his ground. His ears still reached for the sky, his nervous head swinging from the timberline forest back to the motionless body of the cowboy, who appeared as if he were dead.

The sun had now settled behind the high peaks of the Rockies. Dark shadows of night were blotting out the high places and every nook and cranny of the valleys below, including the rock slide, the forest and a lone horse, who stood on the alert; bridal bit still in his mouth, a cowboy saddle still cinched on his back.

An animal with mustang genes boiling in its veins, the appaloosa was a tough one to break to the ways of man. It became a hidden treasure of the river tribes whose camps were not complete without several of the coveted animals tethered close by their tepees.

Though of wild heritage, Bandit stayed as close to the body of his good friend as was possible. He loved this human who had treated him with such kindness and respect, deep inside his animal mind he knew the human loved him as well.

The horse had inherited the traits of the wild ones, a keen sense of smell, exceptional hearing and the eye sight of an eagle. Not to forget the sense of discerning danger, that well might be a foal-hungry cougar or the two-legged humans who had harassed his kind with their raw-hide lassos and long guns that shoot to kill; it did not matter which.

A pair of wilderness-honed eyes spotted a presence emerging from out of the shadows of an early morning dawn, creeping slowly towards him. In the flash of an eyelid Bandit's body went on the defensive, all set to explode in his hoof-pounding ways.

Suddenly, and for no apparent reason, he settled down, trembling from the tip of his nose to the last hair on his tail.

Whatever it was inched closer to Bandit, uttering a strange, yet soothing sound, reminding him of his old friends the mourning doves, who would waken him each morning with their mind-soothing songs of the wild.

The presence was now by his side, a dainty hand gently caressing his neck and mane, still cooing the strange wild tune. Only then, chattering strange talk that he had never listened to before, the horse felt the cowboy saddle removed from his back and dropped to the ground, which caused him to shift around some, favoring his injured fetlock.

The presence standing beside the horse turned out to be an Indian maiden. She spotted Bandit favoring the injured leg, and after carefully lifting it, began feeling and massaging until she understood what had happened.

The eastern sky was now softening, the sun of a new day ready to burst forth in this desolate valley. She released Bandit's injured leg, watching as he gently returned it to the ground, knowing that it might take several weeks to heal. She then removed the bridle from the horse, and stood back watching to see what would happen.

Bandit took one long look at her, then limped over to the seep for another drink, after which he began to graze in a ravenous fashion.

With the sun now above the eastern horizon, the native girl scouted the small opening in the forest looking for Bandit's rider. Finding no clues of anyone being there, she returned to the slide and discovered Smokey Harrison where he had fallen.

✶ ✶ ✶ CHAPTER 4 ✶ ✶ ✶

Lying flat on his back in a hastily constructed shelter, lay a badly injured cowboy who had came mighty close to cashing in his chips. Kneeling beside him was a young woman of the forest, about the same age as Smoky Harrison, dressed in buckskin clothing including the moccasins on her dainty feet. Her long black hair hung down to her shoulders, adding a pleasant background to a comely auburn-hued face. Her dark eyes were piercing keen, as those of a lobo wolf on the hunt. They never strayed far from the face of the cowboy, watching for any life signs from the silent figure that lay helpless on the ground.

Much like those made by a startled chipmunk, faint sounds came from her lips followed by a mournful tune. It was a vivid reminder to someone who might hear the strange-sounding tune of a mourning dove, serenading the arrival of the sun.

After finding the cowboy she cleared a pathway between the shattered chunks of shale, dragging him by his booted feet down on to the grassy clearing. The girl then erected an improvised shelter from the branches of a spruce tree, an art that she had been highly proficient at ever since a small child.

She inspected his body, finding several broken ribs, a severely damaged shoulder and a nasty gash on his head. As she worked strange sounds came from her mouth, a click of her tongue intertwined with a chirp—almost a subdued whistle.

She arose from the shelter and with Smokey's canteen in hand, walked over to the seep, returning with a supply of cool mountain water. She cleansed his face with water-soaked moss taken from a tree, and dampened his lips, which opened enough for her to pour drops of the life sustaining liquid down his fever-wracked throat. With much patience she continued to do this, drop-by-drop, her ingrained intuition of such things assuring her that it could do no harm.

Dove That Sings, and that was her Indian name, remained by his side, never straying far—only to check on the poultice she had tied on Bandit's damaged fetlock with a leather string, Then, gathering twigs for the small fire that she kept burning night and day, the Indian maiden would return to her vigil beside the busted up cowboy.

After a scout into the surrounding woods for the herbs she needed, she went to work doctoring Smokey Harrison. A tree moss poultice was prepared for the head wound, held in place by the cowboy's bandana. The same medicine was used on the badly lacerated shoulder, bound in place by two leather strings that were taken from the satchel that was fastened to her dress. Made from the same tanned hide as her dress, this was the girl's *possibles* bag that held her meager possessions; blending in with her buckskin attire as if it wasn't there.

How to treat the broken ribs puzzled the girl, she had never before been confronted with this sort of thing. When her hand moved across them she could tell they were broken, a distinct grating noise could be heard and felt, resulting in the unconscious cowboy to moan in his stupor from the excruciating pain.

Finally, she pulled the cowboy's belt from his jeans, and cinched it as best she could around his damaged rib cage.

The hours turned into days, the days into a week, and still Dove That Sings remained by the cowboy's side; nursing him as best she could. She found the tasks to be endless. The blanket she had found behind the cowboy saddle must be kept snuggled around his shock-ravaged body. Often at night, she would discover him suffering from a bad case of the chills, his badly-used body not up to the sudden drop of temperature in this high mountain meadow. It was then she would lift the blanket and snuggle in beside him, the warmth of her body flowing into his tortured soul.

The herb poultices she renewed on a daily basis, and most of all, soothing his fever-wracked face with cool water-soaked tree moss.

She did not forget to give him water to drink, from a drop at a time until he began to swallow with much vigor, his body soaking up the life-sustaining fluid—it was all that was keeping him alive!

* * * *

One day Dove That Sings was returning from a scout in the woods, having been gathering tree moss for Smokey's poultices, and assuring herself that the appaloosa horse hadn't drifted too far seeking graze. She was crooning the wild tune that was so much a part of her when she stopped in her tracks, and stood as quiet as a field mouse sensing danger. Her keen ears were on alert status, straining, seeking what had startled her so.

An inherited sense of survival was working for her now, keen ears picking up the strange sound that was foreign to this isolated place. She was packing Smokey's rifle, had been for several days after noticing it shoved in the scabbard on the cowboy's saddle. She had never fired one in her life, in fact this was the first time she had held one in her hands. Yet, somehow it gave her confidence, a sense of security that she could not understand.

The strange sound she could hear again, a voice that was strange to her ears, it was a human voice she was sure of. Click-clicking her chipmunk talk, she hurried over to be with the cowboy, to protect him from harm if needed.

Dove That Sings was panting when she arrived at the shelter, and after dropping to her knees looked down at the cowboy whose eyes were open wide staring up at the girl.

She gasped in awe, and it was a pleasant surprise, creating a happy smile that spread across her face.

* * * *

Smokey Harrison's mind was slowly returning from the fearsome abyss it had been entrapped in for so long a time. His eyes were now open, yet they could not see much of anything. A cloudy void is all, devoid of any and all objects that might be out there in his line of vision.

He attempted to move, and cried out, a fierce agonizing pain forcing him to lay quiet once again.

It was then he sensed an object moving out from the haze. It was that of an appaloosa horse lunging down through the mutilated rocks, and a cowboy being thrown down into the same debris that had terrified the horse. Tortured words, though weak in sound, escaped his fever-chapped lips. "No! No Bandit—don't get yourself all crazy like—!

"Listen to me you doggone son-of-a-gun, settle down 'fore you get us into one hel-luva wreck!"

Smokey's words faded back into some unknown place. With a groan of pain, the cowboy settled back in his blanket, his body was shaking, his tortured mind in utter turmoil.

His eyes were still open, his mind attempting to sort out where he was, what he was doing here in this wilderness shelter, and why he was in such pain. He recognized the spruce bough shelter as what it was meant to be, and his six-gun rigging tucked next to his bed. His old friend Bandit, he could never forget, who was standing outside the shelter, a young woman was standing beside him—a dainty hand resting on his tousled mane.

"Is that you Laura?" he asked, his cowboy drawl now back to its normal self. "Why did you come back?

"I reckoned you must be back home at the horse ranch by now, a breakin' broncs with ol' Kelly, that new husband of yourn."

This one-sided conversation, as short as it was, had taken a toll on Smokey Harrison, whose chin slumped down onto the blanket—his eyes were closed, a body-healing sleep overcame him once again!

Dove That Sings had been exposed to the white man's talk when just a child, and listened with much interest to the strange words that were spoken by the sick cowboy. She was thrilled to see the start of his recovery, yet at a loss as to how she would converse with him. She did recognize some of the words that came from his mouth, also knowing that to carry on a conversation with him would be a difficult thing to do.

She knew that he had been near deaths door, and that his road to recovery would test the mettle of them both. On the other hand she had enjoyed nursing the sick cowboy, and would continue to do for as long as she was needed.

The girl's parents were *yakima*, a tribe far to the south of the *medicine line*. It was while there she enjoyed her early childhood, playing with the others of her age, and also learning the ways of her ancestors. This knowledge was endless with survival being the mainstay of the People. Food to eat, clothing to wear, and a shelter over their heads were at the top of the list.

She was an avid learner, and soon had mastered the art of healing, gathering herbs and plants—using Mother Nature's covert secrets as her own storehouse of knowledge.

Due to the death of her parents, and the tribal wars that were taking place at this time, she was spirited away from the *yakima*, to be used as a pawn amongst the tribes. The distraught maiden found herself being traded from one clan to another, eventually winding up as a slave with a militant clan of the *kutenai* people, here north of the 49th parallel.

She was a mature seventeen snows when first arriving at the main camp, and as such was treated with much respect. There were several males in the camp who coveted her as their wife, and even though they already had one wife, some were greedy and boasted of two or three. These same greedy ones collected wives as others would do so with horses, a symbol of riches and esteem to flaunt in the faces of their less affluent peers.

She refused all their advances and was eventually taken into the Chief's tepee and treated as a slave. This was her punishment for not accepting the various proposals of marriage that had been offered her. Once here, under the watchful eyes of the Chief's jealous wives, she was expected to do all the menial tasks of the camp, and was beaten if she refused. She knew in her heart that it would be only a matter of time until she would be forced into a marriage that she did not want.

Dove That Sings mourned to return to her old home back where she had been stolen from, to the place where she had been born, to be among her own people, the *yakima*. One night she was able to slip away in the darkness, leaving the *kutenai* camp behind her. Using the stars as a guide, her nose was pointed into the south, towards the great *medicine line* that divides old *grandmother's* land from that of the great *white father*. Once across the Medicine Line she knew that she would be home free.

It was imperative that she cross over the magic line, to be back in the land of her people where she would no longer be a slave. No longer would she be forced to sleep with the dogs outside the tepee door, no longer would she be fed rancid scraps of rotten meat, meat that not even the feral dogs would eat. And to suffer the humiliation of being roughed up in the night by the women of the camp, as she lay helpless tied to a tree.

The *kutenai* squaws were savage and mean. As was their custom with defenseless women stolen from other tribes, they took great pleasure in beating her with willow-stick whips, kicking her unmercifully and even urinating on her where she lay helpless amongst the dogs.

Curled up in a fetal position to better ease the pain from the nightly beatings, Dove that Sings was silently weeping, her pain-wracked body surrounded by sleeping dogs. She knew in her heart that she must escape from this place, or die trying. No longer could she endure the shame and humiliation of being treated this way!

One day as she was cleaning up after dressing out a deer, she was able to hide a skinning knife under her buckskin dress. That night as she was being escorted to the tree, to begin another night of beatings and sleeping with dogs, she brought out the knife and stabbed the woman in her heart, and it was one of the Chief's wives.

Dove That Sings fled into the forest, and after retrieving a secret cache of supplies that she had earlier hidden near the camp latrine, she took off on a journey to freedom. She knew they would come hunting her, and slaughter her on the spot if she were found,

To once again be free was a great blessing to the girl, and using all of her skills of survival, she trotted at a tireless pace far into the forest.

It was still dark when she came upon a stream of water. She wasted no time in chucking her clothes. Her captors had not allowed her to bathe or keep herself clean, yet another form of their punishment she had been forced to endure.

She soaked and scrubbed for a long time, cleaning the filth and grime from her body and long black hair. Using damp sand found along the creek shore, the girl then scrubbed the filth from her buckskin dress and moccasins, eventually feeling like her old self once again.

To be clean again made the girl happy. She no longer reeked of feral dogs and rotten meat, and this was another blessing that Dove That Sings would never forget!

Suddenly, and with no apparent reason, her head reared high with a jerk, flared nostrils twitching as she stared into the dark night. A strange, yet vague sound had alerted the girl to something stirring in the forest. She stood quiet as a mouse, almost afraid to breath,

Once again the sound could be heard, much stronger than before. It was then she knew! It was a familiar, yet lonesome melody uttered by one of her best friends. A frightening tension eased from her body, a happy smile was spreading across her face as she began clicking her chipmunk lingo.

An early rising mourning dove was announcing to the residents of the forest the arrival of a new day. Though it was still dark as sin, the dove was cooing a message for her to be up and about to greet the arrival of the sun.

Traveling as true as a bee returning to the hive, Dove That Sings continued on her southward journey. Off to her left was a dense forest, and to her right was a towering mountain pass, a jangled mass of fractured rock stretching up to the summit. She stopped for a brief rest and to refresh herself by a clear mountain brook that she had been following for hours on end.

It was then she spotted the horse, a highly sought after breed back in the *palouse* camps of her birth. The mottled-rump on the breed she could never forget. The horse stood with an empty saddle, head drooped low, facing the base of the rock slide. With much caution she moved in close, sensing the appaloosa had been injured.

It was there she discovered Smoky Harrison all busted up, helpless and alone.

Dove That Sings must help this man she reasoned, clicking her chipmunk talk. Even though he is a white man this *palouse* girl must do what she can to save his life.

* * * *

Smokey Harrison looked long at the Indian girl, and liked what he saw. Though dressed in the clothes of her people, she appeared neat and clean. He could tell that her long black hair had been well cared for, and her face, though void of make-up, was darn pleasant to look at.

"Reckon I owe you for saving my life," he told her. It was only now that he was able to sort out in his mind all that had happened to him. "Many thanks for your kindness, reckon I'd have been grub for the lobos by now if you hadn't cum along when you did."

"My name is Smokey Harrison ma-am." and extended his hand in friendship, a custom of the time.

The girl was at a loss as to what he was saying, yet she was sure he was speaking to her. Shyly she accepted his hand, though she knew not why, and felt a thrill course through her body.

Thirty days had passed since the Indian maiden had discovered Smokey's broken body. The cowboy was up and about now, walking some and striving to strengthen the muscles in his mistreated body.

Each day the cowboy improved, his young body regaining the strength and vigor he had lost from the wreck on the slide. The swelling on his damaged head had shrunk back to normal, no longer was there a nerve-wracking, agonizing pain. Thanks to the moss poultices that Dove had daily prepared for his damaged shoulder, it too was healing nicely. His broken ribs were showing improvement, though far from being healed.

The faith of the girl of the wilderness, and the knowledge of her herbs and plants, were working their magic on Smokey Harrison's recovery. He knew this and wondered how he could ever repay her.

The girl was kept busy from sunup to sundown. Attending to the camp chores, venturing into the woods for a fat spruce grouse, perhaps even digging out some wild turnip bulbs or those of the illusive sego lily; a common source of food at the camps of her people.

She had added on to the shelter, making room for her to sleep along side Smokey, and giggled when remembering when she had slept under the same blanket as he. Fearing he might not approve, she hadn't told him what she had done, even though it was a means of keeping his chilled body pleasantly warm and on the road to recovery.

When the darkness of night lured them to the shelter and their respective blankets, Smokey would help her with the

English talk, and she in turn would help him understand her own language.

He asked her if she would mind if he called her Dove, not that Dove That Sings wasn't her full name, and the appropriate one. It was just that he was used to talking like his peers, the cowboys of the open range, and the easy manner they had of abbreviating such long titles. Some figured them as lazy, others accepted their talk as—just cowboy talk!

The girl was silent for a moment, broken by the clicking of her chipmunk talk. She raised herself from the blanket, resting on an elbow, and stared long at the cowboy who lay next to her. After figuring out how to answer him, she spoke. "...yes, Dove will be happy if you wish to do this!"

It wasn't long until they both had made great strides in understanding each other's talk, and in so doing had made life much easier for them both. By the means of sign language and a smattering of pigeon-English, Dove told him of the renegade *kutenai* bunch who had held her as a lowly slave, and how they had treated her.

"Smokey was furious at hearing her story. "I reckon that bunch o' pot-lickers need a good tunin' up," he said.

"A good thing I wasn't around—there would a bin one helluva hullabloo take place in that camp for certain!"

Dove listened with much interest, and shuddered under her blanket—feeling the wrath of the cowboy.

Finally, she asked, "...ww-hat is—pot-licker...?"

The cowboy lay quiet, busting at the seams to better control himself when suddenly the dam broke and out erupted a burst of hilarious laughter. Dove listened with interest, wondering what she had done wrong, when suddenly she too began to follow his example. Together they laughed with abandon, an uncontrolled mirth echoing far into the dark forest.

Smokey soon had to stop, his damaged rib cage no longer able to handle the unexpected exertion. Several days would pass before he was able to recover. He did explain to her the phrase he had used was cowboy slang, intended to compare the unfortunate recipient to a hungry dog!

They both lay quiet, recovering from the unexpected outburst. Somehow they felt at ease, they both felt a bond tightening between them. After another stretch of silence, Dove turned to the cowboy—she knew that he was still awake.

"Smok'ee," she said. "Dove must make talk with you."

Smokey stirred some in his blanket, then replied, "Sounds good to me Dove, tell me what is on your mind."

"You are now my husband—and Dove is now your wife—it is the custom of the *palouse,* my people!

"...when a man and woo-man...sleep in the same lodge together for five suns...they are then known as married people...this shelter is your lodge Smok'ee—I have slept in your lodge for many suns—one moon has now past.

"Dove is now your wife!"

Smokey Harrison reared up from his blanket, shocked no doubt, and gazed long at the girl. "I'll be a gol-darned whippersnapper," he said, still struggling to digest what the girl had just told him.

"If that don't beat all! He was still gazing at the maiden laying in her blanket, watching the glow from the camp fire embers reflecting in her dusky eyes; and he noticed tears were waiting to flow.

After a long period of silence, he suddenly erupted with a cowboy yell that spooked Bandit, who had been close by loafing in his nightly spot not far from Dove's cooking fire, the fire light was a comfort to the lonely animal.

After several yahoos and yippees, Smokey took Dove in his arms for the first time, whose tears were now flowing.

She now knew that Smokey had accepted her words, and was thrilled that they now were man and wife. She never returned Smokey's hug, knowing that to do so would cause him more pain at the site of his sore ribs.

She did however return his kisses!

After they had calmed down some and settled in their blankets, a mischievous Dove asked him another question, "Smok'ee! What is this strange thing you call a whippersnapper?"

The cowboy was at a loss as how to reply. He had never thought about it much, only to say, "I don't rightly know, Dove.

"Reckon it is just a term I picked up from the nesters and range riders back at my folks ol' spread along the Big Bend, "I reckon it could have several meanings, like the talk you have been teaching to this cowboy.

"It is sometimes used as a cuss word, other times it could be a warm, friendly greeting spoken to a long lost friend."

One more time she questioned him about one of the difficult words that he frequently used. "Hullabaloo!"

Smokey scratched his head on this one, sorting out in his mind how to make her understand. Dove patiently waited for him to reply, Smokey was grinning when he spoke, "Well you see Dove, a group of people sometimes get in a fight—there are two sides—the good guys and the bad ones.

"The bad guys are the ones who usually start it. In no time at all fists are flying, sometimes bottles and chairs as well, if it happens to be in a saloon. There is much shoutin' and cussin' a goin' on, a swingin' of clubs and shooting six-guns too!

"Many of them find themselved badly injured, a few are gunned down and die where they fall.

"It is one helluva hullabaloo to get mixed up in!"

Dove appeared satisfied at the answers he gave her, and snuggled back beside her husband, who was plumb wore out after explaining the meaning of these tough English words.

They no longer slept in separate blankets, one was more than enough for now!

One morning Smokey awoke to the sound of Dove's clicking talk. She was out by her cooking fire preparing their first meal of the day, the aroma coming from his beat-up old coffee pot was driving him crazy.

Dove was always up early preparing her husband's breakfast, it was the custom of her people. First thing she would do was check the small campsite and the surrounding forest for danger, her nose twitching, her chipmunk chatter speaking to any that might hear, including the wild ones who would sometimes answer her back.

Feeling that all was safe and secure, she would find Bandit and bring him back to their makeshift shelter. Bandit appeared pleased to be close to the humans, and would watch with interest as the girl kindled the fire and hustled about preparing the morning meal. Dove's wilderness medicine had worked its magic. Bandit's injured leg was now healed, he was fit as a fiddle and raring to continue the journey

He watched as Dove walked to the stream which was close by. It was there she would attend to her morning rituals, and after chucking her clothes she would cleanse herself in the cold mountain water, all the time clucking her chipmunk talk. After caring for her hair with a hand-crafted brush that had been given to her by a black robe from the *palouse* mission school, she would return to the shelter and wait for Smokey to crawl out of the blankets.

She was happy to see him emerge from out of the shelter, shirt in hand, and saunter down to the stream. "Mornin' darlin'," he would say in passing, "you're sure a lookin' right purty today.

"I reckon ol' Smokey will wander over yonder and get cleaned up, sure can't stand much o' that cold water though— gives the chills to my busted up ribs that are mighty hard to shake."

Smokey was Bandits best friend, having both been together since the horse was just an orphan mustang colt. On seeing Smokey head for the stream the horse would follow him, and after quenching his thirst, watched with interest as the cowboy took his morning bath.

When the cowboy and his horse returned to the camp, they were greeted by the aroma of brewed coffee, a pair of plump mouth-watering grouse sizzling on a spit and the soothing chatter of Dove's chipmunk lingo.

After the meal, Smokey and his new wife were sitting by the fire, absorbing the wonder of it all. The sun had now crept over the eastern horizon, putting to flight the mysterious shadows of the night. The squirrels and chipmunks were making their presence known, chattering their lingo which pleased Dove immensely. "I reckon them little critters are a talking to you Dove," Smoky said in a teasing manner.

"They are my friends Smok'ee," she replied. "The talk they make tells Dove many things…like the strange persons…who are close to our camp. Her eyes were closely watching, her nose was twitching, and her ears were straining to pick up the slightest sound.

The clicking of a startled chipmunk could now be heard, its volume increasing by the second. "Listen Smok'ee, my friend is telling us these men are of the People, bad ones, who wish to take Dove back to their hidden camp.

"It is in this place they will beat her, and tie her with the dogs again—a shame that Dove cannot allow them to do!"

Smokey's dander was on the rise, he was standing now buckling on his six-gun, preparing to face them head on.

"Don't you worry none darlin', your husband will not allow the miserable sidewinders to harm you again.

"Crawl back in the shelter—here's my rifle—shoot them if you have to!" and he had just recently showed her how to handle the Marlin, and to aim it straight and true. Dove was an avid learner, and was soon shooting as good as her husband.

The girl did as she was told, and had no sooner entered the shelter when a blood-curdling whoop could be heard. Riding out of the forest came two Indian warriors, riding paint-daubed ponies.

Dove who had been watching through a gap in the spruce boughs, gasped in shock. She recognized the paint ponies and the riders as belonging to the *kutenai* renegades, a ruthless, cruel group of people who delighted in murder and mayhem. She knew all right, Dove had been there as a slave and was a living witness to their savagery.

Smokey Harrison was checking the loads in his six-gun, preparing himself for a fight. Then he gave a start, walking up beside him stood his new wife, a determined young lady risking her life to stand beside her husband, and together face the wrath of the evil renegades.

With another whoop that sent a chill rippling down Smokie's spine, the two warriors charged across the small clearing, one brandishing a war spear, the other waving a tomahawk; both ready to unleash the deadly weapons.

"Time we stopped them Dove," Smokey shouted, his voice on the rise, "else we'll both lose our hair.

"You take the one on the left, I'll pick off the other one."

Two guns fired in unison, two dead Indians fell from the paint ponies they had been riding, and two young newlyweds were wrapped in each other's arms. Dove That Sings was crooning her favorite tune that reminded Smoky of a mourning dove serenading the end of a long hazardous day.

With the noose of his lasso looped around the dead ones ankles, the other end knotted securely around the saddle horn, Smokey and Bandit drug the bodies back into the forest where he covered them with brush and spruce boughs. Least I can do, he reckoned, knowing that if the renegades had caught them unawares, both he and Dove would have been skinned alive, their tortured bodies left for the lobo and raven to fight over.

On his return, they packed up their meager belongings and prepared to continue Smokey's trek to the eastern prairie. Dove never cared where Smokey traveled, as long as he took her with him!

"Them too Injun hosses will come in mighty handy," Smokey reasoned, knowing Dove had already chosen one to ride. "The other we'll use as a pack horse to bring along our grub and blankets, and what not.

"Sure hope we can soon find us a tradin' post in these here mountains, else we might starve plumb to death."

Dove knew this would never happen. With her ingrained knowledge of survival in the wilderness, she knew they would never want for food.

They were low on the basics though. Smokey's meager salt supply was depleted by Dove's craving for the valuable mineral, and the coffee was near gone—two were now drinking it instead of one. Other items, flour, bacon, beans, jerky and such, they could do without, relying on Dove's knowledge of the great outdoors to keep them alive.

Leaving the rock slide behind them, the young riders rode away to find their destiny. Smokey Harrison who had finally taken a wife, though with tongue in cheek, he reckoned Dove That Sings had entrapped him with the strange marriage custom of her people.

It was of no matter, he adored Dove, who in turn worshipped the cowboy with all her heart. She had saved his life, and was more than happy to do so. He in turn saved her from the clutches of the cruel renegade Kutenai, which was a great blessing to them both.

From breaking daylight until far into the day, they traveled, reveling in the majesty of the mighty Rockies. As night time drew near, they would locate a suitable campsite, one that would offer them shelter from the elements, grazing for their three horses and fuel for the cooking fire.

One morning while Dove was attending to her morning rituals, Smokey was able to shoot a deer which had wandered in close to camp. It was a yearling muley, whose tender meat was a delicious addition to their scanty food supply—all it lacked to make it more so was salt!

They traveled slow but sure, breaking trail through virgin country that no one had set foot in before. Through dense forests, down into steep rugged canyons, and then up top again. Often they were forced to scale high ridges to see what they would be riding into next. Then, while the horses were taking a breather, they would dismount to stretch their legs, at the same time admiring the grandeur of this magnificent world of mountains.

After one of the more grueling climbs, Smokey and Dove were sitting on a ledge with their legs dangling off into space, they were absorbing the peace and quiet of this special place while munching on venison jerky, freshly prepared by Dove from the meat of the mule deer.

"Reckon this must be right next to heaven," Smokey said, his voice disturbing the solitude.

"*Great Spirit* is here!" Dove replied, waving her arm in all directions, even extending it straight up into the sky.

"Dove must leave an offering to the *holy one*, before we leave this place—it is a custom of the People!"

With that spoken, she removed a packet of tobacco from her possibles bag and sprinkled a generous amount on a nearby flat slab of stone. Then, the remainder of the coveted weed was flung off into space, to be whisked away into oblivion by a playful mountain thermal.

Smokey Harrison was plumb upset watching her throw away all that tobacco. If he had only known! His own supply had been smoked up weeks ago, leaving him to suffer. It had been an agonizing time—one helluva time in fact.

Removing his pipe from a saddle bag, he showed it to Dove, who smiled and recognized it for what it was. "Got any more of that tobacco in your satchel?" he asked.

"Your husband could sure use a pipe full 'bout now—bin a coons age since I've had a good smoke."

Having a difficult time to fully understand his cowboy lingo, she was still smiling when she took the pipe and placed it beside the tobacco on the flat rock. She was thrilled as could be, reasoning that her husband had offered her the pipe to be a part of the sacred offering to the *Great Spirit*.

Smokey was plumb irritated, a painful experience in fact, to watch her placing the pipe beside the tobacco. This hadn't been his intention at all. In his own cowboy manner he had merely asked her if he could smoke a pipe full.

Unable to stand it any longer, he stooped low by the stone and tamped his pipe full of the sacred weed. Then, with a sulfur match taken from his pocket, lit the pipe and inhaled a mouthful of smoke into his lungs. A relaxed expression settled across his face, a look of contentment too!

Dove That Sings was shocked at first, watching her husband light up the pipe and all. Her offering was to the Great Spirit, and not to be smoked by her husband. Preparing to give him a good lecture on the ways of the People, her attitude suddenly changed.

"You are now a sacred person Smok'ee." she said, clicking her chipmunk talk. "My husband has made medicine with the *Great Spirit*—who has shared his tobacco with a cowboy.

"My husband has smoked the sacred smoke—and will now be a sacred person to his wife—*Dove That Sings.*

Before their departure from the high mountain spur, Dove gathered up the tobacco from the flat stone, dropping it back into the packet from whence it came. It was only then, with a proud smile on her face, she handed it to Smokey.

"You must take this tobacco too, Smok'ee. It is medicine from the *Great Spirit*, who is now your brother."

Smokey accepted the tobacco, and though still in a daze from all the words she had spoken, and their meaning, he refilled his pipe, stoked fire to it and headed back down off the ridge with a smile on his face.

Riding relaxed in the saddle, his teeth still gripping the pipe stem, he was smiling when he spoke. He talked to his pipe the way he was accustomed to talking to his horse.

"I reckon this is as close to heaven as I'll ever get," he said, tucking the now cold pipe back in his pocket. "It ain't bin all that bad though,

"After Dove finding us both in one hell of a fix, like she did, Bandit, I reckon if she hadn't cum along with her wilderness medicine and savvy, we'd both a bin knockin' on old St. Peter's gate by now.

"I'm sure one lucky hombre, she must be one of the Great Spirit's special angels, a loving, pretty little gal, who was sent down here to be my darlin' wife!"

An appaloosa gelding who was known as Bandit, due to his wild ways when just a colt, perked up his ears at the sound of his name being spoken. The horse appeared to understand, and blew a snuffled reply. Sounding like a horse's version of an aborted sneeze, it took the combined effort of the gelding's nostrils and lips to let Smokey know that he agreed with what was being said.

Dove, who had been bringing up the rear—riding drag—had been able to hear part of his last sentence. She never could make out all of the words, but recognized the following phrases...'special angel'...'pretty little gal' and 'my darlin' wife'. To listen to Smokey talk about her this way pleased her immensely.

One day, as they topped over a high ridge of eroded sandstone, the two riders were greeted by a panorama of brown-hued rolling hills. In the background was a vast expanse of green, becoming as one with the sky along the distant horizon. The rugged Rockies were now behind them, the foothills and prairie were no longer an uncertain destination.

Heaving a great sigh, Smokey Harrison was sure relieved their long trek was coming to an end. To the cowboy, this new country spread out below had became almost a myth, not really certain that it even existed. But now he knew. He was seeing it with his own eyes.

The day was long spent before they made it down off the ridge. "Time we wus huntin' us a camp site," Smokey drawled. Our hosses are plumb tuckered out, bin a long day for ol' Smokey and Dove too."

Dove gigged the Indian pony towards a cluster of willow, beckoning her husband to follow. She was clicking her chipmunk talk as she rode, sensing there was water close by. Smokey was at a loss as to know how she could find water, good clean water too, water that was fit to drink!

He was now riding beside her when he spoke, "You've done it again Dove, when are you going to tell your husband how you do this?"

Dove was smiling, still making her chipmunk talk. "It is a way of the People, Smok'ee.

"It is medicine, good medicine that has been given Dove— by *Great Spirit*—whose tepee is up in the sky!" and she signed to the heavens as she spoke.

"*Sacred God* sits at the door of his tepee, watching his people. He is sometimes happy with his people—he is sometimes sad with what he sees!"

Tweaking the end of her nose, Dove was crooning her strange music when she answered his question, "It is my nose that tells me this thing, Smok'ee!

"Dove That Sings—smell water—sometimes far away!"

She was tweaking an ear as she continued her talk. "Water speaks with this *yakima* girl—sometimes ear hear this water telling me to come—and play with her!"

The call of a mourning dove echoed along the small creek basin nestled along the front range of the Rockies. Nearby in a wilderness shelter, two young people slept the sleep of the weary, snuggled together as well they should be.

The tune of the mourning dove echoed near the camp, the inquisitive creature wondering if he was the only one still awake in the aspen woods. The tune awoke Dove. Smiling, she left her bed and cooed an answer to the wild one, then returned to her husband and their blankets.

A peaceful silence settled over this wild place, the two who cooed the lonesome song of the mourning dove were now fast asleep.

✳ ✳ ✳ CHAPTER 5 ✳ ✳ ✳

Smokey Harrison and his lovely nymph of the forest spent several days camping at the willow clearing, refreshing the horses that were enjoying the good graze that grew here in such abundance. After the skimpy pickings in the mountains, they reckoned this was a Garden of Eden in comparison.

Dove discovered a modest beaver dam not far from camp. It was here they would bathe and scrub clean their travel-stained clothing. Each evening they would go skinny-dipping enjoying the luxury of an endless supply of water. With a mischievous grin Smokey would tease her, "Reckon this must be how Adam and Eve lived in the Garden, a runnin' around buck-naked and all!"

Not understanding his humor, Dove did not attempt to puzzle over his words. Back at her childhood home along the Snake River there was no such thing as bathing suits. To swim in the raw was a natural thing to do.

Several days passed, and with the horses in much better spirits, they continued on their southern journey. Bandit even attempted to buck Smokey out of the saddle, which was the first time for a long stretch of country.

Following an unknown creek which was twisting and winding a path out through a break in the mountains, they eventually rode up to a trading post. It was a modest structure compared to the ones Smokey had dealt with back across the mountains.

Lee's Trading Post a rickety sign read. Though smaller in size, there were two more created out of the same pine-slab material—*we buy furs—whiskey for sale.* Reining in at a hitch rail, they secured their horses and then walked over to see what was there. "Follow me Dove, let's go see what we can find."

Dove was hesitant to do what her husband had asked. Her eyes were as big as saucers, she was clicking her chipmunk talk, something that happened when she was startled or entering foreign territory,

Never in her life had she been inside a trading post, to do so now would take a bunch of courage and grit.

However, after much persuasion from her husband who had taken her hand, they walked in together. Dove gasped in surprise. Never had she witnessed anything like this before. There was so much to see, she just stood rooted to the dirt floor, attempting to absorb all of the merchandise that was arrayed from the ceiling to the floor, and all points in between.

An old timer greeted them at the door. He wore a slouch hat, was smoking a pipe and his clothing appeared as if they had not been around soap and water for a long dry spell. "My name is William Samuel Lee," he said, at the same time lighting a coal-oil lantern to better break the dark shadows of the windowless room.

The old timer appeared as if he wanted to visit some, which never bothered Smokey any. He had been away from civilization for such a long time that to hear another's voice besides Dove's was like coming home after a long ride.

"I had me a tradin' post down yonder, on Lariat Cross crik," Lee said, after stoking his pipe. "'bout a hundred miles to the south, as a crow flies—close by the Yankee border," and he gestured into the far horizon as he spoke.

"I dun real good to start with, had good business with the mounted police, and the Bloods who were mighty good trappers. The settlers were scarce as hens teeth, a few Mormons dropped by now and then is all.

"It was me and a clan of Bloods who gave the name Lariat Cross to that mountain stream. Heard tell that some folks decided to change the name—they now call it Lee's Creek—the Mormon settlement down that way is named Lee's Creek too."

Wiping a tear from his eye, he continued his talk, "Makes an old trader feel dog-gone good having something like that named after him, sure a humbling feelin' though. Anyhow business dwindled off to next to nothing, so I pulled up stakes and brung my tradin' post up here—lock, stock and barrel.

"I reckon the old log trading post might still be a standin' down yonder. If you folks happen to run across it why use it as your own!"

"Don't rightly know how far we're a goin' Mr. Lee, we'll sure know when we get there."

"There's a lake on down the trail aways—name is Lee Lake," he said proudly. "A good place to camp if you're of a mind to."

"We're runnin' low on grub—reckon we'll have a look see at what you got to offer.

"My name is Smokey Harrison," the cowboy added. Turning to Dove who had remained speechless, he introduced her as his wife.

"My pleasure to meet you folks," the old timer said, doffing his hat to Dove. "Not many folks stop here anymore—reason I'm closin' down and movin' yonder across the prairie to the Cypress Hills.

"You folks arrived at the right time. I'll give you a good deal today, save me a packin' it across the prairie with me!"

Once again the cowboy took Dove's hand and together they began to do their shopping. By the looks of things Lee's business had been slow as he had said, finding a well stocked trading post, even if it was all crammed into the small log structure.

First it was food Smokey was after, finding salt and sugar and flour too. Then beans and bacon and hardtack biscuits packed in a tin. He did not forget coffee and tobacco, with sulphur matches thrown in for good measure. And a two-man tent, ammunition for his two guns and a Bowie knife for Dove, complete with a fancy tanned scabbard adorned with the beadwork of the Cree.

Dove was overjoyed with the knife, and promptly strapped it around her waist with a leather string. While Smokey was taking the provisions out to the pack horse for the trader to do his ciphering, Dove finished her inspection of the post. Suddenly she froze in her tracks, her hand on the hilt of her new Bowie, staring with awe at the mounted head of a bull elk fit snugly into a dusty corner.

On Smokey's return, he noticed Dove, who was clicking her chipmunk talk and staring at the six-point denizen of the forest. Taking her hand, he explained. "This animal is not alive Dove, it is dead. The head and horns have bin mounted this way for people to see.

"It is a great honor for white eyes to shoot one of these animals, big medicine for all to see!"

To change the subject, Smokey led her over to the clothing section. He reckoned Dove needed something to wear besides her buckskins. He found her a pair of jeans and several shirts to go with them, making sure they were of the right size. Then a tiny pair of boots and a cowboy hat, a black one the same color as the one he wore. He found her a warm coat made by the famous Hudson Bay Company, followed by a bottle of perfume with a tantalizing scent. Only then did they leave Lee's Trading Post.

After settling up with Samuel Lee, and Smokey had paid him with gold dust taken from the plump satchel that held his share of the partners mining venture, he shook the old timer's hand. "Bin a pleasure a dealin' with you Mr. Lee," he spoke with respect to the friendly old timer. "Reckon it's time Dove and I should be a headin' down the trail."

With a wink, the trader Lee spoke once again to the cowboy, "This here pack saddle I've got cinched on your paint Injun pony here, I'm throwing in on the deal, don't see how you can carry all this stuff without the proper equipment, 'sides I've got several more a kickin' around here somewhere."

After showing Smokey the intricate secret of proper packing and how to use the diamond hitch, the trader stepped back to inspect his work, a broad smile spreading across his whiskered face.

It was now late afternoon, the trader Lee was reluctant to see them leave, and it was plain to see that he was hoping they would stay and visit. "You folks are welcome to camp here for the night," he said, "an old trader could sure use the company."

"Reckon we'll mosey on Mr. Lee, appreciate your offer though. "We're a huntin' us a spread of our own down yonder on the prairie. Bin thinkin' of startin' a horse ranch like my old pard Kelly Tucker has done over west o' the Rockies."

The small pack outfit made it to the south-eastern shoreline of Lee Lake before nightfall, and set up camp in a long-used stop over for migrating Indians. While Smokey was erecting their new tent, Dove was kindling a cooking fire using the sulfur matches to ignite the dried willow sticks that she had gathered.

"Fire sticks—good medicine," she said, gazing in wonder at the burning twigs. Never before had she seen matches until she met up with her husband. "Much better than *yakima* fire sticks—hard work to get fire, must do this for long time," and rubbed her palms together in the age-old method of fire by friction.

After a hearty supper, Dove just could not wait any longer, and brought out the new clothes that Smokey had bought her. After chucking her buckskins, she tried on the cowboy jeans and found that they fit her slim figure. Then it was the shirts, whose different colors thrilled her to no end.

The boots and black cowboy hat she would never part with, and there was something else, a small bundle tucked beside the shirts. Opening it she discovered a pair of lace-fringed bloomers, a bright red neckerchief and a bottle of perfume, which was Smokey's surprise.

Holding the bloomers up with both hands, puzzled as to what they were used for, she closely examined the two leg holes and the larger hole at the top. Clicking her chipmunk talk that she used when confronted with a mystery such as this, she turned to Smokey who was doubled up in convulsive laughter, tears streaming down his cheeks; the spasm of laughter causing his tender rib-cage to scream for him to stop.

Then to add to the hilarity, Dove stuck her head through the large hole, her eyes peering out through a leg hole, still at a loss as to what this strange article of clothing was used for.

Laughter is good for the soul they say, but as Smokey watched Dove go through this last maneuver, he was surely blessed. He tipped over backwards, both arms wrapped around his screaming ribs, laughing until he was sick.

"No more Dove, please no more! I can't handle any more of this." With that said, he arose and with the bloomers in hand attempted to show her how to use this feminine piece of negligee. Hip-hopping from one leg to the other, he managed to pull the bloomers, one small hole for each leg, on up around his belt, then turning to Dove, using sign language to show her what they were meant for.

He discovered that she was now laughing, suffering the same fate as her husband, laughing until she was sick. Not so much from the bloomers, but from the spectacle of Smoky's hilarious dance with the lace-trimmed unmentionables.

They continued their journey into the southeast following well-used Indian trails. In doing so they encountered the odd wilderness stump ranch, an occasional squatter shack and now and then a makeshift hunting camp used by the Blackfoot.

Proudly Dove wore her new cowboy clothes, "Dove is now cowboy like you Smok'ee," she fondly told him one day.

"This one no longer *yakima* girl—no more like People, who use tanned deer skin dress and feather in hair!"

It pleased Smokey to hear her talk this way, he was sure enough proud of her. And as he admired her auburn-hued face, framed by her shoulder length hair—the black hat he had given her became a perfect match for her lovely profile.

"You are one beautiful little gal, Dove. I'm sure happy that you found me when you did.

"Reckon you saved ol' Smokey's life, and to become my wife is a blessing I never thought would happen!"

"There is much love for Smok'ee in this one's heart," she replied, looking long at his whiskered face.

He turned to her, and grinning his cowboy smile that she loved so much, Smokey said, "Reckon I love you too darlin'!"

One day, while stopping at one of these deserted camp sites to prepare a meal, Dove appeared uneasy, and while Smokey was caring for the horses, she couldn't settle down. She moved about the site with caution, her nose was twitching and she was clicking her chipmunk talk.

When Smokey returned after tethering the horses out to graze, he noticed that Dove was plumb upset. "What's wrong darlin?" he asked.

"You look different, your face is pale like you had just seen a ghost."

Returning to stand beside him, she looked long at his face before she spoke. "Smok'ee, this bad place—evil spirits hear—they want us to go away!"

Smokey had never seen her act this way before. Looking into her eyes he knew that she was plumb serious, and reckoned it wasn't the right time or place to tease her about such things.

"What makes you say this Dove," he asked, watching her twitching nose, listening with interest to her chipmunk talk.

"Come Smok'ee, Dove will show you!"

Taking his hand, she took him to the edge of the small clearing and pointed into a copse of birch willow. "See Smok'ee, this is what upsets me so!"

The cowboy took one look, and that was enough!

Lying side by side were two skeletons. One was tiny, that of a baby, the other was an adult with one arm around her child. The scattered remains of the clothing was sufficient for them to know that it had been an Indian mother and her baby.

And that was not all. Two arrows dangled from the woman's rib cage, evidence enough of the way she had been killed. The babe had received the same treatment, yet another arrow was positioned in what had been the wee ones heart.

Dove insisted they leave this evil place, and as they rode away munching on jerky and hard-tack biscuits, she offered Smokey a small scrap of the unfortunate mother's dress. "See, Smokey!

"This woman was *kutenai*—Dove knows this beadwork, your wife a slave in their camp for many suns."

Smokey remained silent, appeared as if he was deep in thought. "Reckon you're right Dove. I am certain them arrows are Blackfoot war weapons, heard tell the two tribes were bitter enemies—couldn't stand the sight of each other.

"The Blackfoot were mighty protective of the buffalo that roamed this country, and to see the Kutenai cross over the Rockies, returning to their camps loaded down with a winters supply of meat was reason enough to go on the war path."

Into the south and east they rode, traveling along the eastern slope of the Rockies, stopping at their leisure to fish, pick berries, explore strange places, and such. They were happy to be together and that was all that mattered. Yet, deep in Smokey's heart, was a desire to find a horse ranch like his old pard Kelly Tucker had found.

Few people did they see, a lone Indian now and then, who appeared startled as they rode by, who most likely was on a vision quest and quickly vanished in the forest.

One day as they were trout fishing at a beaver pond, they were startled by the appearance of a lone white man. He appeared as if he had been away from civilization for a considerable stretch of time, long-haired and bearded, his clothing in decrepit condition, but he was a cheerful sort.

He approached the Harrisons, the palm of his hand open wide in the peace sign of all wanderers, including the natives of the region. "How-do," he said in a raspy voice. "Mind if I join you and set a spell? I haven't had the pleasure of visiting with the likes of you folks for a long dry spell."

The coffee pot was bubbling on one of Dove's smokeless fires, and she was frying fresh-caught trout in Smokey's old battered skillet. "Reckon you must be hungry stranger," Smokey said. "Sit a spell, we'll share our grub with you, least we can do!"

Listening to Smokey's talk resulted in Dove frowning, and clicking her chipmunk lingo. "It is only two coffee cups we have Smok'ee," and they were empty bean tins. "No problem Dove—we'll make out!" her husband replied with a grin.

The stranger ate like a savage wolf, devouring trout after trout, until Smokey was forced to throw in the line and start fishing all over again. "When was the last time you et stranger?" Smokey asked, frowning as he watched the fourth tin of coffee go down the gullet of the bearded loner.

"Can't rightly tell stranger," came the reply. "Bin livin' on berries and little ground critters for a mighty long stretch."

"Why you do this Smok'ee?" Dove asked. "Why you give this one our fish and coffee?" She once again began her clicking lingo, showing her displeasure of his doing so.

"Dove darling, I reckon you don't know!

"When we were just small kids a livin at home, we were trained in the ways of the Code of the West. Never let a stranger go away hungry! Treat them with respect—the same way as you would like to be treated if you were a walkin' in his boots."

Dove clicked her chipmunk talk once more, not really understanding what he was telling her.

"By jove!" the stranger said, interrupting their talk. "Sounds to me like a family of chipmunks are living here." and brought out from his pocket a wire snare and began uncoiling it in front of Dove's startled eyes.

"Sure make me a good supper." he muttered, already smacking his lips in anticipation of the juicy meat.

"No! No!" Dove screamed. "Do not eat the little ones, they are Dove's medicine—they are Dove's friends."

Smokey was watching with interest from where the stranger had been squatting, and as he stood up, a willow branch upset the sweat-stained hat from off his head allowing the cowboy to witness a sorry sight. A round scabbed-over wound, showing where the unfortunate fellow had been scalped; and lived to tell about it.

"He crazy man," Dove said, as she watched him leave the fishing hole.

"I reckon so," Smokey replied. "He's lost the top-notch from off the top o' his head—reckon he tangled with one o' these Blackfoot, who left him this way—figurin' that he was dead!

"The poor devil don't seem to know where he's a goin', or where he came from. I reckon an experience like that would drive most people plumb loco too."

"Smok'ee," Dove asked. "What does this word—loco—mean?"

Autumn was now creeping into the forests and prairies, turning the leaves into an eye-pleasing golden hue. The grasses on the prairie were changing too, into a dusky-hued shade of brown. This change of seasons caused the Harrisons to look for a winter camp site.

Still traveling along the eastern slope of the Rockies, they eventually arrived at a wilderness river. This water shed was known to the Blackfoot as the *mokowanis*, meaning Belly, referring to a long ago tribe who once lived here, and were regarded as beggars of food; hence the tribal sign a rubbing gesture across the abdomen.

This early tribe was known as the *atsina* people, a detached segment of the *arapaho*, and were regarded as the ones who are always hungry, referring to themselves as *belly people* or *big bellies*.

Several miles up the Belly, the adventurous couple discovered what they had been looking for. A dense lodgepole forest grew down to one side of the river, on the other side was a broad grass-covered prairie, consuming several acres of forest.

Used for unknown years by the native American people, the flat prairie had received an Indian name *beebee flats,* out of respect for an old Blood chief whose name was Beebee.

Dove That Sings was thrilled with their winter camp in the lodgepoles, and together she and her husband soon had built a comfortable lodge to spend the winter in. She was now heavy with child, and back to wearing her buckskin dress, looking forward to the arrival of her husband's son. She just knew it would be a son, her secret medicine had told her so.

Smokey was equally satisfied, knowing that if Dove was happy, he would be happy too. It was now time for him to go hunting and bag some winter meat, with all the elk sign scattered around he reckoned it should be easy pickings.

Early the next morning, after kindling Dove's cooking fire, he put on the coffee pot and began oiling his Marlin, He felt somewhat guilty, having neglected cleaning the gun for quiet a spell.

"Reckon ol' Smokey must take better care of you," he muttered. "You are a good faithful friend," he was speaking to his 30.30. as if it could hear what he said. "You have saved my bacon on more than one occasion," least I can do is keep you clean!"

Dove had now left their winter lodge, and was listening with interest to Smoky's conversation. "Why do you talk to this gun?" she asked.

Her unexpected voice startled him some, and looking up with an embarrassing smile, he found that he was uncertain as to how he should answer her. "Reckon I'm just a talkin' to an ol' friend." he said, and continued cleaning his rifle.

"Look at me Smok'ee! Dove has just found a new name for her husband.

"The *yakima* people and your new son will know you as the one who—talks to his gun.
"Smok'ee big medicine now...*gun talker...*!"

Smokey Harrison, alias *gun talker,* was up at the crack of dawn the next morning, and with his rifle in hand slipped away into the shadows. One of his coat pockets was stuffed with jerky, in the other with ammo for the .30.30. He hunted in earnest until night time returned to the land of the Belly. He hadn't fired a shot, from the Marlin, in fact he hadn't seen anything to shoot at.

Grumbling to himself, knowing that he had a long walk ahead of him, he reckoned he should head back for home; a winter lodge on the bank of the river. It grew downright chilly after the disappearance of the sun, and after pulling his coat collar high, a disappointed hunter headed back down river to be with Dove.

From far up river came the mating call of a bull elk. Echoing an answer, yet another wooer of the night whistled a challenge. He too wanted in on the wild and wooly action, and was working himself into a feral rage, determined to fight for his share of the romance of the wild ones.

Smokey Harrison reckoned his wilderness home was just ahead. Then he heaved a weary sigh knowing that he was right. A dancing light was reflecting from off the lodgepoles that sheltered the camp. He knew the reflection was from Dove's cooking fire, who most likely had piled on a heap of logs; a signal fire for her husband to see.

Moving in close, Smoky suddenly stopped and froze in his tracks, he was certain he had heard the sound of a man talking, and the sound of laughter too. That a man was in the camp, he was sure of!

His heart skipped a beat, and then it was two. "Dove!" he whispered, wishing he had never left her alone.

"What has happened to my Dove? If she has been harmed—ol' Smokey's a declarin' war, be he-ell to pay along the Belly!"

Levering a cartridge into his Marlin, Smokey injuned up to the camp so he could see, ready to declare war if needed. The fire was blazing bright, as he had reckoned, and there sat Dove on the stool that he had made for her, hewed from a windfall fir tree that had been downed by a bolt of lightning.

She appeared to be listening to the talk of a stranger, a tall, slender man clad in buckskins and wearing a muskrat cap on his head. There was a faded sash around his waist, where hung an impressive knife, encased in the same muskrat fur as his cap.

He was standing by the fire, leaning on a long gun—smiling at Dove, who was staring past the stranger at the appearance of her husband, who was moving in behind him—his Marlin ready for war.

Dove gasped in shock, her hand then covering her mouth. She remained silent, listening to her husband, who appeared angry and upset. "Don't move stranger—if you expect to see another sun!

"Drop that long gun you're a leanin' on—and reach for the stars!"

The stranger did as he was told, and watched as Smokey moved over beside his wife, gun ready and blue flame still flashing from his eyes.

"You all right Dove?" he asked, never taking his eyes off the buckskin clad intruder.

Dove, who had been in shock finally recovered her voice, in fact it was loud and shrill "No! No Smok'ee, do not shoot this man. He has done no harm to Dove.

"His name is Trapper Joe—he is our neighbor—tell Dove what is a neighbor."

Smokey relaxed his vigil of the trapper, settled down some and set his long gun against a stump.

"This trapper has been kind to your wife, Smok'ee. He has told Dove many strange things—stories of this place of many trees, where he has his tepee and traps the beaver and wolf."

Smokey walked over to Trapper Joe, and offered his hand in friendship. The trapper, somewhat relieved, accepted the friendly gesture, knowing this was a man to ride the river with. He would make a good friend, the trapper just knew it.

"Come on over by the fire, from that delicious smell that's a driftin' around the camp, reckon Dove has brewed up one of her hunter's stews."

Dove, who had been listening to her husbands talk, was beaming with pride as she dished up two heaping bowls full, giving one to her husband, and the other to their new neighbor.

"Best meal I've ever et," Trapper Joe said, after cleaning up the third bowl full. Looking at Dove he continued his talk, "You can cook at my fire any old time."

Then, looking at Smokey, he spoke with a wink, "Dove cooks mighty fine stew Smokey Harrison—you're one lucky fellow, lucky indeed."

After the meal Dove retired to her blankets. Smokey and Trapper Joe sat by the fire, smoking their pipes and swapping tall tales with each other. Eventually, Smokey became sleepy, just couldn't keep his eyes open. The long day hunting in the forest was taking its toll.

Suddenly, much later, an exhausted hunter awoke with a start. He looked around in confusion, at a loss as to where he was, and why he was here. Standing beside him was a smiling Dove, her hand resting on his shoulder. "Come to our blankets Smok'ee, your Dove needs you to keep her warm."

"Reckon you're right darlin'—I cannot keep my blasted eyes open," his sleep-dimmed eyes were scanning the clearing. "There was someone here, a trapper I believe.

"I wonder what happened to the story telling son-of-a-gun?"

"Oh, Smok'ee!" his wife was giggling as she spoke. "Trapper Joe go from our camp long time ago, he say he go home now, and smoke by his own fire."

Early the next morning the cowboy was up and about at his usual time, kindling the fire, putting on the coffee pot, and checking on their horse remuda, consisting of his gelding and the two Indian ponies.

After wading the shallow crossing, he found them close by grazing in knee-high forage. As was his custom, he talked to Bandit as he groomed the winter growth of hair, using a rusty well-used curry comb given to him by the trader Lee. Then with the horses in tow, he returned to the shallow crossing of the river. This rocky crossing of the Belly was within a stones throw of the Harrison winter camp.

Daylight was now chasing away the shadows of the dark forest. Entering the camp, he was startled by a strange bundle on the ground beside the entrance to the pine bough-woven winter lodge. "A strange one sure!" he said. "It wasn't here when I left a short time ago."

A closer look revealed a freshly killed quarter of venison. There was no doubt about the meat being fresh, the flesh was still warm and steaming in the crisp morning air.

Dove had now left the lodge, she too was shocked to see fresh meat, and looked at Smokey in wonder. "Have you been hunting this morning?" she asked. "This part of a deer was not here—when Dove take you to our blankets."

"No, no Smokey did not do this," he answered, looking deep into her eyes. It was then she knew that he was not teasing her, as he was prone to do.

They both remained silent, puzzled as to who could have left this welcome addition to their food supply, when a thought entered Smokey's mind, "Dove listen to me. Do you reckon the trapper could have done this?"

She looked up in surprise, smiling as she spoke, "Yes! Trapper Joe has done this kind thing. He is now neighbor, who bring this meat—trade, for supper Dove cook him last night.

"Smok'ee, when will you tell Dove what is a neighbor?"

"Reckon maybe I will, even though you already know what it means. You see, a neighbor might be living next to you in the next tepee, or in a wilderness camp fifty miles away.

"As a rule these neighbors are good friends, and treat each other as such, sometimes they are not friends and can't stand the sight of each other. As my old mother once read to us kids from out of her beloved Bible, '...do unto others as you would have others do unto you...'

"I reckon you and the trapper are good neighbors, you fed him when he was hungry. in his own way he is repaying you in kind; a fat juicy hunk of venison for your cooking fire."

The trapper was a good neighbor, though a lonely one. He dropped by often, knowing that he would be fed a meal, sometimes two; always bringing a small gift for the Harrisons. Sometimes a brace of ruffed grouse it would be, other times the tanned pelt of a mink or martin.

One day when Smokey was out hunting, Dove ventured out of the lodge and discovered a large, well muscled wolf tied to a nearby sapling with a leather string. To her it was a wolf, the color was right, the stature of the animal was right, and the fangs of the animal appeared to be those of a wolf.

She stood transfixed, staring at the animal, who was laying in the grass staring back at her. She knew it would be a friend, a long hairy tail was wagging, thumping the ground, surely a sign of friendliness.

Dove moved closer to the animal, cooing and clicking her chipmunk talk, causing the inquisitive animal to move his head in wonder. Cautiously she reached out her hand and caressed his head, ruffled his ears and scratched him on his shoulders.

Standing now, a long tongue returned the favor, kissing her on the hand, a tail wagging with joy. "You must be hungry," she cooed, noticing the animal's rib cage was showing through the taut hide.

"Dove will find you a piece of venison," she said. "My husband Smokey has not yet found a *wapiti* for us to eat. After her return with a generous piece of the meat taken from the trapper's deer, she spoke again.

"This one will take the leather string from your neck," noticing the tightness of the knot. "You may stay with us, if you are a good wolf.

"You will be one of our clan for a long time!"

The dog, and he was of the shepherd breed, closely resembled his wild cousin, the wolf. Dove would always suspect the trapper as the one who had left the animal tied by her lodge, and would forever believe that he was indeed a wolf.

On Smokey's return, and he had bagged a *wapiti*, he met an excited Dove at the door of the lodge, standing beside her was the large friendly shepherd, a smile on his face—his tongue hanging low.

"See who has come to live with us!" she said, excitement written all over her face. The *palouse* girl then told her husband of all that had taken place since his departure early that morning.

"It's sure a mystery all right," Smokey said, admiring the dog, who was now standing beside him.

"I reckon though it was the trapper who gave us this gift, Dove. Most likely showing us what a true neighbor is like, knowing this wolf will be a good companion to you, and our new son who will soon be with us."

"I have given this wolf a name," she said. He will be known to us as—*grizz!*

"His pretty hair is the same color as a bear—big one that stands like a person, and roars scary words at us!"

Smokey and Trapper Joe became good friends. Often the cowboy would tag along as Joe made the rounds of his extensive trap line, educating his friend in the ways of fur bearing animals, and how to catch them in his traps. He showed him how to remove the skin with a sharp knife and how to stretch and dry, preparing the valuable pelts to be sold at the nearest fur dealer; perhaps the big rendezvous in the early summer.

Late one evening Smokey returned to camp to be greeted by an excited Grizz, who was dashing back and forth between the lodge and Smokey. "Dove! Has something happened to Dove?" The big dog yipped a strange greeting, now standing at the door of the lodge, tail wagging, waiting for the cowboy to come.

Uttering a growl, as Smokey brushed past him and entered the lodge, the dog followed him in. A candle was burning near the bed, allowing him to see Dove covered with her blankets, and a strange wee bundle wrapped in her arms.

Raising her head to see who was there, she was weeping and crooning a strange tune. "Smok'ee! Is that you?" she weakly spoke. "This one offers thanks to the *Great Spirit*—that you have come back to your *Dove That Sings!*

"Come to Dove and see—she will show her husband his new son—who has come to live with us, and become a big strong hunter like his father."

Smoky dropped to his knees beside his wife, the dog was close beside him, intently watching that no harm came to the woman and her new one. She offered the bundle to her husband, and settled back into her blankets.

There were tears in his eyes as he looked into the face of his new son. The wee one was only a few hours old, yet his eyes were open staring at his father. Dark eyes like those of his mother, and dark curly hair.

That night, no prouder man could be found along the eastern front of the Rockies than Smokey Harrison, who was now a father, holding a new son in his arms; a son whose tiny face wrinkled into a scowl, and then began to cry.

He returned his son to Dove. "Our son is hungry Smok'ee," she said, a faint smile was on her face. "I must feed him now—with the milk of a new mother.

"*Dove That Sings* is hungry too, she has been waiting for her husband to come back to lodge—and feed her coffee and the meat of a mighty *wapiti*."

The proud cowboy hustled right out to the cooking fire, adding more fuel to the glowing embers, and prepared his wife the first meal of that long grueling day. Not forgetting Grizz, who received a raw chunk of fat and gristle, Smoky entered the lodge one more time, bringing Dove her supper.

As was the way of the People, Dove was up and about the following day appearing none the worse for wear. Smokey remained close to camp, never out of range of her voice, or the off-tune bark of Grizz, alerting the camp of impending danger.

After several days had passed, Dove appeared uneasy, not her usual happy self. "We must give our son a name," she told Smokey. "So the *Great Spirit* will be happy,

"He is sad when one of his Spirits has no name!"

"Reckon I agree with you Dove, haven't thought about it much though."

"Dove has a name to tell you, she has given much time in finding it. I wish to name him after you…out of respect for his father…which is you, Smok'ee!

"He shall be known by *palouse* people as…*Little Smoke*… you my husband will know him as…little Smok'ee.

"Dove that Sings now has two Smok'ee's—one big hunter, and one little one who will learn the ways of his father."

The cowboy remained quite, mulling over Dove's talk. After a long pause he looked up at Dove and agreed with the Indian name. "Reckon little Smok'ee sounds like a real fine name," he said.

"Reckon I will know him as Smokey Junior though. It will make me happy to have my son using his father's name—Smokey Jr. Harrison."

The long nights of winter gave way to a change of the seasons. It was now spring in Belly river country, late spring when Dove told her husband of her plans. Little Smoke was growing like a weed in a flower garden, clad in tiny buckskin clothing fashioned by his mother.

One night as all three of them settled into their blankets, Dove remained awake. She just couldn't settle down, tossing and turning, finding that sleep had been taken from her by the Spirits.

"Smok'ee, is my husband awake?" she whispered in his ear. "Dove must make talk with husband."

"Reckon so," he grumbled. "I am now! What is it that is troubling you so?

"You bin a buckin' around in these blankets most all night, like a maverick steer with a tail-full of cockle-burs."

"I must leave you, Smok'ee. *Great Spirit* tell Dove to take *Little Smoke* back to *palouse* People. It is his wish that our little one—be raised in the ways of his ancestors—and become a big strong brave!"

Dove That Sings was weeping bitter tears as she talked. Smokey was thunder struck, speechless and angry that Dove wished to take his son away from him. Finally, after finding his voice, he replied, "I can't let you take my son away from me!

"I will not allow Dove to do this thing! After all we've bin through together, how can you just ride away like this?

"The two people I love best, my darlin' wife and our son, Little Smoke?"

Dove's tears continued to flow, Smokey's eyes were damp too, and remained so for a long time. Though Dove loved her white-eyes husband with all her heart, she knew she must answer the urging of the Spirits, or forever be shunned, even cursed by the Holy Ones, who were the inner most essence of her primitive religion.

Grieving, like he had never done so before, Smokey Harrison knew that she would leave him, possibly never to return. The call of the Spirits was much stronger than the love for her husband.

The evening of her departure was a tough one for both Smokey and Dove. She was weeping bitter tears, he was hugging his son so tight the little one began to cry. The tears of a father now mingled with those of his son.

Dove was up top of the Indian pony she loved so well, the other pony was patiently waiting, a pack on his back secured by a diamond hitch. Smokey handed the little one up to his mother, who positioned him inside a blanket-lined cradle board, the child facing the ears of the trailing pack horse.

Crooning her mourning dove tune, Dove That Sings rode into the south seeking an unknown destiny. The last sound Smokey could hear of her voice was the talk of a chipmunk, chattering a goodbye to a broken-hearted cowboy.

Traveling at night, Dove That Sings navigated like her ancestors of old, her nose in line with a distant star.

* * * CHAPTER 6 * * *

Leaving the land of the Belly, Smokey Harrison rode far across hill and prairie, struggling to erase the bitter memories of the past that haunted him night and day.

Hidden deep inside his inner self, the cowboy sensed that he was looking for the illusive pot at the end of the rainbow, that he was sure he had once found, only to have it snatched away from him by the Spirit protectors of Dove That Sings.

From the western Rocky Mountains to the badlands across the eastern prairie he traveled, Bandit enjoying every mile of it. The big gelding mustang had been cooped up far too long at the Belly river camp on Beebee Flats, and was happy to once again have his friend up top in the saddle; a freedom for them both, riding with the wind.

Trailing behind, his tongue hanging low, came a shepherd dog. Although he had followed Dove to the first camp on her journey to the south, she had sent him back to be with Smokey. Grizz had obeyed her command, and though highly disappointed, was doing his best to catch up to his other good friend.

The dog, the horse, and the man were now together. A team of three friends who not even the devil himself could break apart. Where one went the other two were not far behind.

Finding nothing but badlands and a desert like environment, the cowboy changed the course of his journey.

Reining the gelding around, a whiskered nose now facing into the west, he continued a quest for a spread of his own.

Smokey Harrison never strayed far from the Medicine Line that divides the land of the whiskey runner to the south, the mounted police and Blackfoot tribes to the north. Seldom would he venture more than a one day ride from this invisible border, stopping often to rest his animal friends, and explore a strange new land of tall stirrup-high grass, and gentle glacier-carved hills bumping into the mighty Rockies.

One day he reined in his bronc at the mouth of a mile-long coulee. And liking what he could see, stepped down from the saddle, ground-tied Bandit and walked over to perch on a huge buffalo-polished chunk of rock; so common place on this northern prairie.

Scores of willow and berry brush clumps grew in the coulee. Chuckling a pleasant tune, a small spring-fed stream wove its way down a winding path to meet up with the prairie. Continuing on, a nameless creek emptied into the river a few hundred yards out.

The coulee was alive with the sound of cackling prairie chicken, the chatter of voracious magpies, and from far across the river echoed the lonesome call of a whippoorwill. Dozens of species of small birds knew this as their home too, flitting here and there, attempting to outwit the parasitic cowbirds, who would invade their nests, and after leaving an egg, expect the song birds to hatch and rear the over-sized nestling as one of their own.

Situated between the coulee and the river was a long abandoned cabin, a line cabin for a huge ranch that had once covered the area, the cowboy reckoned. It appeared to be in rough shape, so were the corrals that were out back of the old structure.

The thing that interested him the most was the grass that grew here along the Milk River. Walking over to Bandit, he put his left boot in the stirrup and swung his right leg high to avoid the blankets and the war bag stuffed with his grub and what not that was secured behind the cantle.

"Reckon we'll ride over by the river," he said, the dog and the horse both perking up their ears. "Have us a look around, could be the start of a ranch like we've been looking for, and the grass!

"Never have I run across grass like this before."

It was late in the day when Smokey rode up to the cabin. After pulling the saddle from off Bandit's sweaty back, he watched the horse lay down and roll his big body back and forth in the thick grass. Then, after standing erect again, the horse would shake himself in an erratic, almost eccentric manner; a custom of the horse and the canine family.

"Reckon we'll camp here tonight, ol' pards," he said, talking to the two animals. "This could be our new home on the prairie."

Smokey found the old structure in rough shape, but not beyond repair. It had been built of cottonwood logs, the roof was constructed from a layer of river brush covered with a generous layer of sod. The corral rails were lodgepole, weathered but still usable. No doubt freighted here from up yonder, at tree-line along the western woods.

Inside was a rust-stained stove, complete with stovepipe and chimney, a table and a set of bunks. The cowboy smiled at several unsightly bundles of seasoned grass entwined with small twigs from a buffalo berry bush stuffed into the far corners, evidence enough of the presence of pack rats.

"Make good kindling for the stove," he told Grizz, who was standing beside him.

The dog was not pleased with the feral scent of the rat, his nose was twitching, a chilling growl echoed around the small room.

"Don't you worry none big guy," Smokey told the dog, who was still showing his displeasure over the foul odor. "We'll put the run on these rascals—right pronto!"

The next morning Smokey Harrison went to work cleaning the cabin. Using the leafy branches taken from a willow bush as a broom, he dusted and cleaned the best he could. Then after finding a rusty bucket out near the corrals, he packed water from the river and continued to transform the cabin into a respectable condition.

As the shadows of night crept down the valley of the Milk River, Smokey was pleased with what he had accomplished. Although not as spic and span as a woman would have been satisfied with, the cowboy was pleased with his endeavors.

"Plenty good enough for this cowboy," he said, knowing that Grizz, who never left his side was listening.

With provisions running low, Smokey knew that it was time to ride to a trading post he had heard of. It wasn't far, a half-day ride into the northwest he reckoned.

The route he had chosen was as the raven flies, up and down several gigantic hills, then leveling off some into a well-used wagon trail that led him to the Whiskey Gap trading post.

He was in luck that day, as the trader was in a good mood. That he was in the whiskey running business was only too evident. "Give you a good deal on some Missouri River moonshine," he said, winking at the cowboy as he talked.

"Best drinkin' likker in the territories," he continued to pressure the cowboy, who was showing little interest.

After the smoke had cleared, and the trader realized the cowboy wasn't after his sippin' whiskey after all, the trading began. Smokey picked out a goodly supply of grub, a generous supply of coffee and pipe tobacco too. Followed by tools and various odds and ends to be used at the ranch, oats for Bandit and even a wagon and team of horses to pack it all back to the ranch in. He paid the trader with gold dust, which lightened the satchel but little.

As he was securing Bandit at the rear of the wagon, the trader sauntered up with a package that he placed in with Smokey's load. "'tis a bonus for your business," he smiled. "Be pleased if you drop by again sometime."

Smokey thanked him, knowing by the shape of the package what was hidden inside. Crawling up into the wagon seat, he was preparing to head back down the trail, when a thought entered his mind. Turning to the trader who was standing along side, he said, "I almost forgot! I'm looking to buy a few cattle, reckon I could handle about fifty head to start with—a starting me a little spread, over yonder by the river." and signed into the southeast."

The trader was scratching his shoulder length hair, and with a smile answered the cowboy's talk. "Reckon I do stranger. Why I happen to have that many I bin a meanin' to sell.

"They are yours cowboy—for twenty dollars apiece in gold."

With a stunned look on his face, Smokey couldn't believe what he was hearing. He gazed long at the high hill that was hiding the southern horizon, still too shocked to speak. "Reckon the price is too much for me," he finally replied.

"I'll give you ten delivered in my corrals, best I can do!"

The old trader was beginning to fidget some, worried sick that he had lost a deal with the cowboy.

"You are a tough one to deal with stranger, but rather than keep them around, I'll take fifteen, cash on the barrel head."

Smokey Harrison knew now that he was dealing with a sharp, conniving man, the honesty of whom was now in question. "You will be paid in gold dust at my corral gates, in two days time—twelve dollars a head—my final offer!"

Struggling to control his rage, the trader knew he had been outfoxed, and could do nothing but accept the final offer, or else keep the cattle as before. However, needing the money to pay for the next load of contraband booze that was due to arrive any day, he had no other choice.

Smokey told the trader to deliver the cattle to his river ranch. The whiskered barterer of goods made the following reply, "Shucks, cowboy. I've been by there many times—why I know the country between the Missouri and the Milk like the back of my hand!

"The Missouri tribes refer to that river as 'the river that scolds all others'. Back in 1805 them eastern explorers named it the Milk River, from the murky color of the water as it chews up the light colored soil."

After the trader signed his name to the terms of the deal, Smokey stuffed it in his pocket and headed off down the Milk River trail. Following the well-worn ruts, he drove within sight of the river, and there found where the trail curved into the south, following along the bank of a winding prairie stream known as the Milk.

Out in front, sniffing out the trail trotted a large shepherd dog named Grizz; proud as could be. He felt like he was doing his share, escorting the wagon and his good friend safely back to the Harrison river ranch.

This was the same trail traveled by the Fort Benton bull trains, their loaded wagons rolling at night to elude the sharp eyes of Canada's new lawmen. The North West Mounted.

After Smokey explained to the trader where to deliver the cattle, the whiskered barterer of goods made the following reply. "The Missouri tribes refer to the river as 'the river that scolds all others'.

It was late in the day before the loaded wagon pulled in by the cabin. After caring for the horses Smokey began packing the grub inside his new home on the prairie. Leaving the remainder of the load until morning he lit his pipe and relaxed, elated over his good fortune.

He was now in the ranching business, his cabin was stocked with supplies and he had the necessary tools to start fixing up the place. But most of all, he now had the start of his own herd of cattle.

Two days later, Smokey was awakened by the erratic barking of Grizz, the lowing of cattle and the strange talk of someone close by the cabin. "Reckon all hell has broken loose out there," he said, and strapping on his six-gun, then pulling on his boots he left the cabin.

The sun was now peeping over the eastern horizon, consuming the dark shadows of a prairie night. A horse and rider were several yards from the cabin, challenged by an outraged Grizz to step down to the ground if he dared. Another rider was in the background, watching with interest Harrison's herd of hungry cattle devour the lush plants that grow on this prairie meadow.

"Grizz!" the cowboy ordered. "Come over here and sit!!

"This man means us no harm, reckon he has brought us our doggies—the trader has kept his word after all."

The big shepherd obeyed his friend, and trotted over beside Harrison, sitting as close to him as he could get; still challenging the stranger with a wicked snarl.

Taking a closer look, Harrison could see a new born calf draped across the lap of the rider. "Reckon one of these here longhorns is a new mama," the young cowboy drawled.

"If you will keep you're dog from eatin' me for his breakfast, I'll bring you the calf."

"Stay!!" Harrison ordered, and walked over by the horse. The young in years cowboy handed down a squirming new born longhorn into Smokey Harrison's arms. The calf was crying for his mama, a pitiful sound that resulted in all hell breaking loose in the door yard of the old line cabin along the bank of the Milk River.

A scene resembling a three-ring circus unfolded before Harrison's eyes. In the background the mother longhorn had heard the voice of her lost newborn begging for her to come. With fire blazing from her eyes she charged the cabin, slobber escaping her open mouth, moaning a scary tune. The young cowboy's green-broke mustang, not used to this sort of thing, became unglued. Bucking off the young rider, and fleeing with great haste for parts unknown; wanting no part of the enraged beast.

At the same time, Grizz had ventured out to challenge this strange creature, having never met a longhorn before, only to turn tail and race back for the safety of the cabin. The young bronc rider was now standing. He took one look at the advancing danger, and headed for the off-side of the cabin seeking safety; closely followed by the dog and the enraged mother cow hot on his heels.

Around the cabin the three of them sprinted, the cowboy, the dog and the longhorn. On the second pass around, Harrison who had been standing in the open doorway watching it all, reached out and grabbed the cowboy's arm; dragging him inside, closely followed by Grizz.

After slamming the door shut, Harrison broke down with a contagious laughter. "That's the funniest thing I've ever seen in my life," he managed to say, struggling to control himself.

"Still breathless from the physical exertion of the past minutes, the cowboy appeared a bit miffed by Harrison's talk. "It weren't funny Mr. Harrison—that she devil was blowing snot all over me and your dog.

"A trying to kill us with those needle-point horns, I reckoned one more time around the cabin and the pearly gates would a bin open wide, ol' St. Peter himself standin' there, hopin' I would make it in time.

"I'll be forever beholden to you for saving my life!"

Harrison once again began to roar with laughter, tipping over on his bunk in mortal pain. Grizz joined in with a dog's version of such mirth, followed by the cowboy who had decided he just as well laugh too.

The cranky old cow had now found her calf, and after licking the baby's face clean, returned to the herd, a wobbly little critter following behind; hoping she would stop long enough for him to suckle.

Harrison and the young rider left the cabin and found the cow and her calf had returned to the herd. Every thing was fine now, Harrison had laughed until he was sick, the highly offended cowboy hustled over by the river to round-up his badly spooked bronc.

The sun was now moving higher in the sky, the herd had settled down making themselves at home. Harrison was in the cabin preparing a meal for the hungry boys, who were over by the river scrubbing the trail dust off their hands and face, and Grizz was laying by the open door, closely examining his new domain.

The boys devoured Harrison's breakfast with gusto, cup after cup of black coffee, followed by sourdough biscuits, fresh fried bacon and anything else that was within their reach.

The meal was no sooner over when the sound of an approaching wagon could be heard. It was the Whiskey Gap trader who had come for his gold. After the trader had the satchel of dust secured deep in his pocket, the boys approached him for their trail-driving wages. "Nothin' doin' boys," he told them.

"I'll take the wages off the tab your folks owe me back at the Gap!"

With that said he crawled back in the wagon and drove away. There they stood, heads hanging low, disappointed as all get out. After a wild and wooly day of rounding up the longhorn critters, followed by a twelve hour drive in the dark, they reckoned they had been shafted by the old skinflint trader.

Harrison had listened with much interest, noting the downcast condition of the boys. "You jaspers come on in the cabin," he said.

"We'll brew a fresh pot of coffee—and have us a medicine talk!"

Resigning themselves to the fact that they were broke, penniless in fact, they entered the cabin to be greeted by the pleasant aroma of brewing coffee and the smoke from Smokey Harrison's pipe tobacco.

With each of them finding a place to sit, a cup of the steaming drink in hand, Harrison began his medicine talk. "I'm in need of a couple of hands to help me build up my little spread here along the river.

"It will be a full time job if you're interested. The pay will be fifteen dollars a month, plus all the food you can eat; until I can get a bunkhouse built, you will have to sleep under the stars.

"I will pay off your folk's debt at the trading post, and within six months time, if you have earned it, you will receive a five dollar raise. By the way boys, my name is Smokey Harrison—if you accept my offer you may call me Smokey.

"What's yours?"

The young cowpunchers were only too eager to accept the generous offer. To them it was like manna from heaven. "My name is Billy," offered the one who was in the foot race around the cabin, "William McGregor—most folks call me just plain old Billy.

"My younger brother here is Boot, Boot McGregor.

"Our family live about thirty miles west of here on a homestead given to them by the Northwest Mounted. Our daddy was one of them English police, who came over from Scotland and joined the force. Several years later, due to health reasons, he was given an honorable discharge, and allotted a hundred and sixty acre homestead."

Harrison could tell the boy was running out of breath from relating the lengthy history of his family, and after refilling their cups, he took over. "Do you have a mother," he asked.

Young Boot McGregor now answered, giving his older brother a respite from his story telling. "God rest her soul, we did have a darlin' mother, who was taken to heaven several years ago—stomach consumption some folks called it."

"She was a half-breed lady, her mamma and papa were both different. Grandma was from the Blood tribe, Grandpa was a fur trader of Scottish birth. Us kids never knew our grandparents, but we respect their memory just the same."

Harrison could tell the boys were all in, struggling to keep their eyes open after an all night trail drive, and suggested they go out doors in the shade offered by the cabin, and get some much needed shut eye.

Out they went, both struggling to keep their eyes open, and both were soon fast asleep.

Close by, his keen nose on the alert, rested a big shepherd dog guarding the boys from any danger that might be lurking in the vicinity. Grizz was especially on the lookout for a cranky old longhorn mama, who had put the fear in him not so long ago!

It was late in the day when the boys awoke, somewhat refreshed yet still looking hung over. Harrison was out with the herd, Grizz was off tracking down strange scents, offering a blood-curdling challenge at the entrance to the numerous badger holes he found scattered across the meadow.

The dog had trailed along with Harrison for a bit, only to change his mind after being challenged far too often by the feisty cows with long horns. With much prudence, the big shepherd would slink away to a safer environment.

Harrison spotted his new cow punchers had finally aroused, and reckoned they would be wanting some supper. With Grizz trotting along side Bandit, the three of them returned to the cabin.

With a sheepish look on his face, Billy McGregor was the first to speak, "Sorry we slept so long Mr. Harrison, its bin a long time since we've had a chance to sleep like this.

"That ole' bootleggin' devil was workin' us night and day—with no pay besides—wouldn't even give us a piece of jerky to eat!"

Harrison was smiling as he listened to Billy's talk, knowing that to have the boys with him would be his good fortune. He had not only plucked the boys from out of the trader's clutches, they had been happy to stay and become his cow-punchers. Good ones too, as proven by their skill at driving fifty head of run-crazy longhorns to his river ranch in the dark of night!

"Think nothing of it Billy, no need to apologize.

"You are true cowboys now, good ones too. I'll ride the river with you both any old time!"

The boys were overjoyed to hear his talk, both smiling from ear to ear. But their big boss wasn't finished his talk. "I want you boys to come in the cabin and eat another meal, then crawl in your blankets for some more shut eye, which you are both in need of.

"Come five o'clock in the morning, saddle your broncs and ride up yonder and visit your family for a couple o' days—have a good visit—cause on your return your home will be right here along the river."

Harrison arose early the next morning to find the McGregor boys had already left, headed for their parent's home up on the edge of the big forest. Grumbling a bit, he was figuring on cooking them breakfast, and watching them drink a pot of coffee as they had done the previous day.

"Them cowpunchers o' mine sure like their coffee, reckon maybe their folks have been short o' spending money," recalling the debt the trader had held against the McGregor family.

"Raising a family without a little jingle in your jeans, must be a tough chore to keep food on the table."

Harrison was once again talking to himself, as he was prone to do before the arrival of the McGregor boys.

Though embarrassing at times, Harrison reckoned all loners are this way. Asking questions of themselves, and suddenly realizing they were answering them as well.

It was breaking daylight when he finished his morning meal, and after leaving the cabin, he realized that Grizz was not there to greet him. "I wonder where the son of a gun could be?" he said, after much searching in vain. "Sure hope he hasn't tangled with that old longhorn again, be in a heap o' trouble if he has.

"That old she devil would kill him in a wink of an eye, if she had the chance!"

Harrison kept busy that day, and most of the next, keeping track of the herd, tinkering at the corrals, and most of all, he was on the lookout for his good friend Grizz. He was overly fond of the big shepherd dog, the only link he had left to his long departed Dove That Sings.

His own beloved family, consisting of a wilderness wife and their six-month old son, who were lured away from him by the whims of a religion from ages long past.

Tears flooded his eyes as the memories returned. Answering a call to her Spirits, Dove had tucked their son into a cradle board, strapped it on her back and then just rode away for another life somewhere. Though he was happy to have found his river ranch, he was lonely, wishing that Dove and *Little Smoke* were here to share it with him.

Leaving the cabin at the crack of dawn, Harrison's plans were to ride down river, check out the grass, and as always keep an eye out for wolf sign. As of late he had listened to their eerie howls in the dead of night echoing up and down the river valley.

The day had advanced into late afternoon before he returned to the cabin, and there stretched out on the shady side of the old structure lay Grizz. The dog appeared to have been here for quite a spell, and was plumb tuckered out, totally spent! Harrison knelt down beside him, and sensing his good friend was mighty close to deaths door, brought him a pan of river water and several strips of jerky.

After much caressing and speaking of pleasant things to the suffering animal, Grizz raised his head, his eyes acknowledging the kindness of his master. Soon, with the assistance of Harrison, Grizz was able to stand and lap at the water. It was dark before he left to prepare his own supper, and was pleased that the dog was now feeling much better.

Still puzzled as to why Grizz had let himself get in such a condition, a thought struck him, and then he knew. He must of trailed the McGregor boys to their parents ranch, and then knowing they were safe and sound, had retraced the trail back here to the line cabin; making sure no harm come to me— Smokey Harrison!

A distance of sixty miles in about sixteen non-stop hours!

Early the next morning Harrison knew the dog had recovered from his ordeal. Grizz never barked as was his way, but was scratching at the door, a signal that Harrison must come and see. He opened the door, and watched Grizz came into the cabin only to swing around facing some unknown adversary, that must be out there in the waning darkness.

The brightness of the stars were losing their shine, the North Star faintly visible in the approaching daylight would soon be at rest, waiting until the dark of night to once again return to the prairie.

Standing at the open door with rifle in hand, Harrison could sense movement about a hundred yards out, and then he knew what the dog was wanting him to see. A small band of antelope was moving toward the river, no doubt to quench their thirst before the heat of the sun forced them to hole up in some sheltered coulee.

It was an easy shot that brought down one of the wanderers of the prairie. The tantalizing scent of roast meat would soon be wafting strong in the line cabin by the milky river.

The McGregor boys returned as they said they would, eager to begin their new life as a cowboy. Billy was proudly packing a pistol on his hip. Boot was packing an old rifle. Both weapons were of British make, used by their father when he was a member of the North West Mounted.

They were both starving after the long ride, and devoured an antelope roast that Harrison had prepared for them. Then to top it all off, swigged down several cups of coffee before they were through.

Much was accomplished that summer, from keeping track of the cattle to repairing the corrals. Even a stack of hay was harvested. Accompanying the haying crew was Grizz, who wandered the meadows scratching out voles, field mice and other small creatures.

Then came the day when he showed much interest at a freshly dug badger hole. He would poke his nose as far down the hole as he could, then come up for air and with his front paws scratch at a furious pace, attempting to enlarge the hole for easier access. At one of his diggings he found himself in serious trouble. With a yelp, he backed away from the diggings, rubbing his nose in the fresh soil he had dug out of the hole.

Drifting out of the hole came a noise foreign to the dog, the unmistakable warning of a prairie rattler. Harrison, who had been watching the antics of his big dog, was close by, and after arriving at the scene attempted to console the big shepherd who was rolling on the ground, then bouncing back to his feet; swinging his head back and forth at a furious pace.

That he was in severe pain there was no doubt. "Well, big guy," he said, "you finally snooped at the wrong hole," closely inspecting the two fang marks on the end of Grizz's nose.

"Reckon you won't be doin' much snoopin' for awhile!" Harrison was worried though and took the dog back to the line cabin. He tethered him on the shady side of the cabin. Then after setting a pan of water within reach, went back to the haying field. "Not much else I can do," he muttered.

The dog suffered for a week or so with a very sore and swollen nose, but was able to survive the poisonous attack of a prairie rattler.

Sufficient prairie hay was cut and hauled into the corrals to see the horses through until the following spring. The cattle would be kept out on the wind-blown hills. The western slopes were swept bare by the Chinook winds that howled down out of the Rockies.

Haying season was now over. Autumn was just around the corner and the mile long coulee was now adorned with the luster of ripe prairie fruit. Chokecherries, service berries and wild raspberries flourished there in abundance. A scattering of buffalo berries and the rosy red fruit of the wild rose could be found as well.

On one of their rare visits to their old home, the McGregor boys mentioned to their family the abundance of wild fruit back in the coulee, whose own berry patches along the mountains had been decimated by a late frost. What few bushes that had escaped the frost had been decimated by a host of hungry bears.

On the return journey back to Harrison's river ranch, they were accompanied by a team and wagon and two giggling girls. Billy was driving the farm wagon, his sister Sage was riding her brother's horse.

Harrison had been out with the herd when the McGregor clan arrived, and as the sun was settling in the western sky he rode back to the river to be greeted by a pleasant surprise. A strange wagon was parked near the cabin, Billy and Boot's ponies were in the corral, accompanied by a team of draft horses. All four of them were munching on a bait of Harrison's freshly harvested hay.

After tending to Bandit's needs, he walked over to the cabin wondering who in the blue blazes could have invaded his home. Closing in on the doorway, he froze in his tracks, hand hovering near his six-gun, preparing himself for a showdown if need be.

He was sure that he could hear laughter—happy laughter of young girls. His wilderness-honed nose picked up another strange sign, the scent of freshly cooked food; and it sure smelled good!

The McGregor boys seldom attempted to cook, when they did it sure never smelled like this! I wonder what's going on here?" he said. "Reckon my cowboy's are back and must be having themselves a party."

With much caution Harrison reached out to open the door, only to find it opening on its own, and their stood a nineteen year old Sage McGregor preparing to toss out a pan of dishwater. She was startled to see the tall stranger, gun in hand, standing much too close to the open doorway. The dishwater came within mere inches of splashing him in the face.

He stepped back, a confused look on his face, watching the girl utter a startled gasp. Her face reddened in an uncontrolled blush, her dark eyes were locked on those of the big cowboy.

There they stood, Sage McGregor and Smokey Harrison, neither speaking, neither stirring. Both transfixed by this unexpected meeting. A moment in time passed in utter silence.

His six-gun was shoved back in the leather, his hat was in his hand when he began to talk. "Reckon I come mighty close to getting' my face washed," he drawled, offering a slight smile as he wiped a few spatters of dish water from off his face.

He admired this slim built girl, she was a pretty one too, her dark hair and olive-skinned features reminded him of Dove That Sings. She was dressed in faded jeans and a shirt to match. On her feet she wore moccasins showing much wear.

Sage still hadn't spoke, her eyes still locked with those of the tall stranger. Then, with a trace of a smile showing on her rosy lips, her eyes began to wander.

The girl from the western hills liked what was standing before her, a tall handsome stranger with a quaint cowboy drawl. It was the manner in which he had removed his hat when first seeing her, a polite gesture that had never happened to her before. And his cowboy clothes—black hat, a six-gun on his hip, spurs on his boots and a faded bandana around his neck; just thrilled her to death.

Sage was still unable to speak, and listened with much interest to the talk of the big cowboy. "My name is Smokey Harrison," he told her.

"Folks who know me call me just plain ol' Smokey—you may call me Smokey if you like."

Finally the girl was able to find her voice. "I am Sage, Sage McGregor the sister of Billy and Boot—your cowboys.

"My brothers have another sister, she is here in your cabin—her name is Aspen, Aspen McGregor.

"We came down here with Billy and Boot to pick berries over yonder in the big coulee. Our folks will be beholden to you if—if you don't mind our intrusion on your ranch.

"The berries will be a great help in seeing our family through the coming winter."

Harrison was touched by the candor of the girl, sensing an essence of honesty and downright innocence in her make up. He assured her that they were welcome to take as much of the wild fruit as they wanted.

He was smiling as he replied to her innocent request, "Reckon there is one condition though!

"You must bake me a service berry pie before you leave— ol' Smokey hasn't et one since I was a kid—back home in my dear old Mom's kitchen."

They were both smiling as they entered the cabin where Sage introduced him to Aspen, who was busy putting the meal on the old plank table. Much like Sage, she appeared shy around the big cowboy, and after smoothing her hair some, looked up into his eyes—a slight tinge of rosy red showing on her face.

To Harrison's way of thinking they could have been twins. They dressed the same, their delicate olive-hued features were the same, the sound of their talk was the same. Sage and Aspen were just dog-gone pleasant to be around, that's all there was to it!

The meal was a big hit with Harrison. He praised the girls for their cooking, told them he hadn't eaten such a fine meal since he was back at his Mom's table, many years ago.

Sage and her sister were pleased over his remarks, and promised to cook for him any old time. His cowboys, gluttons as they seemed, were equally taken with their sister's cooking, having thrived on it back home before they became cowboys.

After the meal the girls went to work, Aspen washing the dishes, Sage cleaning up the leavings from the table. The boys wandered up by the corrals, Smokey left the cabin to smoke his pipe.

It was a pleasant night, the light of a harvest moon reflecting from off the silent flow of the river. He felt at peace here, for the first time in a very long time he was at peace. He was sitting on a bench made by Boot, who had carved it from the wood of a cottonwood tree.

The lad was handy with an adz and a saw, and had made several improvements to the cabin, including wooden pegs for the walls; the same on the outside where hung such paraphernalia as ropes and bridles, and other trappings and gear common to a cattle ranch.

The glow from a recently purchased coal-oil lantern escaped through the open door. The pleasant chatter of the girl's could be heard, only to be broken by happy giggles. They even sang several verses from a song, a song that Harrison hadn't listened to since he was a youngster.

'Love At Home' was a song that his dear old Mom would sing to us kids—he remembered.

His reverie was broken by the voice of Sage, who was standing with her sister by the bench looking at him. "May we sit by you, Smokey?" she asked.

"Please do," he replied with a start, somewhat disconcerted over his lack of good manners.

Harrison had been sitting in a relaxed manner, his legs were crossed and stretched out before him. He had tossed his black hat on to the toe of one of his boots. "Reckon my mind was a thousand miles from here," he said.

"That purty song you gals were a singin' took me back in time to my childhood home. It was far to the south of the Medicine Line, the Yankee border you know. The one you see yonder across the river."

He was sure enough in a melancholy mood, his wandering mind, strengthened by the influence of the girls; just wouldn't let him be. There were three of them sitting on the bench now, with Harrison in the middle. It was a tight squeeze with Sage on one side of him, Aspen was sitting on the other; he sure didn't mind the feminine company! The close proximity of the two young girls was sure a comfort, good medicine for Smokey Harrison's tortured soul.

All it took was a question from Sage, followed by another from Aspen, for Harrison to begin his story. He told much of his life history up to the time of Dove That Sings saving his life. He appeared reluctant to continue, the hurt of losing Dove and *little smoke* was still a sore spot in his heart, and would remain so forever, he reckoned.

Sage and Aspen were good listeners, though saddened when he told of Kelly and Laura, and his eventual brush with death at the bottom of the shattered rock slide on Kutenai Pass. "There must be more?" Sage asked.

"What happened next?" questioned Aspen.

Firing up his pipe, he spoke with a quiver in his voice. "Reckon I might as well tell it all to you girls, sure can't keep it bottled up inside me much longer."

Looking at Sage, he added, "The rest of the story will not be a pleasant thing for me to share."

"We will respect what you tell us," Sage told him.

"No one will ever know but Aspen and me!"

Requesting Harrison to wait for her, Sage scurried inside the cabin and returned with a pot of coffee and three cups.

Why he was divulging this traumatic time of his young life he would never know. Yet, deep in his heart, he sensed that he would be better for the doing. There they sat in the moon light, two young girls on the verge of womanhood, and an equally young cowboy struggling to create a new life on the prairie.

The words of his story came slowly to start with. Then as Harrison's memory came alive, they flowed from his mouth like a tumble weed bouncing across the prairie!

He continued his story with Dove finding him all broken up and on the verge of death. How she had faithfully nursed him back into the land of the living, he could never forget.

And then Dove's ancestral theory of marriage was still a question mark in Harrison's mind. His Christian upbringing said no, Dove's tribal customs, taken from the knowledge they had preserved of the ancient ones—said yes! However, he had accepted this tribal marriage, and was happy by doing so.

He told the girls of their journey across the Rockies, to find the eastern prairies was their quest. And then meeting the trader Lee, and Trapper Joe who helped them settle along the Belly River. It was there Dove gave birth to their child. It was a boy who she proudly gave the name of *Little Smoke*.

And then one day, like a bolt out of the blue, she had left to return to her people—taking *Little Smoke* with her. "It dern near broke my heart," Harrison said.

"Don't reckon I'll ever see my son again!"

Harrison remained quiet, tears streaming down his cheeks, the girls were both weeping as well. Up high in the mile long coulee, echoed the lonely wail of a lobo wolf, and close by the river a dove of the wild sang a mournful tune.

Sage McGregor was holding one of the cowboy's hands. Not to be outdone by her older sister, a timid Aspen was also gripping a work hardened hand.

Sage then stood up and gave him a warm hug, on the far side sixteen-year old Aspen was doing the same. The three of them were weeping together. Finally, breaking away from the girls, Harrison was the first one to speak. "Reckon it's time we call it a day, you girls can sleep in the cabin, I'm a headin' out to the stack yard and sleep in the hay.

"I have always enjoyed the scent of freshly mown hay!"

The stars were sparkling in the heavens, a young cowboy's active mind was reliving the events of the past day, when suddenly he reared up from his blankets realizing he hadn't seen his faithful dog for quite a spell.

The arrival of the unexpected guests, and the influence of their feminine nature, had distracted him from the whereabouts of Grizz, who had always been close by, tail wagging and happy as could be.

Harrison was standing now. "Grizz!" he shouted. "Grizz, where are you?

"Come and sleep with me in the hay."

Expecting the big dog to move in out of the darkness, tail wagging with joy over the invitation, Harrison was greeted by nothing but a deathly silence. No Grizz could he see, no familiar bark could he hear, nothing but an ominous silence.

A cold chill rippled down Harrison's spine, a lump was in his throat and a tear in his eyes—something bad has happened to the big shepherd!

He just knew it!!

* * * CHAPTER 7 * * *

Early the next morning the McGregor girls were ready to start picking berries. Breakfast was over, the team was hitched to the wagon and the girls were up on the weathered seat all set to cluck the team into action. Harrison rode up on a frisky Bandit, who was buck-jumping on the spot, eager to head down the trail to somewhere. The big gelding was chuck full of get up and go, and was happiest when out on the trail, his nose facing into the wind.

Various tasks had been assigned the cowboys, who had ridden away before first light. There were no fences on the prairie, resulting in the small Harrison herd topping the list.

"Keep them within a half-day's ride," Harrison had ordered. Knowing that eventually they would drift far from the home ranch and become vulnerable to the predators of the plains; the kind who could be walking on four legs, or two!

"Keep an eye out for Grizz," he ordered. "I can't find him anywhere, could be he's got himself in a heap of trouble."

"We could hear him barking up in the big coulee last night," Billy offered. "We haven't seen or heard him bark since!"

Harrison planned on staying close by the berry pickers, knowing the bootlegger trail ran just a half mile west of the line cabin. He also was familiar with the type of unsavory characters the whiskey-runners were, and how they would treat two young girls, who were alone while picking berries.

Good morning ladies," he greeted with a smile. "Reckon you could use some company?" knowing darn well what their answer would be. They were all smiles, and assured him they were happy to have him with them.

He hadn't checked out the coulee for several days, reason enough to be on the lookout for smugglers, who could be holed up in the brush waiting for the dark of night to continue their illicit journey.

And something else, as of late he had found fresh bear droppings and tracks moving up river. The frightening claw impressions in the sand were the clue. Harrison knew at first sight they were those made by a grizzly bear. Knowing the young girls would be vulnerable to both of the above mentioned, he reckoned he should stay with them; in case of trouble.

And if that wasn't enough, there were rattle snakes thriving in this portion of the western Territories.

Sage was at the reins of the team, and after maneuvering up the coulee a few hundred yards she was forced to stop. The faint trail they were following became plugged with dense brush. Out they climbed, giggling and happy as young girls are prone to be. They were in awe at the prolific growth of berry brush that thrived from the top of one side of the coulee, down and up top on the other.

With buckets in hand, they began harvesting the wild fruit that grew here just waiting to be picked. This delicious fruit was known to very few excepting the native Indian and the bear family.

Smokey Harrison remained concerned, patrolling the long coulee for any sign of danger that might threaten the McGregor girls. A slight trace of a trail led up the coulee, used by mule deer and other cloven-hoofed animals, including elk. Bandit was enjoying the challenge of busting through the dense brush, and bulled his way through, his whiskered nose pointing for the stars.

Nearing the top, the big horse suddenly stopped, refusing to take another step. His ears were on alert status followed closely by an outraged snuffle from his nostrils, both were the gelding's warning of imminent danger ahead. Harrison struggled to keep him under control, the horse was determined to swing around and flee back down the coulee. It was then he caught a whiff of what was upsetting Bandit so, a foul, feral scent reeking of wild things and wild places.

From the dense brush ahead, a bone-chilling squall challenged the horse and the man. A commotion in the brush, followed by the appearance of an outraged animal closely followed by two furry pups, set the hair rising on the back of Harrison's neck.

"Indian Devil!" gasped the cowboy, who had lost control of Bandit—who had now turned tail; plunging hell bent for leather back down the coulee, not stopping until reaching the startled girls.

Smokey Harrison was plumb upset, not only had he lost control of his trusted horse, he had lost his hat in the wild melee between a cowboy, a horse, and a mother wolverine protecting her pups.

His long hair was waving in the breeze. his shirt was in tatters from the wild ride through the brush, and his bruised pride had been severely tested!

"Reckon we tangled with a wolverine," he told the wide-eyed girls. "That old she devil was on the fight, downright cranky too.

"Why I even lost my ten-dollar Stetson!"

Sage was struggling hard not to laugh at the disheveled looking cowboy, or to sympathize with him—deciding on the later. Knowing the ways of the wolverine from her childhood days spent exploring in the big forest, she knew that he was lucky to have not been hurt much worse. His shirt was not only hanging in tatters, there were many deep scratches and bruises on his body, the berry brush had taken their toll as well.

"She walked over by him and spoke, "You are all scratched and bleeding Smokey, the berry bushes have not been kind to you!"

After removing the remains of his shirt, Sage gasped at what she could see. Still embedded in his body were the needle-sharp thorns of hawthorn brush, which had broken off the mother limb in Bandit's mad dash for safety. The hawthorn was equally at home in the coulee with the choke cherry, growing side-by-side as a close neighbor.

"Oh, Smoky!" you are hurt bad." she said, knowing that she must remove the thorns as quickly as possible.

"This will hurt you—you must be a brave cowboy and let me do this."

"Go ahead Sage," he growled. "The sooner the better I reckon."

Sage removed the thorns, Harrison clenched his teeth, and with beaded sweat dripping from his brow never uttered a sound. Then from her possible satchel, she brought out a salve concocted by her Blood mother. It consisted of the chewed inner bark from a diamond willow tree, blended with various secret ingredients known only to the Woodland Cree. Sage's Mom had been a distant cousin of these people, and familiar with many of their medicines and customs.

It was a healing substance—a gift from the ancient ones.

It was then Aspen walked out of the brush, in one hand she held Smokey's hat, in the other she held Grizz's collar. She offered both to Smokey and spoke, "This was around the neck

111

of your wolf dog—he is back there," and pointed back in the direction she had came from.

"Your dog has been in a fight, he is dead!"

Aspen led Harrison and Sage to where lay the mangled body of Grizz. The big cowboy was devastated. There lay the body of his faithful friend, killed while defending his territory from some savage beast—a grizzly by the looks of it.

Smokey Harrison uttered a curse as he looked at the mangled body of his dog. Then began to cuss even louder, realizing it must of been the wolverine mom the dog had tangled with—the fearsome Indian Devil!

Smokey Harrison buried the body of his dog near the entrance to the mile-log coulee, the last vestige of his life with Dove That Sings.

Much later that day the McGregor girls had filled all their berry buckets to the brim, and decided they should leave for home bright and early the next morning. Once back in the cabin, Sage began fussing around the old kitchen stove. She remembered Smokey had asked her to bake him a service berry pie.

Sage McGregor's delicious pies were a welcome treat at Smokey Harrison's supper table that night. She had baked only three, one to be eaten for supper, the other two were for her newly found friend Smokey Harrison, to enjoy in the days to follow. She watched in disgust as the three pies disappeared before her eyes; having been eaten by five hungry people.

After the meal Harrison went outdoors to sit on his bench where he could smoke his pipe in peace—it wasn't long until the McGregor sisters were there too, one sitting on each side of him, eager to hear more of his stories.

The girls were up early and prepared a hearty breakfast for their two brothers and their cowboy boss, after which they harnessed the team and were ready to go. Harrison had tugged the cinch tight around Bandit's belly, and with one hand on the horn, swung aboard the saddle. He informed the girls that he too was ready to ride.

"I decided to escort you home," he informed them. "Reckon I've got an uneasy feeling about you girls traveling thirty miles all by yourselves; alone on this wild and wooly prairie.

"You don't mind my company—do you?"

The girls were overjoyed to have Smokey come with them, and told him he was more than welcome. With a happy smile on her face, Sage McGregor clucked the old team into action and pointed the horses into the west.

Billy and Boot were left at the ranch to ride herd on Harrison's long horn cattle.

Sage proved to be an excellent teamster, maneuvering the McGregor wagon up and down the rolling hills, crossing streams, and evading the ever present badger holes. Often she would stop the rig and allow the aged team to take a breather, making sure the precious cargo was protected from the sun, and only then, accompanied by Aspen, the two girls would crawl from the wagon to walk around some, stretching the kinks out of their legs.

Harrison would ride beside the wagon for a spell, making small talk with the girls, enjoying the sound of their happy laughter, and most of all, absorbing an ingrained sense of innocence that was so much a part of the two sisters.

And then he would ride on ahead checking out a passable route for the cumbersome wagon.

"I wonder where Smokey could be," Aspen asked her sister. "He has been gone for at least an hour!"

"He'll be back soon," Sage assured her, knowing that Smokey was doing the same as Boot had done on their journey down to the Harrison ranch—scouting out a passable trail.

The sun was high overhead when the little one-wagon caravan reached the land of willow and aspen, and after rounding a dense thicket of diamond willow, the girls discovered him hunkered down by a modest camp fire, his coffee pot sending forth a delicious smell.

"Light and set, you pretty gals," he invited with a big smile. "ol' Smokey has got the coffee ready to drink—reckon you could scratch around in that wagon and find us some food to eat?"

"This cowboy is starvin' plumb to death!"

Sage was the first to respond, and in no time at all climbed back in the wagon, and returned with enough sandwiches to satisfy all three.

"I'm sure glad you fixed this lunch for us," Aspen said, and began to devour her cold venison sandwich. Smokey was doing the same, leaving Sage hoping there would be enough left for her.

After eating his fill, he fired up his pipe and settled back on the seat of the saddle he had just pulled off Bandit's sweat-stained back. "Sure enough peaceful here," he said.

"After livin' out on the treeless prairie for a spell, these here trees look mighty good to me—reminds me of my old home."

"We were born and raised around trees Smokey. I feel the same way as you do, I sure am lost when I cannot see a tree!"

It was near midnight before they reached the McGregor place. The dogs were barking at the intrusion, a donkey brayed into the night and even a rooster aroused by the hullabaloo, crowed an alarm from his roost in an old shed.

The horses were put away in the corral with the donkey, the girls scurried into the old log house and found their beds, and after the racket had settled down; the cowboy rolled out his blankets under the stars.

His tired body was finally at rest, and as he gazed up through the forest canopy, he felt at peace. The soothing music of a nearby creek was good medicine for his weary soul. His eyes closed, and remained that way until the sun once again returned to the aspen forest at the mouth of Lobo Canyon.

* * * CHAPTER 8 * * *

Smokey Harrison awoke at the crack of dawn and after stretching a kink out of his back, reached under the blanket and removed a fist-sized rock that had been the cause of his discomfort.

Tossing it into the creek, he muttered, "Take that you blasted rascal—hope you drown good and proper like—a pestering me all night like you have!"

Still under his trail-worn blanket, he relaxed once more. Then, after hearing a strange noise and sensing that something was close by, he sat up with a start; the blanket was sent flying, his six-gun appeared in his shooting hand!

"Well I'll be damned!" he said, "reckon I almost gunned you down."

There sat a grinning Sage. Sitting beside her was a large collie dog who was also grinning, her tongue hanging low. Blending in with the black fur of their Scotch mother sat her litter of pups, one of which settled back on four feet and wobbled toward an astonished cowboy.

"Well I'll be forever damned," he spoke once again, watching the little one nearing his blanket.

"I've never seen the likes of this!"

He watched with interest as the pup's nose bumped into the messed-up blanket. Then with his rump resting on the ground, the little one reached up with his front feet scratching for help.

Sage McGregor still hadn't spoken. Though still smiling, she was watching with interest the cowboy who had picked up the little ball of fur. Holding it in one of his big hands he was caressing the pup with the other.

"He is now yours Smokey, a gift from our family to you for being so kind to my brothers—and, and to Aspen and me.

"His name is Lobo!

"He likes you Smokey. He is only six-weeks old—and already he knows that you will be his good friend!"

"Well thanks a whole bunch Sage, reckon I sure appreciate the kindness of you folks.

"And you Sage, will you be my good friend too? Friends are mighty hard to come by these days!"

Sage was blushing when she answered his question, dreading the fact that it would show on her olive-skinned complexion. "Yes Smokey Harrison, I will be your good friend!

"I will be your friend forever!"

Still holding the little bundle of fur against his whiskered cheek, he spoke again, "Reckon I am the luckiest hombre on the wide open prairie, I now have two very good friends—before you gals came down pickin' berries—I was all by my lonesome."

"Come to the house now Smokey, I want you to meet my folks, they are just a dying to see you.

"Besides the coffee will be ready to drink and breakfast will be on the table."

Off they went, two young friends happy to be together, followed by a proud collie Mom, her pups trailing behind her. In the coat pocket of the cowboy, squirming until a tiny head was showing, was little Lobo; a newly found friend of Smokey Harrison.

Old whiskered Angus McGregor met them at the door. "Come into our 'ome," he welcomed, "...tis a pleasure to meet you my lad!..." He was beaming from ear to ear, and thanked the cowboy for the kindness shown to his family. And for the berries he was thrilled beyond words.

"...'tis indeed a rare thing to happen...in this wild glen that we live in, to have a friend like you gracin' our door...

"You will be welcome to share our hearth stone any time that you might be in need of a friend.

"And you lassie," he said, pointing his finger at Sage, "must come in and help your sister preserve this delicious fruit for our winters use."

With a wink and a raise of his bushy eyebrows, he took Smokey aside and spoke so his daughter could not hear him. "My darling Sage has nothing on her mind lately but marriage. Oh, she's old enough all right, bin doin' nothing lately but mooning around, wishing she could find herself a husband!"

Smokey was at a loss for words, in awe at the old Scotchman's frankness of speech. It sounded to him as if Sage's father had offered her hand in marriage, with no strings attached.

The breakfast turned into a real feast, a Scotchman's way of greeting a new day. Could be, as it often was, the only food they might have until nightfall. Later in the day, while the women folk were still busy canning the berries, Smokey wandered over by Lobo Creek and sat by the chattering mountain stream. He just had to ponder over what had been happening to him as of late.

For the remainder of his stay with the McGregors the pup had been returned to his mother to enjoy a last suckle or two. Smokey was happy with the gift Sage had given him, and knew that it was her way of telling him that she really cared.

And he cared too, dad-burned it, he really cared for Sage McGregor. He was restless at the ranch, something was missing, a yearning in his heart for female companionship was getting more than he could handle.

Later that night they had a chance to walk in the twilight, to be near the creek and its friendly chatter is where they wanted to be. "I've got to head back to the ranch," Smokey told her. "Reckon my cowboys will be a needing me by now, most likely think I've left them for good."

"I wish I could go back with you," Sage replied, "I would be happy to cook and scrub, and do other chores. To be able to ride with you on the big prairie would be a dream come true!"

Once again a hint of marriage had been offered him. In her own way this delightful lass from the McGregor clan was telling him something, something that he reckoned he should pay attention to. After a deep silence on Smokey's part, he suddenly knew.

He too was lonely, as was Sage McGregor. He too would welcome her into his life, knowing Sage's desires were the same as his.

"Will you come back to the ranch with me, as my wife?" he asked, somewhat shocked that the all important question he had been mulling over in his mind had really happened.

"Sure enough make me a happy cowboy if you can."

With a squeal of delight, a shy Scottish girl accepted his offer of marriage, and they sealed the start of a new life together with plenty of hugs and a kiss. "I don't know where we can find a preacher to say the good words though," he said, worry spreading across his face."

Sage was giggling when she replied, "No need for you to worry none, Smokey Harrison! My father will marry us. It is a custom of the highland clans back in old Scotland for the laird of the clan to perform a marriage ceremony for his own daughters."

As laird of the wee clan of McGregor in this western wilderness, he indeed had the authority to tie the knot for the cowboy and his daughter, a custom dating back to the time of the ancient Celts, and even the Picts of old Caledonia.

Old Angus McGregor was proud and happy on hearing the good news, and as the berries were preserved for the coming winter and out of the way, he gave his consent to Sage and Smokey to become man and wife.

Early the next morning, dressed in his plaid kilts, Angus McGregor appeared at the door of the house ready to perform a sacred Scottish ceremony. Though a bit moth-eaten and wrinkled from long storage, a well known symbol of Scotland would highlight the marriage; the proud tartan of the clan of McGregor.

As a finale to the wilderness wedding, he brought out his bagpipes, and though suffering from a shortness of breath, played several lively tunes, including music for dancing; in which all who were there participated in the traditional Scottish reel and the Highland fling.

Welcoming a new member to their clan, they danced until they were weary, only then did they enter the big log cabin to a sumptuous wedding feast consisting of roast mutton and all the trimmings. Aspen and her sister and most of the clan had spent a long night preparing the food for Sage's wedding. Old Angus even broke the seal on a bottle of Scotland's finest. It was Scotch whiskey as could be expected.

That night the newlyweds spent their first night together sleeping under the stars. Lobo creek was singing them a happy tune, accompanied by a lonesome owl hooting from a nearby tree.

Down out of the high hills they traveled, heading for the prairie river that was home to Smokey Harrison's ranch. Both Smokey and Sage were bone-weary from the long ride, having celebrated most of the previous night with Sage's lively Scottish clan.

It was twilight when they rode into the corral that was home to the horses, the small ranch yard appeared lonely and deserted. No cowboys could they see, no sound could they hear but the howl of a lonesome wolf; followed by the chatter of a coyote family.

Billy and Boot, who never went home with the berry pickers, much preferred staying at the river ranch. Until Smoky returned they were top guns of the Harrison spread, riding the range caring for a herd of wander-lust longhorn cattle; not knowing of their sister's sudden marriage,

Smokey's face was troubled as he spoke, "I wonder where our cowboy's are Sage?" noting the corral was empty of any saddle stock.

"Not like your brothers to stay away this late. Billy and Boot are always here by this time—hungry as a pair of starving bears a wanting their supper."

With keen eyes sweeping the horizon for some clue to his cowboy's whereabouts, Smoky told her, "I reckon our cowboys have run into a heap of trouble somewhere!"

Sage was in tears, her voice quivering as she spoke, "Oh no, Smokey!

"This can't be happening to us. I sure hope my brothers haven't got themselves hurt—or, or something even worse…!"

Comforting Sage as best he could, the two newlyweds left their horses at the corral and turned towards the cabin. Sage had a small bundle in her arms. Packed inside were the only possessions that she could call her own, and it was a small bundle; very small.

But she was a proud Scottish lass, walking beside the big cowboy who was now her husband, and knew that not far down the trail—there would be better days to look forward to.

Finding the door open, Smokey struck a match and lit a lantern that hung on a rusty nail beside the door. Taking a long look inside, they found the place in a shambles, ransacked from one end to the other.

"Oh!! Oh Smokey, your nice home is, is just ruined," Sage said, her tears were still flowing.

"What ever will we do now?"

After salvaging several tattered blankets, Smokey replied, "Reckon all we can do is wander over to the stack yard and sleep in the hay."

At first light the next morning, after making sure that Sage was still asleep, he returned to the cabin and started cleaning things up. "One helluva mess," he grumbled, as he threw out what was not salvageable, keeping anything that was still of use. It was then he noticed long brown colored hairs scattered at random about the cabin, streaked with an odd tint of silver.

Then he knew that a grizzly bear had paid him a visit, and raised hell inside the cabin while looking for who knows what all. Smokey was mad, damn mad in fact, and after cursing a blue streak, stopped his cussing when noticing that Sage was standing in the doorway. "Reckon I lost my cool," he said, attempting to voice an apology for his breach of good manners.

"Don't worry about it Smokey, together we can get the horrible bear smell out of our home." Sage meant what she had said, and began cleaning and returning, as best as she could, the old structure to its former condition.

Sage had finished her scrubbing, and after Smoky had reinforced the latch on the cabin door, they both agreed it was time to ride out on the hunt for Billy and Boot. They should have been back by now, something was amiss that troubled the big cowboy. The whereabouts of Sage's brothers was a mystery that had to be solved.

Munching on jerky as they rode away, Smoky drawled, "Reckon when we get back from finding our cowboys, you and I Sage darlin' are a ridin' over yonder to the Gap and do some tradin' with that Yankee trader.

"That darn bear cleaned out our food supply Sage, what he never ate is not fit to eat, scattered all over the floor like it was; tainted with bear scent and droppings."

The newlyweds rode on with Smokey doing most of the talking. To have Sage as his wife was a great blessing, and for her to be his riding companion was even better.

"The trader told me that Whiskey Gap was named for an American whiskey post." he told her, "that flourished in the area before 1874.

"Goin' on ten years since that Missouri river bunch began crossin' the border with the pig swill they call whiskey."

Riding east and south, Smokey was pointing for the last known grazing ground of the herd, which was along the Yankee border. There was good grass there that only the buffalo were aware of. The big bison of the prairie never stayed in one place much, their restless ways urging them on in a never ending migration, allowing the grass to regain its former nutritious nature.

The sun was high overhead before the young riders arrived at the grazing grounds, only to find it barren of any longhorns. Smokey stepped down from the saddle, and after they both tipped their canteens, he wandered around some checking for a possible clue as to what had happened. Sage was like his shadow, never far behind.

"I reckon whatever happened took place last night," he said, showing Sage the cattle droppings that were not yet crusted over by the heat of the sun.

"And notice these here tracks! Our longhorns were spooked into action by something that sure enough put the fear in them.

"Bin one hell of a rip-roarin' stampede happen here, crossin' over into Yankee land too!"

Sage walked out into the devastation left by the passing of the cloven-hoofed stampede, the short grass chewed to shreds. With a hand shading the sun from her eyes, she was gazing long at a dark object that appeared out of place far across the prairie.

"Come see Smokey, there is something way over that way," and pointed in the direction she had referred to.

He was now standing beside her, and shading his own eyes, said, "I sure can't tell what you're a lookin' at Sage—my little wife must have the eyes of an eagle!"

To satisfy his wife's curiosity he helped her into the saddle, and after stepping into his own, they rode into the southeast to check out what had alerted Sage to a possible clue to the mystery of her missing brothers.

It was then the cowboy spotted a pair of vultures soaring high in the sky. Familiar with the ways of this cruel scavenger from the clouds put the fear in Smokey's soul. "Let's ride Sage, put the spurs to your hoss and follow me."

Across the mile-long grazing grounds they raced, both fearful of what they might find.

The unknown dark spot on the prairie was a downed pony, still alive but struggling to stand, thrashing a sweat-caked neck and feebly moving its legs. Three legs are all that moved, the fourth was broken below the knee.

But that wasn't all! Trapped beneath the dying animal lay Billy McGregor, one foot hung up in a stirrup, unable to squirm his way free. He had tried several times only to settle back in agony, the pain from his ankle more than he could handle.

Sage vaulted from her saddle, screaming as she moved in close and found her brother still alive; just barely!

LOBO CANYON

Recognizing that help had finally arrived, Billy could see it was his sister who was screaming and appeared to relax some, knowing that help had finally arrived. From the time when he was a small boy he had trusted his big sister, and now in this time of need she was here by his side when he needed her most.

Smokey was standing beside Sage, spooked beyond words and knew what he must do first. A shot rang out on the sun-baked prairie. The suffering pony was now free from the misfortunes of his short stay at the Milk river ranch.

He uncoiled his lasso and looped the noose around the pony's neck, then tied the other end to the horn on Bandit's saddle. Swinging aboard, he spoke to his frightened wife. "Sage darlin' you must help me."

"Bandit is going to pull Billy's horse up off his body, when this happens tell me if his boot is hung up in the stirrup. If it is free let me know, and then Bandit will pull the hoss out of the way."

"I'll do my best Smokey," she replied, still upset and fearing for her brother's life, whose mind had drifted off somewhere into a shock-induced coma.

"I know you can do it Sage! Bandit backs up real good, we'll have your brother away from there in no time at all."

To witness a cowboy and his horse in action is a sight to behold. Having a horse trained to keep the lasso snugged tight on a fighting animal, is one of the basic elements in the making of a good rope horse; a right handy horse to have around at a round-up corral, or at a branding out on the open range. And Bandit was one of the best.

As if the big gelding knew what he must do, he began to slowly move backwards, tightening the lasso, and then after another cue from the cowboy's spur, backed up another step which slowly raised the dead horse from off of Billy's body.

"His boot is free!" Sage shrieked.

After which Smokey vaulted to the ground, charged down the taut lasso and pulled Billy out of harms way. With a word from the cowboy, Bandit stepped forward causing the lasso to slack off; allowing the forward part of Billy's pony to settle back to the ground.

Sage dropped to her knees beside her semi-conscious brother, a canteen in hand, allowing small amounts of water to drip into his mouth. Using Billy's bandana, she soaked it with water and cleansed his sun-burnt face. Then, with the maternal instinct of one who cares, continued to dribble the life sustaining fluid into his open mouth.

The boy was in rough shape, suffering from a badly bruised body, an injured ankle and heat exhaustion. And if that wasn't enough, the dreaded shock had made its presence known as well.

Smokey was plumb upset, venting his anger at the badgers. "Damn the confounded critters!" he cursed, and was now standing beside the badger hole that was the making for Billy's wreck.

"Why its two feet straight down," he muttered, Fate had played a hand with his young cowboy, he reckoned. The age-old adage of 'being at the right place at the wrong time' rang true for poor Billy.

He had heard of such wrecks before, but this was the first time that one had happened so close to home. He knew that it wasn't the horses fault and couldn't put the blame on Billy, who must have been riding like the wind to get around the stampeding longhorns. The horse and rider never had a chance to foresee the deadly trap that was lying in wait just ahead.

The more he mulled over the mishap to Billy, the more irate he became. His cursing became more fluent, and ended with a final blast at the hole-diggers, damning them all to the gates of purgatory itself.

Cooling down some, his attention was drawn to the sharp croak of a vulture that had been keeping a close watch on Billy and his horse, and had drifted down from the sky to check out the site of an unexpected feast.

"Git outta here, you blasted vermin eater!" he shouted, his anger still simmering right near the surface.

"You'll get to gorge your belly soon enough, but for now you leave us be."

The big cowboy then drew his six-shooter and fired a warning shot at the over-eager scavenger, who with great haste flapped its way back up into the ever changing thermals.

The sound of Smokey's gun echoed far across the prairie, startling a small family of antelope. A mule deer grazing near a small seep looked up in wonder, keen eyes surveying the far horizons for danger; and a grizzly bear, stopped gorging herself on the remains of a longhorn steer to check on the whereabouts of her two cubs.

Several miles south of the Medicine Line at the mouth of a prairie coulee, Boot McGregor sat in the saddle of his weary horse watching a small bunch of longhorns. The wild Texas cattle were jaded and worn, after running most of the previous night in a crazy stampede.

It was the nature of the beasts to run crazy like this, as the young cowboy had found out the hard way, and tired as he might be he was determined to stay with them, waiting for Billy to show up and give him a hand in trailing them back across the border to the big boss's river ranch.

His brother should have showed up by now! They had been riding together when the herd bolted in terror—Billy had ridden one way—Boot had taken the other side, both attempting to circle the cattle and stop the stampede. But his brother had never showed, leaving Boot to do nothing but follow the running beasts as best he could.

The young cowpuncher had stayed with the herd, and now as he stood guard on the remains of Harrison's longhorns he could tell they had settled down some, and had began to graze the lush coulee grass. But he must remain as vigilant as an old she bear guarding her cubs! It wouldn't take much of a ruckus to send them off on another insane run across the prairie.

He was struggling to keep his eyes open, having been without sleep for the last twenty four hours. Both the horse and rider were bone-weary and hungry. His horse as was the cattle, were ravenously eating the Yankee grass. But Boot wasn't as fortunate, his jerky satchel was empty as was his water canteen, and had been for most of the night.

He knew both he and his horse were in dire need of water, he also knew they must find the life sustaining liquid soon or suffer an agonizing death. His throat was bone dry from breathing in the manure-saturated dust kicked up by the running cattle. He had no other choice but to keep his pony's nose pointed into the dust cloud, a means of keeping track of the herd in the dark of night.

And as the sun rose higher in the sky, the sweltering heat became a burden to be reckoned with. Boot knew he must leave the cattle and ride back to the river while he was still able. His tongue was now badly swollen and getting more so by the minute, to speak would have been impossible for the boy to do. Sure no fun he reasoned, to be without water this way—suffering from the pangs of a mind-eating thirst.

But dog-gone it all, he was a cowboy. His big boss had often told him that when the going got downright hard to handle, that he should 'cowboy up'!

"To be a good cowboy," he told them, "takes a lot of grit and guts. So when you boys get in a tight spot, remember what I'm a telling you—Cowboy Up!"

Young Boot McGregor was proud to be a cowboy, something that he had desired to be since a small boy. He idolized Smokey Harrison, and forever would be this way. He had taken in two young mountain boys, green as grass in the springtime, and taught them the ways of the open range and how to be a cowboy.

The young puncher was in a bad way, and though he was reluctant to leave the herd, he reckoned he should ride out on a hunt for water and find his brother Billy. He attempted to climb back up in the saddle, but found that he was unable to do so. The severity of heat exhaustion and the lack of water were taking their toll on his dehydrating body.

The phrase 'Cowboy up' entered his mind. It was if Smokey was standing there beside him, encouraging him not to give up, to keep fighting as a cowboy should, and be much better for the doing.

Close by was a small rise on one side of the coulee, could be a vantage point to view the vastness of the prairie. With the words 'cowboy up' strong in his mind, the boy began to crawl up the slight slope. Once on top he collapsed in the grass, his weakened body spent from the exertion.

After a bit, the boy stirred some, his mind in a mysterious haze, wondering where he was and how he got to such a place.

Above all else he sensed a presence standing near him. Billy has found me after all, he reckoned.

My brother will help me! I just know he will!

To his dying day Boot McGregor swore this strange phenomenon was true.

The boy's unseen benefactor continued to rule his mind, perhaps it was a dream, perhaps it was not, who knows? But it was directing the dying boy to do what must be done.

129

He was standing now, mindful of the presence close by.

Then, in a blink of an eyelid a horse was there, so close that he could have reached out and touched it. None other than Boot McGregor himself was in the saddle, standing high in the stirrups, scanning the far horizon for any clue to his lost brother. The hard to distinguish rider then settled back down in the saddle watching with interest something far across the prairie.

Boot too was watching from the ground where he stood, and after rubbing his bloodshot eyes to make sure it wasn't a mirage, he reckoned the dark spots were two horses heading his way.

A six-gun was drawn, three shots were fired into the sky—a signal of trouble—that Smokey had drilled both he and Billy on in case of trouble such as this. He relaxed some and waited for a reply. It could have been brought about by the scorching heat of the day, or the condition of his dehydrated body that caused his mind to doubt what his eyes could see.

Perhaps it isn't two riders after all, his troubled mind told him. It might be two stray longhorns that were left behind in the midnight stampede. Another possibility is grizzly bears, of which there were many on the prairie at this time. Who were often seen on the prowl, their nose to the wind sniffing out the scent of an easy meal.

His mind wouldn't let him be until he was sure of the answer.

The body of the young cowboy now lay quiet on the high point of the coulee, yet in the maze of his turbulent mind, he could once again see no other than himself sitting astride his saddle horse, a smoking six-gun in his hand.

A lone rifle shot—followed closely by another, echoed across the prairie. To Boot McGregor it was like manna from heaven to hear the coded message. It was just one more of the big boss's savvy ways to let his cowboys know that help was on the way.

The lad opened his eyes, in a daze from the sequence of events that had taken over his inner self. He looked around for his horse that had been standing in this very spot, and discovered that it was still down yonder by the longhorns, greedily munching on the forage that grew there. Turning once more towards the prairie, he could see the two riders were much closer now, and recognized one as his big boss Smokey Harrison. The other he was not sure of, but somehow he knew that it wasn't his brother Billy.

Before continuing on the quest to find Boot and the herd, Smokey improvised a shelter for Billy McGregor. Making use of a sage brush cluster and Billy's upended saddle, the shelter was complete with a saddle blanket for the roof, and protected on three sides by his oilskin slicker. The makeshift shelter would protect him from the rays of the sun, even a late afternoon thunder shower if one should happen by.

"I need Sage to come with me," he told Billy, who was showing favorable signs of improvement. "Could be we'll find Boot in trouble, needing some doctoring much like yourself.

"You know Billy, Sage and I are now married. Old Angus tied the knot for us while we were up at your ranch, remember? I am now a member of the McGregor clan; you and I are now brother-in-laws."

"Yes I know," the boy replied, a happy smile spreading across his face. Sage reminded me that I was now your brother-in-law while you was fixin' me this shelter.

"I sure thank you both for saving my life. I reckoned I was a goner when you two rode in together, like you did."

"And I want you to know Billy, that Sage is one of the finest ladies I've ever had the pleasure of knowing. I love her you know, and always will."

Sage, who had been kneeling beside her husband was listening to his words, and was more than pleased. She too loved her new husband, and would forever do so!

After seeing to Billy's needs, Smokey and Sage rode out to find Boot. They discovered the grazing grounds barren of any longhorns, with no sign of Boot McGregor.

The chewed up grass left no doubt as to the direction the spooked longhorns had taken, it was an easy trail to follow.

And then the three gun shots, though far away and faint to hear, Smokey knew that Boot was in trouble and needed their help. He was pleased to know that Boot had remembered to do this. It was one of the first lessons in survival he had given the two brothers after hiring them on as cowboys.

"Boot must be in serious trouble Sage, reckon he needs our help really bad!" he shouted above the racket of the pounding hooves.

"Put the spurs to that little pony you're a ridin' darlin', our run-crazy herd must have crossed the river. From the sound of his signal he is far across the border and is now in Yankee land."

The two horses were running at top speed when the Milk river cowboy pulled his rifle from the leathers, and returned an answering signal to a young cowboy, who was in dire need of help from anyone who might be in hearing distance.

Not slowing down much at the river, the two horses charged into the milky stream, buck-jumping across to the other side. They continued on, crossing over a fenceless border into the territory of a wild and wooly territory known as Montana.

"There's the makin' of a coulee up yonder Sage," Smokey shouted to his wife, whose little pony was struggling to keep up with Bandit.

"Reckon we should ride up that way and check it out."

✶ ✶ ✶ CHAPTER 9 ✶ ✶ ✶

Far back in the ages of time, a phenomenon of the prairie was created by the convulsions of an unsettled earth. It was here on the prairie, a short distance from the northern territory, three massive mounds of rock and glacier-refined soil were thrust up into the sky.

The Blackfoot referred to the hills as Sweet Pine, to the early explorers they became known as the Sweet Grass Hills. These prominent landmarks were unique in nature, running parallel with the border of a close neighbor—the northern territories of a British colony known as Canada. The farthest west of the mammoth-sized hills became known as West Butte.

Concealed from view by a growth of aspen trees and berry brush, a secluded camp lay hidden in a deep coulee along the northwest slope of West Butte. Shadows of the approaching night were moving up from the prairie, the sun had now settled behind the Rockies seeking a long night of well earned rest.

The border here was wide open, lawmen from either country were non-existent before the arrival of the new territorial police—the English inspired North West Mounted.

The camp was a make-shift affair, a rustler's hideout rarely used, but handy when needed as a cooling off spot to escape the prying eyes of an irate settler from the territories; who might be missing a team of horses, perhaps a milk cow herd, even an entire herd of longhorns!

A camp fire lit up the rustler camp, casting a twinkling glow into the surrounding aspens. The scent of brewing coffee was evident in the small clearing, merging in with the aroma of a newly introduced roll your own tobacco—Bull Durham. Four hardened rustlers were inhaling the addictive weed with a questionable pleasure.

They had just finished a supper of roast sage grouse, and were boasting of their latest venture at cattle rustling across the border in Milk River country. Course laughter resounded across the small clearing, a way of making fun at the two young cowboys who had tried to stop them.

"Just like a pair of school boys," one of them said. "We had them out foxed all the way—like takin' candy from a kid."

"Not quite!" Whiskey Bob broke in, the leader of the small gang of rustlers.

"We missed part of the herd, remember? Don't recall of seein' much of the one rider, but the other one sure had some smarts—and got away with part o' them longhorns right out from under our dusty noses."

"You're right Whiskey," replied Dutch, the second in command of the outfit. "It was the dust all right, I still can't breath proper.

"Take a good shot o' whiskey to get me a feelin' better."

Whiskey Bob and Dutch were cast offs from the bloody war that raged between the States, a wild and wooly affair that saw brother face off against brother; splitting many families asunder. One of them might be wearing the uniform of the blue coats, the other could be in favor of the southern rebels.

Two more gang members sat sipping the fiery moonshine, both half-breeds of questionable origin.

And then there was still another, old Soupbone, who had been assigned to guard the rustled longhorns. It was here, where the narrow coulee gave way to an open piece of grass, boxed in by thick timber and wind battered spires of sandstone; the old timer was stationed to keep the longhorns from heading back down country. It was a simple job for the old timer, yet an important one.

Old Soupbone was a lacky of sorts, as well as the cook. He didn't mind the lowly chores that had been passed his way, as long as he had tobacco for his pipe, a blanket to roll up in and a hefty jolt of moonshine on occasion. Soupbone's philosophy was that an exposure to moonshine was not a deadly sin, rather good medicine for his aching old bones.

The liquor the gang was guzzling was rot-gut at its finest, not fit for a rabid skunk to drink, yet it bothered them none. With only a swallow or two left in the jug, they ceased bending their elbows at the sound of Whiskey Bob's roar.

A command from the big boss was reason enough to sit up and take notice, of which they were prompt to do. "You breeds, leave a swaller or two for ol' Soupbone," an outburst of words of which left the illiterate rascals scratching their heads. "or else he'll poison us for sure at our next meal!

"You!" he said, pointing a dirt-stained finger at the breed known to him as Hawk. "Git up yonder and change off Soupbone, reckon it's time for him to roll up in that blanket o' his and call it a day.

"And you," he continued his talk, his rheumy eyes now locked in on the other. "Head down yonder and hide in them quackin' trees.

"Could be that ranchin' outfit down yonder is hot on our trail by now, all red-eyed and ready for a fight.

"I've got a feelin' they'll be a huntin' us really soon.

"Dutch, you and I must hit the sack, and get us a few hours shut eye. I've got a hunch we'll be movin' out around midnight—could be we'll have a fight on our hands if we don't!"

It became as black as the ace of spades on West Butte. The rustler's camp became quiet, no sound could be heard except the inquisitive chirp of a night bird, and the convulsive outbursts of the snoring outlaws

Much later, and it was nearing midnight, when a disturbance from below erupted, awakening four booze-drugged outlaws.

That there had been gunshots fired they were sure of, the number of shots that had disturbed their sleep they weren't sure of!

✶ ✶ ✶ CHAPTER 10 ✶ ✶ ✶

Perhaps it was luck Smokey and Sage tracked down Boot McGregor, perhaps it was the skill of an experienced range rider, whichever way it was, had sure enough brought them to the little rise above the coulee.

They both were shocked to see the condition Boot was in. Sage scrambled from her saddle with canteen in hand, and knelt beside her suffering brother. Her hands were trembling as she cleansed his face, and as with Billy, began to give him small sips of water.

"Oh, Smokey I just don't know! Boot is in worse shape than Billy was—and he is burning up with a fever—what should we do?"

"Why you're doin' just fine Sage. Keep up what you're a doin'—there's no one within a hundred miles of these parts can nurse a person back to health, like you can.

"In my way of thinking water and grub is what he needs," Smokey continued to praise her. "And tender lovng care like you gave Billy!"

Boot McGregor's young body would not stay down, and though he was weak as a new born kitten, he recovered his senses and was up walking around; thanks to his sister Sage Harrison.

After a couple of hours of making sure Boot would be all right, Smokey spoke, "Reckon it's time we were movin' on—a chasin' them cattle rustlin' devils that took our herd. There will be hell to pay when your sister and I catch up to 'em!"

With a slight smile on his face, Boot answered his boss. "They never got them all!

"I got some of them hid real good, back up the coulee," and gestured up beyond where they were standing. "I managed to get them this far before I took sick."

"Well I'll be…," Smokey managed to say, in awe at Boot's words. "You must have followed my advice and 'cowboyed up'—done a good job of it too.

"Your sister and I want you to know that we're both dog-gone proud of you and Billy, and what you have accomplished here—and doing it all by yourself."

Not through with his praise of the young cowboy, Smokey added, "You'll sure do to ride the river with any old time!"

The trail of the rustled herd led far into the east, pointing toward a massive landmark on the prairie. Though it was a serious venture the Harrison's had been caught up in, they were happy to be riding together.

To the riders of the open range time and distance have no meaning. They always rode prepared, as did the Harrison outfit. A canteen full of water, sometimes two, and a satchel full of jerky stuffed in a saddle bag, along with plenty of spare bullets for their guns.

There was no such thing as a barb-wire fence. They rode as the crow flies, in a straight line from one destination to another. The Harrison eastern boundary was situated roughly, who knows how many miles, half-way between the whiskey post at the Gap and the buttes of sweet grass to the east.

The Harrison home ranch was situated along the north fork of the Milk River, a country mile from the old Whiskey Gap trail.

To those who rode from the north fork to the south fork in either direction was a long day in the saddle; often it took part of another.

The sign left by the herd was easy to follow, showing the cattle had been pushed to the limit. The strange butte appeared closer by the hour, the sign of their cattle heading in a beeline for the big mound in the sky.

The day was long spent when they stopped at a small spring of water, the horses were in need of a rest, and so were Smokey and Sage. Smokey kindled a small sage brush fire, Sage dug out the coffee pot and soon they were relaxing, a hot drink in one hand, a strip of jerky in the other.

The saddles had been pulled from the horses, the jaded animals were only too eager to have a roll in the grass, and after taking a long drink at the spring, both began munching on the short grass that grew here.

"Appears as if these hombres are takin' our cows over yonder—by that big butte on the skyline," Smokey said, munching on jerky as he spoke.

"Reckon so," Sage replied, who was quickly learning the cowboy slang of her big husband. "That big hill looks almost like a baby mountain, don't you think?"

Smiling a broad grin, Smokey replied, "Never thought of it that way Sage, but dog-gone it, you're sure enough right."

He could tell Sage was tired, reason enough for their stop. Besides the butte was not far now, an hour's ride at the most, and he suggested Sage stretch out in the grass and have a nap.

She readily agreed, and was soon sound asleep, rejuvenating a young body that had been used hard this past sixteen-hours of hard riding.

Sage and her pony felt refreshed after the short rest, and so did Bandit who liked nothing more than to be out on the trail, his nose pointing into the wind. While it was still light enough to see, Smokey reckoned they should stay with the well-defined trail of his rustled cattle.

Still able to see the outline of the trail, twilight had settled across the land before they arrived at the western butte, where it began a gradual zig-zag climb up towards a brush-covered ridge. "Reckon our cows are up in that brush," Smoky told the lady that rode beside him.

"We are so close now that I can almost smell 'em!"

"Me too," Sage whispered back, and they were both right. As is the case with a cattle drive of this nature, the trail they leave behind becomes littered with the liquid droppings of a disturbed group of animals. A nerve-wracking time it must be for the cows to be driven away from their home range to an uncertain future.

"Reckon we should ride up to the brush and hide our hosses, then make like a pair of Indians on the hunt for enemy scalps—which will be our plan!"

All went as planned, and after concealing the horses, they both sat nearby in the dark, amazed at the brilliant display of stars.

"You all right Sage?" Smokey asked. "Hope you're not freezing—when this is all over, you and me are riding to the Gap and buy you some decent clothes."

"I'm fine Smokey," she replied, and cuddled closer beside him.

"This wool shirt you gave me is keeping me warm," she giggled, not letting him know that it was the musky scent of her big husband's body, deeply embedded in the material of the shirt, that kept her temperature on the rise.

Soupbone was up and about when he heard the rifle shot. He always arose early, kindling the fire, putting on the coffee pot and preparing a meal for four hungry outlaws. "That Hawk injun must o' fired that shot," he reasoned, knowing the other three were sawing logs right here in the camp.

"Wonder what's a goin' on.

Cautiously the old timer approached his snoring boss, waking him from his sleep, then stepping back to avoid a fist in the chin, worse yet a smoking gun. Soupbone was right in being cautious, watching as Whiskey Bob reared from his blanket, raving and cursing a blue streak, and he was hung over from the drinking binge of the night before.

"Who woke me?" he roared. "Was that you Soupbone?" his vision now had cleared enough so that he could see his cook standing in the shadowed clearing.

"Boss, boss listen to my talk, Hawk just fired a shot from his rifle—could be he's warning us of...!" Two more shots interrupted his talk, resulting in all hell breaking loose in Whiskey Bob's outlaw camp.

After a long silence Smokey became uneasy. He sensed that something was not as it should be, that a presence was close by, and reckoned that it was time to declare war on who; or whatever it might be.

"Stay here Sage," he said. "Be quiet as a mouse. I'm going to scout around some, there is something over yonder I want to check out," and he left her his six-gun which he had just recently trained her to use.

"Be careful Smokey, don't get yourself shot!"

An odd noise greeted him as he started out, sounding like the spitting hiss of an irate bob cat mixed up with the grumbling of distant thunder. It had him stumped for a minute or so, and then, as he closed in on the ruckus he could tell that it was someone snoring.

H.K. JENSEN

He continued on, spotting a shadowed figure sitting with his back to a tree, slumped over as if he had fallen to sleep. A long gun was held across his lap, a tobacco-stained finger was on the trigger and the gun was cocked ready to fire.

Smokey moved closer, his own rifle ready to do the same, when a breed known as Hawk awoke with a startled jerk—and in one swift motion raised the barrel of the gun and pulled the trigger. A red-hot chunk of lead whizzed past Smokey's whiskered cheek, at the same instance he pulled the trigger on his trusty Marlin..

"The son-of-a-gun was playing possum on me," he mumbled as he watched the outlaw tip over to the ground, the round from the rifle had traveled straight and true.

"Are you all right, Smokey?" Sage screeched, who had crept up behind him, her own six-gun aimed at the downed outlaw sprawled in the grass. And then, faster than a blink of an eyelid, she too fired, her bullet whizzing close by her husband, who had turned at the sound of her voice to see his wife standing behind him. A smoking gun was clasped in both of her dainty hands.

"Tears were hard for her to hold back, cold chills had invaded her body when she spoke again, "He was pointing his gun at you again, Smokey. I knew he was going to shoot you in the back!" she had been following her husband, not wanting to be left behind.

"I killed this man, didn't I Smokey?"

"No Sage, it was me that killed him, you just made sure that he was dead."

The sky was softening along the eastern horizon, allowing the Harrison duo to see more clearly. The crashing of brush and the bellowing of Whiskey Bob, left no doubt in their minds that a war had been declared.

The small clearing where Hawk had gasped his last breath, was riddled by a stream of bullets, spraying this way and that, attempting to flush out the unseen rancher and his sharp-shooting wife.

Though the three men were still suffering from a moon-shine hang over, the bullets they were shooting were for real, forcing Smokey to grab hold of Sage and force her to the ground. "Stay down," he told her. "'fore you get yourself killed.

"Pick one off if you get a clear shot, I'll do the same. Together we just might come away from this fight with our hair intact!"

The fight with the outlaws was over in mere minutes. Holding a sobbing Sage in his arms, together the young ranchers surveyed the carnage of the fierce battle. Smokey had been hit, a flesh wound is all, though the dripping blood had made it appear much worse. Sage had come through it all unscathed, except for a ragged hole in the arm of the wool shirt she wore, made by a wild shot from a dying outlaw's smoking gun.

Whiskey Bob, Dutch the younger, and a half-breed with no name, died where they had fell. Their sinful ways were over and done with. They were now up in the sky pounding on the pearly gates of old St. Peter's domain; begging to be let in.

Sage's tears ceased to flow when she spotted the blood on Smokey's shirt. "You've been shot," she moaned, "I didn't know!"

"It's nothin' much Sage—a flesh wound is all—the blood does look a little scary though."

The rancher's wife removed her husband's shirt, and in no time at all began her doctoring. It turned out to be just a flesh wound next to his ribs, and though downright sore to the touch, he was grinning at his wife who was fixing him up with a bandage and what not.

Finishing up the knot on the bandage, Sage stopped with a subdued gasp and said, "Smoky, don't make a move! There is someone standing over by them aspens, and he hasn't got a gun!

"Don't shoot him, Smokey! His hands are in the air, and he is acting kind of friendly like."

Smokey, with gun in hand, swung around to face off with another unknown adversary, only to find old Soupbone standing there with his arms raised to the sky.

"You belong to this cattle stealin' bunch?" he asked, not yet sure of the ethics of the man. "Tell us your name, so as we know who we are talking to."

Soupbone appeared nervous to be here with a shirtless Smokey and his attractive little wife, and finally said, "Most folks know me as just plain old Soupbone, I bin a cookin' for this wild bunch—never knowed they was such a rustlin' outfit when I hired on."

Not only did the two Harrisons make him nervous, the sight of the four dead outlaws only made him more so.

Not really knowing if he should shoot him, hang him or let him go his way, Smokey relaxed some at the insistent urging of Sage.

"Hear him out Smokey, please do. The least we can do is listen to his story."

Heaving a sigh of relief, Soupbone began to talk. He told them of his involvement with Whiskey Bob's outfit, that he had been hired on as cook of the camp, caring for the horses and other odd jobs that were handed his way.

After a few weeks at his new job, he discovered they were outlaws and rustlers of cattle and horses, and with the threat of being shot on the spot, he was forced to become involved in there shady doings.

"Them longhorns you folks are looking for are close by, up yonder above the camp," and pointed towards the boxed in canyon.

"Be not much of a chore to move them out, and point them back towards your river ranch from where they came from." Smokey liked what he was hearing, and after another careful scrutiny of the old timer, he was satisfied that he was telling the truth. With the approval of a well-pleased Sage, Smokey offered him a job as handyman around the ranch, and to assist her with the cooking that was becoming a time-consuming chore. Her desire was to spend more time with her husband. Riding the range together would be like a dream come true.

Soupbone was overjoyed at Smokey's offer, and gladly accepted his new calling.

After gathering up the guns, saddles and such, they rolled the four cadavers into a small ravine, and covered them over with rocks and debris that was scattered about the area. Then the six horses were brought in from where Soupbone had them cached, their saddles cinched back on—five were saddle stock, the other had been used as a pack horse to carry food, camping gear and other fixings.

They were now all set to move their longhorns back to where they belonged. With a mounted Soupbone on the far side of the uneasy herd, they poured out of the box canyon, and flowed on down off the butte, their noses pointed into the west and home.

The longhorns had become homesick for the wide open prairie, cooped up like they had been. There was no need to push them as they never looked back.

A small caravan headed into the west—three mounted riders, a loaded packhorse and four saddle ponies trailing behind with empty saddles.

A long tiring day, and even a longer night later, the trail drive arrived back on Harrison range complete with the stolen longhorns. The two cowboy brothers both heaved a happy sigh of relief when the main herd showed up on the distant prairie. Though still physically drained from their separate ordeals, they rode out to meet their sister and her husband Smokey Harrison.

It was just this very morning, realizing they were still in the land of the living, and together once again, they had ridden out and retrieved the portion of the herd that Boot had snatched away from Whiskey Bob's outlaw gang.

It was an exciting time for the entire crew to watch the two herds merge into one. Smokey and Sage were sure pleased and proud too, of how Boot and Billy had handled themselves through this crisis, and knew that from here on out, the two brothers would show much more respect for a scorching prairie sun.

With the herd settling down, the Milk River cowboys, and one lovely cowgirl rode on to ranch headquarters for a well-deserved rest and a first meal of the day. Without being asked, Soupbone set right in to helping Sage prepare a meal for the hungry bunch, and it was a good one too—fried antelope steaks, sourdough biscuits and wild onions—all washed down by a pot of ranch-brewed coffee.

All that were there were impressed with the old timer they knew as Soupbone, Billy and Boot knew right off that he would be the making of a good and trusted friend. Sage was thrilled too, knowing that her burdens would now be lightened, and he was a good cook also.

The days grew into weeks, the weeks into months, with no more trouble from the night riders such as the Whiskey Bob gang. For now, word had circulated across the territory to stay clear of the Milk River outfit, a right salty bunch willing to fight back.

The demise of Whiskey Bob's outfit put a chill into the bones of others of the rustling profession—they had heard by means of the tumbleweed grape-vine of a young rancher and his sharp-shooting wife, who had shot the hell out of Whiskey Bob's gang.

"Best not mess with that bunch!" the word spread, "else you might wind up as old Whiskey's gang did, shot to pieces!" If caught by the new North West Mounted, the Yankee rustlers would be taken to Fort MacLeod for a trial, only then would they be deported to Fort Benton, there to be hung by a territorial marshal.

If caught on the Montana side, they were often hung on the spot, saving the trouble of a trial. Which ever side of the Medicine Line they were caught on, the punishment for horse and cattle rustling at this time was one and the same—hung by the neck until they were dead!

Smokey and Sage had ridden into the Gap, and returned with provisions for the ranch, even warm clothes for Sage, all of which were secured on the back of the pack horse they had confiscated from down yonder at West Butte.

"Do you think it was right for us to take their horses and guns, like we have done," Sage asked.

"It is the fortunes of war!" Smokey replied, smiling some over her innocent question. "Little enough payment for all the trouble they caused us. Besides Sage, them hosses would have just joined up with the wild bunch, and the saddles and other gear would have remained where they lay, rotting into a pile of dust from the passing of time and the elements."

"That makes good sense," Sage smiled as she replied, her worry about the confiscated contraband now settling down some.

"The horses were most likely stolen from some poor grass-roots settler," Smokey continued to enlighten her on such things. "The horse gear and guns were likely taken from others they had gunned down in the same ruthless manner common to most outlaws."

Sage's mind was still not clear on her husband's philosophy of cattle rustlers and how to punish them for their sinful ways. "Would you have hung them Smokey?" she asked. "I-if we hadn't shot them all dead!"

"Yes Sage, we would have stretched their necks real good—it is an unwritten law of the open range."

"Thank you Smokey, for having patience with your backwoods girl," she shyly replied.

"This hanging business is now much clearer in my mind.

"However, old Angus would have uncoiled his black-snake whip, then ripped of their shirts so he could lash their bare backs. Not stopping until the skin hung like moss on an oak tree."

She then told Smokey of long ago times, when she was just a child. Her father would relate to her and her siblings stories of Scottish history. Stories of how the English armies had beaten the Clans into submission, how cruel they were to the women and children, and how they slaughtered the Clans as if they were sheep. And yes, hanging was one of their favorite methods of subduing a proud people.

Smokey listened with interest to her story, and though he sympathized with the plight of the ancient Clans, he was still a bit disturbed over her questions about lynching the bad guys. A well deserved punishment for those who rustled horses and cattle in his way of thinking.

On the other hand he was pleased with her concern over the safety of the ranch, knowing the cattle were the life blood of such a venture, and without them, they would eventually starve out, fading away into nothing.

She now understood that the longhorn cows meant the same to Smokey, as sheep meant to old Angus. It was a livelihood for a family, a means of keeping food on the table and clothes on their backs.

Smokey was now able to realize that his wife must have a paranoia of sorts tucked deep in her mind; dating back to her father's bedside tales of the ancient Clans. To be hung at that time was a dreaded way to die, stripping the victim of his pride and self respect, as well as his life. To her Scottish way of reasoning, the same applied today. Not as yet realizing the bad guys had it coming.

He reminded her of a Bible quote, '*an eye for an eye*'. He went on to compare the quote to that of a cowboy being left afoot while out on the prairie, or on an arid desert, it didn't really matter which; suffering an agonizing death from the intense heat and the lack of water, his horse having been stolen out from under him by outlaws.

Smokey was determined to explain to her the comparison he was attempting to portray in her mind. "Think of this Sage, as an example of what I'm trying to show you. Think of a dark night on the prairie. A cowboy is rolled up in his blanket, sound asleep, when thieves sneak in and steal his horse and rigging, including the saddle which holds his gun, food and canteen.

"Here's one more example to ponder. A cowboy is riding alone when he spots another rider, or riders approaching from the far-reaching prairie. He reins in his hoss for a friendly chat with the advancing strangers. Being downright lonesome for the sound of another's voice, he trusts the incoming riders to be a friendly bunch; only to be greeted with drawn guns.

"After being set afoot, all he could do was watch them leave with his horse, guns and canteen, knowing that he was miles from nowhere, and with certain death staring him in the face!"

"The fate of the thievin' varmints if, and when they are caught, is to be strung up to the nearest tree.

"...*an eye for an eye*...Sage, can you now see what I have been trying to make you understand?"

The two remained silent, deep in thought until Sage broke the silence. "Yes, Smokey. I do understand much better—forgive my ignorance—please do!

"I didn't know about these things you are telling me—I just didn't know!"

Smokey was more than happy to forgive her, and while holding his wife close in his arms, assured her there was nothing for her to forgive.

The normal routine of a cattle ranch had returned to the Harrison spread. The McGregor boys had recovered from their narrow escape from death, the wild stampede now pushed far back in a secluded corner of their minds.

Old Soupbone was an instant hit with Smokey and his two cowboys, going out of his way to make life easier for the three Milk River cow punchers. He enjoyed caring for the horses, saddling and unsaddling them was no problem at all for an old retired cowboy, such as Soupbone. He insisted the animals be rubbed down and curried, doing it himself if Billy and Boot had forgotten.

He was a godsend to Sage as well, whose life was made much easier from his knowledge of the cooking profession, and his willingness to share the burdens of such a chore. Oft' times he would tell her to leave the meal for him to prepare. "Ol' Soupbone will cook supper for you tonight," he would say.

"Crawl on that pony o' yourn Mrs. Harrison, ride out and find Smokey—who should be headin' back to the ranch by now," not telling Sage that her pony was standing outside the door, already saddled and ready to ride.

"I'll cook them steaks for you tonight, might even stir-up a batch o' sourdoughs while I'm at it."

Sage was thrilled that he would do this for her, knowing that his prowess with a fry pan and cook stove was just as good as her own, if not better. They became good friends, the boss lady of the kitchen and an old cowpoke known to all as Soupbone. If the occasion ever arose, she would champion him, and he in turn, would do the same for this kind lady who treated him as an equal.

The talent of the old timer amazed them all, and when they found out he was right handy with a hammer and saw, he was put to work building a bunk house. Boot was also this way, and he was soon assigned as Soupbone's helper.

The Lobo pup was growing like a weed, and soon responded to the mysterious urging of his inner self. It had to be an ingrained gene from some ancient ancestor that inspired him to guard the ranch yards. Slowly but surely he increased his territorial boundaries, now venturing several hundred yards out onto the open prairie. Harassing the gophers and badgers, stalking field mice and voles; eating them too. Like all members of the canine family, he would mark his territory with the usual dash of urine—a sign for all intruders to keep out!

All at the ranch adored the maturing Scotch Collie, knowing that he would become a valuable asset, and good friend to have around. Lobo worshipped Sage, and if the occasion arose, she knew that he would protect her with his life if necessary.

Sage had mothered him since he was a tiny bundle of fur, training the little one to lap milk from an old cracked saucer.

She had improvised him a bed in an empty hardtack tin, and the Lobo pup was soon relishing the leftovers from Sage Harrison's kitchen. Old Soupbone too was an admirer of the pup, and would slip him scraps of meat, and other delicious morsels—on the sly of course!

The bunk house was soon finished, not an elaborate structure, yet a castle to the cowboys, who up to this time had been sleeping under the stars. It was complete with three double bunks and a well-used pot belly stove.

Soupbone was proud of the bunk house, whose bare walls were soon adorned with the various trappings of a working cowboy. Lassos and spurs, a worn out hat and a boot with no heel, even several Blackfoot war arrows they had found while riding the prairie.

The most prized trophies of them all were the tail feather from a golden eagle and the antlered skull from a long dead mule deer. The McGregor boys couldn't be considered as pack rats. Yet, to break the monotony of the long, lonely days riding the prairie, they were always on the alert for such finds.

Soupbone still was not satisfied, and suggested a few changes to the cabin that would be of great benefit to his good friend Sage McGregor. She was thrilled with his idea, and the very next day a team and wagon was sent to Whiskey Gap.

Trading posts were few and far between at this time, the Gap being the closest and handiest for the Harrison ranch to deal with. The traders, and there were two, had openly stocked their shelves with the Missouri river whiskey. This all changed with the arrival of the North West Mounted in 1876.

Even though their main interest was dealing in illegal whiskey, the traders were now forced to remove the whiskey from the shelves. The American made booze went underground. The goods of a normal trading post were now on offer.

The traders were out to make a buck, and often bought and sold livestock, even freighting in rough-sawed lumber from a Yankee saw mill. Smokey knew this and had taken home one load for Soupbone's bunk house project, and was now returning for another.

Soupbone was at the reins of the lively team. The two draft horses were full of get up and go this morning, having been too long without a good days work, they were stepping right out in a grand old fashion.

He knew that Soupbone could have managed without him, yet he was hesitant to let him go alone, knowing of what might happen. Though not seen often, he knew the Blackfoot were still a bunch one didn't want to fool around with. For this proud people to be subdued and confined to a reservation was bad medicine as far as they were concerned. One never knew when a band of militants might leave their tepees, seeking revenge on any white-eyes they could find

Smokey often rode ahead, scouting out a suitable trail for the wooden-wheeled rig that was following behind. He was concerned, and well he should be. The old Whiskey Gap trail he was traveling was not only used by the whiskey smugglers, it was a well traveled route used for untold centuries by the natives of the region; a branch of the 'Old North Trail'!

The Blackfoot tribes were known for their savage dispositions, and were sure a bunch one didn't want to fool around with, as Smokey well knew. To discover strangers traveling on their trails at this time, would soon enough stir up a war party of militants, eager to be once again on the warpath.

Continuing on with great caution, they made it to the old trading post with no mishap, although Smokey had sighted several lone riders perched here and there on the top of some distant hill.

With a heavy load of lumber aboard, the Milk River outfit started back to the ranch, winding there way through the winding hills, anxious to arrive home with their hair still intact.

Smokey had been riding ahead when it happened. At the sound of a war whoop, and then there were more, he turned in the saddle to see what was happening. And their riding beside the wagon was a half-naked Indian, all decked out in war paint, and brandishing a feather-decked war spear.

The Indian's feet were wildly kicking the ribs of a small paint pony, urging the fatigued animal on to a faster pace. Smokey reckoned the savage wanted a clear shot at old Soupbone.

Cold chills rippled down the cowboy's spine, knowing what might happen. Then after reining Bandit around to face the oncoming wagon, an amazing thing happened. Old Soupbone who was doing his best to stay out of reach of the warrior, reached down between his legs and brought out a blacksnake whip.

The Indian was whooping like a crazy man, screeching vile threats at Soupbone, who was expecting to be scalped at any minute. The outfit was speeding down a slight incline when he went into action.

With one hand gripping the reins of the terrified team, the other holding the handle of an uncoiled blacksnake, he stood up and cracked the whip; which stung the rear end of the little paint pony.

The Indian was promptly bucked off, leaving him sitting on the trail, gesturing all sorts of obscene gestures at the departing lumber wagon. After assisting his camp cook to stop the run-away team, Smokey spoke in a harsh tone, "Hand me that whip of yourn, I'm a goin' to teach that rascal a lesson!"

"I don't know who he belongs to, or where he came from, but I do know where he's a goin'"

The Indian appeared to be just a teenager, and watched with fear at the white-eyes charging towards him, a whip in hand and roaring with rage. Although groggy from the unexpected buck-off, he was still able to spring to his feet and raced off the trail for the safety of a deep coulee that wound up through the hills; leaving his war spear laying where he had fallen.

The big gelding was known as a better than average rope horse, and caught up to the fleeing youngster in record breaking time, allowing Smokey to do his thing. He did not rope him, but using the weapon for what it is meant for, snapped the whip at the fleeing boy several times before he reached the coulee. Each crack of the whip landed on the seat of his pants, resulting in howls of rage and old-fashioned pain.

"Take that!" Smokey muttered, as he watched him vanish in the depths of the coulee. "Next time I'll rope and hog tie you, might just leave you lay for the wolves to fight over."

On his return to the wagon he paused to pick up the war spear, and gave it to Soupbone who was still in awe over what he had just witnessed. "Might do to hang in the bunkhouse," he told him, a broad grin spreading across his face. "It will be a reminder of you and your black snake taking on a war lance."

The frightened team had now settled down, the load of lumber once again was on the move. The next stop would be the home ranch.

The old timer had now settled down too, his frayed nerves were slowly returning to normal. Smokey was riding along side the rolling wagon when he spoke, "I reckon you was a lucky hombre Soupbone."

"I sure admired the way you and your whip stood up to that young hellion like you did—it was a sight to behold—keeping control of the team with one hand, the other using that whip of yourn to save your life."

155

After a hearty laugh from both the teamster and the cowboy, they continued down the trail, both silent and deep in thought.

To count *coup* against a dreaded white-eyes would have been big medicine for the young vision seeker, Smokey reasoned. This must have been the young ones plan, and he came mighty close to accomplishing his quest.

He is most likely hidden in the big coulee, Smokey reckoned, sulking in the tall grass, watching his pony trailing behind the white-eyes wagon, and he had watched his war lance taken as well.

And Smokey was right. The boy was in tears, still suffering the pain from the vicious black snake attack. More painful than this would be when he returned to his family's tepee in disgrace. He had lost his brother's pony, and his father's war lance. And to make matters worse, he hadn't even come close to receiving the sacred vision he had been sent out to find.

* * * CHAPTER 11 * * *

The end of an eventful year, full of adventure and intrigue, was drawing to a close in the lives of Smokey and Sage Harrison. To celebrate this first anniversary of their marriage, the McGregor Clan had planned a bountiful feast at their ranch high up in the western hills. To add zest to the lavish party, a new baby girl had been delivered into the Clan by a proud, but very tired Sage Harrison.

As her time drew near, Smokey had taken Sage up to be with Aspen, who was a home-grown midwife. She had been trained in the age-old art by her Mom, who in turn had been trained by her own Mom back in the Blood camps of her youth.

Smokey was thankful they had arrived in time. He was right handy in delivering a colt or a calf, but was hesitant to be close by when a baby was on the way. He reckoned if this ever happened, he most likely would come down with an extreme case of the shakes.

Being told the baby wouldn't arrive for a couple of more days, and he had been shooed away from Sage's bed by the women folk, he rode back to the ranch, only to return the next day bringing Billy and Boot with him. At the arrival of Smokey and the two brothers, they discovered Sage with the new baby in her arms.

"See Smokey, what I have for you!" she said, her voice still weak from the trying ordeal she had just been through.

He knelt by her bed, overwhelmed but yet thrilled, at the sight of his new baby daughter. Though tears were flowing down his cheeks, he managed a reply, "She is a spittin' image of you darlin'—I now have two beautiful women to love—you and our new baby girl!"

He recognized that she was in dire need of a restful sleep, and after kissing them both, he silently left the room to join the Clan in a joyful celebration that would last for several days.

At the insistence of her sister Aspen, the little one was given the name of Willow. The official christening ceremony was attended to by the patriarch of the Clan, old Angus McGregor.

Old Angus was as proud as a peacock looking in a mirror, and to add a bit of flavor to the proceedings, brought out a jug or two of well-aged whiskey that had been stashed away for just such an occasion. The birth of a baby in the Clans was celebrated the same as if it had been Christmas. Little Willow was his first grandchild, and as such was treated as if she had been the baby Jesus himself!

After two days of revelry, Smokey reckoned he and the boys should head back for the ranch. Before leaving, he spent as much time with Sage as he could, and was startled when she asked him to hold their new daughter. "Take her Smokey," she said, offering him the tiny bundle.

"Willow wants to get to know her father—from here on out she will recognize you by your scent—one whiff is all it will take. For the rest of her life she will never forget you."

"You reckon I smell bad?" he asked, feeling slightly miffed.

Sage burst forth with a happy giggle, the first time she had done so since the birth of Willow. "No, no Smokey! I'm sorry if I have hurt your feelings.

"I love your smell, it has a mixture of many different things. Along with the scent of your body that I adore so much—there is a vague aura of horses and cows, tobacco smoke from your pipe, and the sweat from my hard working husband."

He was more than willing to change the subject, and accepted their baby, fearful that he might squeeze her too hard, perhaps even drop her on the ground.

Sage stayed with her folks for another week before she returned home to the ranch. She was happy to be back with her husband, and thrilled with her new baby, Willow Harrison.

The little one was an instant hit with old Soupbone, who having had no children of his own, was as caring as if she had been one of his own.

Knowing that Sage must need a break after the tedious chore of birthing a baby, he volunteered to take over the duties of chief cook at the ranch. He prepared two hardy meals a day, and had a lunch prepared to eat when the sun was high in the sky. The sun would tell him that it was noon and time for a coffee break. Along with the coffee, a sourdough biscuit was added for good measure; adorned with a thick slab of roast antelope meat.

Smokey was never far from the ranch, popping into the cabin now and then to keep Sage company. Also, to Sage's delight, he was now holding his daughter more often, in awe at her tiny features, who on occasion offered the making of a wee smile at her big cowboy daddy.

Even the Lobo dog knew there was someone new in the family. Since the return of Sage and the baby, a new delicate scent tickled his nostrils whenever he was near the cabin. The collie longed to see the baby, and one day he did just that.

Early one morning he discovered the door was ajar and just walked inside, following the pleasant scent into the bedroom. And there, snuggled next to her sleeping mom, lay a wide awake Willow gazing up at the smiling face of Lobo. The dog was panting, as do all members of the canine world, reminding one of a happy smile with the extended tongue and all.

The new scent was strong here, an innocent, friendly scent, one that the big collie would never forget. Two pair of brown eyes stared at each other—Lobo's and little Willow's—both fascinated by the other.

And though no sound had been made, a bond had been created that would remain with them both for as long as the sun set in the west. Lobo became uneasy, knowing that he was treading on forbidden ground, and after his tongue flashed across Willow's cheek, he turned and trotted back outside.

Willow had received her first kiss from a friendly male, a furtive kiss that would be known to no one but Lobo and little Willow Harrison.

Billy and Boot adored their new niece, and when not riding the prairie could be found at the cabin, taking turns holding the new member of the McGregor clan. Often they drew straws to see who got to hold her first, other times they simply drew a card out from a deck of cards—the low card became the loser.

Two more years slipped into the past, allowing a peaceful atmosphere to settle across the open range of Milk River country. The Harrison ranch prospered, the herd was increasing as well as the cowboys, whose job it was to ride herd on the longhorns.

Billy McGregor was now foreman of the twelve-man crew, his brother Boot was second in command, answering only to his brother Billy and brother-in-law Smokey Harrison.

Although Smokey was kept busy at the home ranch, he never missed a morning of riding out on the range with his cowboys. He enjoyed this daily ride, giving him a chance to talk over the tasks of a growing ranch with Billy and Boot. Several hours later he would be back at the cabin and his makeshift office on the kitchen table.

It was here he could be close to Sage and Willow, who were thrilled with his presence. Sage hovering in the background with a friendly word, supporting her husband as best she could as he settled in to keeping track of the financial matters of the ranch.

Smokey wasn't fond of keeping books, yet knowing that it was a must for the ranch to succeed he gritted his teeth and sharpened his pencil. Hiring and firing cowboys was becoming more common, as was the ordering of supplies and equipment.

More important than all the rest, was staying close to his darlin' Sage who once again was heavy with child. It was an exciting time, knowing that three-year old Willow would soon have a sibling to play with, yet a trying time for Sage.

Like all expectant mothers, her nerves were riding a fine edge, concerned over the welfare of the new one that was coming, as well as for herself. Birthing a baby on the prairie was a risky venture, no doctors within a hundred miles and midwives were few and far between.

One morning she seemed troubled, just couldn't settle down. "Smokey!" she said, "Will you send one of my brothers up to Lobo Canyon—and have him bring Aspen down to be with me.

"I would feel much better if she was here, and I can tell our new baby isn't going to wait much longer!" How she knew, nobody knows except those who are in such a fix, but somehow Sage knew it was going to be a hard birth; needing all the assistance she could get.

"Holy Smokes!" Smokey replied, standing up from the paper-littered table, a surprised look appearing on his face. "I sure never reckoned it would be this soon.

"Billy is still at the corrals—bin a workin' with a green colt o' his."

Out the door he went, almost at a lope, and returned with Billy who was equally concerned about his sister Sage.

"Take that gelding o' mine," Smokey roared. "Bandit can eat up the miles like no other hoss on the prairie, I'll stay here with Sage."

And Billy did just that. Swinging aboard the saddle, he put the spurs to the big gelding and pointed his nose into the west.

With her dogs doing most of the herding, Aspen McGregor was moving the sheep flock out to graze the lush meadow grass. She then returned to the big two-storied cabin, an intense concern showing on her pretty face. She was worried sick over the condition of her sister Sage, who was due to give birth to a new baby any day now; might even be hours as far as she knew!

Aspen had been pacing the floor for days, worried sick of over the condition of her sister Sage. Sensing that the time for arrival of the new babe was here and now, she spoke to old Angus for the umpteenth time. "Sage is alone!" she told him, her Scottish temper rising, "with no one there to help her!

"I am riding down to be with Sage, and help her through this trying time in her life!"

"Well go then Lass," he said, finally giving his consent. "You are gifted with a knack at birthing the babies, and have a soft spot for your sister in your loving Gaelic heart too."

Aspen wasted no time in packing a satchel full of the necessities that she might need, then after stepping into the saddle on a patiently waiting pony, she headed for the eastern prairie leaving Lobo Canyon behind in the dust.

The pony was fresh and ready to run. With no let up the girl continued on, following a faint trace through the forest, until finally reining in the pony at a small rivulet of water pooling near the base of a balsam pine.

The cool water was welcomed by both the girl and her horse. She gazed around in wonder, realizing that she could now see the hills of waving grass, the tree-line of the big forest fading away behind her.

She knew they were making good time when spotting the grass covered hills, and took advantage of the stopover to stretch her legs and allow both herself and her pony to quench a nagging thirst.

The pony was greedily savoring the cool spring water, when with an unexpected move, raised its head with a jerk, both ears on the alert—paying close attention to a nearby willow thicket. The pony's nostrils were flaring, inhaling a strange scent that Aspen was unaware of.

The girl was startled too, and realizing that danger could be lurking nearby, quickly stepped back into the saddle; only to be near unseated by the action of the frightened animal. All that saved her from getting thrown to the ground, was the sheep-skin wrapped horn on the saddle, both of her dainty hands were hanging on for dear life saving her from a buck-off.

After securing her feet once again in the stirrups, Aspen hung on to the horn as best she could. The normally docile pony was streaking for the open prairie, with a long-haired tail flying straight out in the prairie breeze.

From behind the frightened pair could be heard a series of savage whoops and hollers. The pony could sense the ruckus closing in behind him, though tiring the pony continued to run.

The chilling war cries were closing in behind her, Aspen knew that she couldn't stand up to whoever was chasing her much longer, and pulled in her heaving pony before it collapsed from under her. Turning her head to see, a gasp escaped her wind-chapped lips at the sight of two half-naked Indians, their bow strings taut, ready to shoot her in the back.

Stealing her nerves for the expected pain of an arrow entering her body, she heard a rifle shot, and looked up to see a charging Billy McGregor. His first shot downed the one moving in close to Aspen, in mere seconds a second shot downed the other.

Reining in a charging Bandit, Billy was in a state of shock watching his sister's horse collapse beneath her. Aspen was able to scramble away from her dying pony just in time, thanking her lucky stars that she was able to do so.

"Are you all right Aspen?" Billy shouted, as he vaulted from a sweat-streaked Bandit, and rushed over to kneel beside his downed sister.

Aspen was weeping bitter tears, watching the death throes of her beloved pony, and unable to answer his question. The little horse had given his all attempting to save his mistress, and had run himself plumb to death.

With one arm holding his devastated sister close, all Billy could do was be patient, and wait for her to settle down.

After Aspen realized that she was still alive and breathing, she was ready to make talk with her brother. To have him here holding her close, gave her the confidence to continue on. "I must go and be with Sage," she managed to say.

"That's where we're a going," Billy replied, "as soon as I pull the saddle off your dead pony, and put it on that Indian pony standing behind you."

And this he did. Then off they went, Bandit and Billy streaking for the home ranch, Sage was close behind, riding an appaloosa Indian pony with the feather of a raven still entwined in its unruly mane and tale.

It was dark when they rode into the ranch. Though there was no way to have timed the wild ride, there can be no doubt that it had been a fast one. Both horses were physically exhausted, heads hanging low. Struggling to recoup the life-sustaining air to their tortured lungs, the horses would eventually recover in time. Time is what it would take, and a bunch of tender loving care.

With her satchel in hand, Aspen leaped from the staggering pinto and ran for the house. Bursting through the doorway, she almost upset Smokey, who on hearing the ruckus outside was in the act of opening it himself, praying that it might be the return of Billy, bringing with him his sister Aspen.

Not bothering to speak, she continued on into the bedroom to find Sage in a delirious condition and moaning in pain. Smokey who had followed her in, was promptly shooed back out, after which she told him to bring her hot water and towels,

It seemed like hours to Smokey Harrison, who was endlessly pacing back and forth on the cabin floor, worried sick of what might be happening to his darlin' Sage, when suddenly he heard the cry of a baby.

After being shooed away by Aspen, he was still a bit reluctant to enter the bedroom, and it was then a terrified scream broke the silence. His nerve-wracked body began to shiver and shake, cold chills were rippling down his spine, not slowing up until they crashed into his boot heels; and it was Aspen who had screamed.

Suddenly the door burst open, and out came Aspen who wound up in Smokey's arms. She was sobbing her head off, and managed to say, "I was too late getting here Smokey!

"We have lost Sage!"

A husband and a sister-in-law, both weeping bitter tears, stood together sharing their grief until another sound drifted out from the bedroom. It was the sound of a newly born baby girl, crying for her Mom who was no longer there!

The body of Sage Harrison was taken back to the McGregor ranch and interred at the edge of the big forest. It was here old Angus had set aside a peaceful site for those of the Clan who had been taken from this life, a journey of wonders as they crossed over into another median.

Aspen took Willow and the baby back with her, and treated them as if they had been her own. She knew Smokey would be upset over their leaving, she also knew that the big cowboy would be unable to give them the care they were in need of at this crucial time in their young lives.

With great misgivings he allowed her to do this, he too realized that he would be unable to fill the void of a caring mother. Deep inside his heart he knew that Aspen would proudly walk in the shoes of her sister Sage, and raise her daughters in the way of the Clan of McGregor.

The entire crew of the Milk River ranch attended the funeral service for the boss's wife, including Soupbone. The old camp cook had made a special effort to prepare himself for such an event, scrubbing his well-worn clothes in the river, and to the amazement of the entire crew; scrubbed himself as well.

Boot McGregor was a self-appointed barber at the ranch, and trimmed the old timer's shaggy beard into a respectable condition.

And then, after Boot had built a casket for his sister's body, it was placed into the wagon box and they were ready to roll. The mounted cowboys were all decked out in their finest duds, riding as escorts for the wagon and the precious cargo that it held.

There was no prouder camp cook in the territory that day than old Soupbone, who was at the reins of an equally proud team, transporting Sage Harrison's body up to the grave site in the pines; once there, the last rites were given by a grieving leader of the Clan, her father Angus McGregor.

The grave site was a hallowed plot of ground to the Clan, a place where they could gather and meditate over the mysteries of life—and feel close to their loved ones who had gone on ahead, breaking a trail for the rest to follow.

✳ ✳ ✳ CHAPTER 12 ✳ ✳ ✳

The flicker of a sage brush fire did little to boost the spirits of the cowboys that night. After enduring another sixteen-hour day of living hell, the three riders were ready to toss in their chips in utter defeat. A decision had to be made this very night on what to do, and when to do it.

Reflecting on the fate of their ill-fated cattle drive, Smokey Harrison was desperate, fearing for the survival of the ranch. It was nearing the autumn equinox and still no rain had fallen on the prairie. The grass, short as it was, became as crisp as a late autumn leaf, crunching under the feet of the longhorns as they wandered far and wide attempting to fill their bellies.

Here in a makeshift cow camp, the shadows of a prairie night crept across the sun-baked prairie, easing somewhat the incessant heat of a late summer day. Followed by the black of night, the only light was from the star-studded heavens and the reflection of a camp fire bouncing off the dust stained canvas of a chuck wagon.

Day after day, from daylight until long after dark, the entire crew had been kept glued in their saddles, moving the starving herd from one place to another. On the hunt to find enough grass to keep them alive; and just barely it would be.

While on a recent visit up to the McGregor's Lobo Canyon ranch to visit Willow and Rose, he was surprised to discover the mountain country had received rain in the form of thunder showers, enough to keep the grass showing a tinge of green.

But here in short grass country it was not to be.

The famished herd were pushed farther into the east, finding conditions in the badlands even worse—nothing but empty water holes and cracks in the arid ground.

"Swing 'em north!" Smokey ordered one day, "could be we'll find grass up in that Saskatchewan River country."

Billy McGregor, second in command of the drive, stood up from the fire ring where he and his brother Boot had been listening to Smokey's talk. "Reckon old Soupbone must be asleep," he said. glancing over at the chuck wagon, knowing the old timer slept underneath the wagon.

"This hellish drive has been hard on him—he's not his old happy self anymore—bin looking mighty poorly to me!"

Billy walked over to the wagon, and finding his beloved friend asleep, tucked the blanket under Soupbone's whiskered chin before returning to the fire.

"I reckon you're right Billy. I'm concerned about him too, Smoky said. "I have insisted that he return to the ranch, ordered him in fact, but he refused to go. He let me know in no uncertain terms that his job was to take care of his friends… meaning you brothers and me!"

After a ten day drive of living hell, the Harrison longhorns met up with the big river; staggering, gaunt and in a weakened condition. To everyone's dismay, nothing was there but the same sun-scorched conditions.

It seemed the entire southwest prairie was in the same fix. No rain, no grass, nothing but a heat-baked land cursed with a hot sun and an endless wind.

Scores of Indians were following the beaten path left by the herd, happy to find and eat the carcasses of the dead longhorns who had fallen by the wayside; suffering a lingering death from starvation and fatigue. What few buffalo that were left had migrated far to the south, finding food down that way where the rains were more frequent.

Members from several tribes had banded together on the hunt for food, Cree, Blackfoot and Sioux, though bitter enemies most of the time, they now rode as one, food is what they were after; nothing else mattered at this time.

Smokey had watched them with great concern, knowing what they were doing and why, yet concerned that it might develop into something more serious. Knowing that to be engaged in an Indian battle at this time would complete the disaster they were already experiencing.

The three cowboys were silent, drinking coffee and smoking their pipes, listening to the lowing of starving cattle and the victory howl of a prairie wolf, who was dining on Harrison cattle.

Smokey was the first one to break the silence. "Reckon we've taken one he-ell of a lickin," he said, watching closely his two top guns, Billy and Boot. His attention then strayed to the wagon and the ludicrous sound of Soupbone snoring up a storm.

"Reckon the old timer is plumb tuckered out, bin' goin' without a decent night's sleep for far too long.

"And you two!" he spoke again. "When was the last time you two had any sleep?"

"Can't rightly say," Boot said, fighting to keep his eyes open. "...'bout the same as you Smokey—none...!"

"Reckon we've lost half the herd," Billy commented, struggling to keep his own eyes open after a sixteen hour shift in the saddle.

"Two more riders left us today, said they couldn't stand anymore of this heat and dust—out of the dozen we hired on— only six of us are left!"

Deep in thought, the three remained silent, a silence broken only by the nerve-wracking snore of a worn out Soupbone.

Finally Smokey began to talk. "We started out on this hunt for grass with about three-hundred longhorns, you reckon Billy we have lost half?"

"Reckon so." Billy answered, "and they're dropping like flies as each day passes.

Another week and there will be nothing left to drive but their shadows."

Though sick at heart, Smoky was not going to give up and just ride away. He had a new plan in mind that just might save what was left of his herd. Early the next morning the herd was pointed into the west, driven by five riders and a camp cook trailing behind in his chuckwagon.

It was late in September before they arrived in the foothills of the Rockies, a much smaller herd, driven in stages by a much smaller crew of cowboys. Three of them were left, Smokey and his two brother-in-laws Billy and Boot, and of course a faithful Soupbone.

Grass was found in the upper foothills, though dry as hay, it was nourishing graze for the fifty some odd cattle that had survived the ordeal.

Smokey Harrison had fought a losing battle with the dreaded drought of 1886, but not for lack of trying. His head was still held high, he and his brother-in-laws had cowboyed up when the chips were down, and brought to safety a remnant of a once promising way of life.

The cattle settled down and were finally content after a summer of living hell, several had gorged themselves on the abundance of graze, and had swiftly died from a condition known as bloat.

And then November arrived. To add insult to injury another calamity swept across the land, the hard winter of

1886-87 rolled in with a fury. Four months of blizzard after blizzard battered the land piling up enormous snow drifts, the temperature stayed well below zero with no let up at all.

In a small clearing along the edge of the big forest sat an old canvas-topped wagon, abandoned and near buried by the deep drifts of wind-driven snow. The mountain meadow which had become the new home for the remaining Harrison cattle, had evolved into a barren surface of nothing but deadly ice-crusted snow.

An eerie silence was broken by the moaning of an incessant wind. The lowing of starving cattle no longer echoed across the clearing, even the creatures of the forest were silent, having found shelter back in the forest—away from the wind!

Far to the south, within shouting distance of the McGregor sheep ranch, struggled three half-frozen cowboys breaking trail for their exhausted saddle horses. Able to walk on the hardened snow, Smokey Harrison was out in front—Bandit was close behind, lunging with every step—breaking through the belly-deep snow as he did so.

Dusk was closing in on the survivors of the terrible winter when Smokey called a halt, giving the cowboys and their horses a chance to ease their aching lungs. "How's every one a doing?" he shouted back.

"Soupbone, are you still with us? he shouted once again, and received no answer. All three turned to check on their old friend, who had been struggling most of the way—but no Soupbone was in sight.

The eerie moaning of a winter breeze pestering the tree tops broke the silence of an ancient forest, prolific with lodgepole pine and giant spruce trees. Then a sharp bark, almost a howl, sounded close by. Could be a timber wolf smelling out the McGregor sheep, Smokey reckoned, or even a hungry coyote lurking nearby. But it was Lobo who appeared out of the gloom, wagging his bushy tail, his tongue hanging low, excited as all get out at finding his old friends from the Milk River ranch.

Although Lobo had wanted to be in on the cattle drive, Aspen had taken him to be with her and the girls at her parent's ranch. The dog greeted Boot and Billy with the same enthusiasm as he had Smokey. Not at all satisfied, his attention was now centered on the incoming tracks, as if knowing there was yet another out there in the darkness; freezing in the snow.

A strange sensation entered the mind of the three cowboys, as if it was Lobo who was talking to them. '...*where is my friend Soupbone? what has happened to him?...*'

He took one last look at the cowboys with an inquiring stare, then uttered a sequence of low growls and took off down the trail to find a good friend. His shaggy form was soon lost in the gloom of that dark night,

"Reckon Lobo will find our camp cook," Smokey said.

"The devil himself couldn't keep the dog away from the old cook, who has fed him leftovers from the kitchen since he was a small pup!"

The crunch of snowshoes in the snow alerted the cowboys of yet another presence approaching from out of the dark night, and then Aspen appeared. With a shriek of joy, she recognized the three cowboys as Smokey and her brothers.

She was bundled up in warm clothes, a rifle in hand and a spare pair of snowshoes was strapped on her back.

"I'm so happy to see you all," she spoke, a quiver in her voice. "We thought you had all died from this terrible winter!"

Smokey could tell she was in tears, and moving beside her gave the guardian of his two daughters a warm hug.

"Have you seen Lobo?" she asked. "He has been upset all evening, barking like crazy, hanging out back yonder by the sheep corrals."

"We've bin through hell and back again," Smokey told her, "lucky to be alive!

"Yes, Aspen! The dog was here. greeted us and then took off back down our tracks lickety split. Old Soupbone's back there somewhere—we just now realized he wasn't with us.

"How the Lobo dog knew this, I'll never know."

Knowing that he couldn't keep Aspen from going on alone to find the old timer, he sent the boys on to the ranch, Billy leading Bandit—the rest would follow. After strapping on the spare snowshoes, he turned to Aspen and said, "I'll lead the way."

They found Soupbone about two-hundred yards down the trail, slumped over in the snow. Lobo was there barking up a storm of his own, making sure that help was coming to help his good friend.

The old timer had died where he fell, Smokey reckoned his over-worked heart had quit him. It was a tough time for Smokey and Aspen, to lose such a good and caring companion. Aspen was sobbing and could not stop. Smokey's eyes were damp from his own tears, which were turning into miniature icicles on his eyelids.

Neither of them spoke, the silence disturbed only by the sound of Aspen's sobbing. Then after a shrug of his weary frame, Smokey said, "Reckon there's not much we can do till morning Aspen. Reckon we should head back to the ranch and get thawed out ourselves."

"We can't leave him here alone Smokey, all alone and in this terrible snow!"

"Nothin' much we can do for him now," he told her. "I'm all tuckered out and so are Billy and Boot—all three of us are all in 'bout the same shape as old Soupbone was,

"We bin sloggin through this confounded snow since daylight this morning!"

"But won't the wolves find his body Smokey, and have him et up by morning?" It was an innocent question she asked, but one full of logic and common sense.

Reaching deep in the pocket of his coat, he brought out the remainder of his jerky ration that had been shared that morning by the four cowboys. "Lobo will stay with old Soupbone till we come back for the body.

"He'll curl up by his old friend and guard his remains from the pesky wolves and coyotes—keep them away until we return.

"Lobo!" he ordered. "Stay! Stay here with Soupbone!"

The dog did what he was told, and with his mouth chomping on jerky watched Smokey and Aspen turn and head back toward the ranch. Lobo was only too happy to stay with his old friend, and after pawing away the snow, cuddled beside him to keep him warm.

But something wasn't as it should be, no amount of cuddling could keep old Soupbone warm. It was then the dog sensed what had happened, and even though he stayed put as he had been ordered to do, he was not comfortable by doing so.

In his own canine way, he voiced his sympathy for his dead friend with a sorrowful tune, accompanied by a lonely howl of displeasure over the fate of an old camp cook who had treated him with such kindness and respect.

After enjoying the first home-cooked meal in months, the three cowboys found a bed and were asleep the minute they hit the sheets. Twelve hours later Smokey and Billy awoke, both feeling like new men. Boot had a fever though and stayed in bed, a severe case of ague had taken control of his worn-out body.

Aspen had arose early, and after preparing breakfast for the family, was putting on her warm clothes to go find Lobo, when Smokey said, "I'll go with you—reckon we can rig up a drag—like an Indian travois—and bring Soupbone back to the ranch.

"It will make me happy to have you with me Smokey," she replied, a happy smile spreading across her face.

Off they went, Smokey pulling a makeshift travois, Aspen packing her brother-in-law's rifle. It was daylight now, and as they neared the location of Soupbone's body they both stopped, sensing that something was wrong.

No Lobo came to meet them, no sound could they hear but the chatter of a magpie family who had collected around the corpse of the old camp cook. "It appears like Lobo must of had unwelcome visitors," Smokey said, pointing out to Aspen the abundance of tracks around the body.

"And it was wolves, a whole pack of them by the looks of things, I reckon Lobo has had one helluva of a fight on his hands—while we've bin sleeping!"

Neither the cowboy or the young lady that stood beside him were prepared for what they discovered—it was a terrible shock to them both. Two dead wolves lay in the snow, torn and bloody, and near Soupbone's body lay an equally torn-up Lobo.

By the confusion of the tracks, Lobo had put up a gallant battle against the savage denizens of the forest, and had been overpowered by a ravenous pack of wolves. The tracks told the story, utter confusion had taken place here. Lobo had been out numbered, and had gone down fighting, gallant to the end as he lay beside Soupbone's body gasping his last breath.

Kneeling beside the dog Aspen was weeping bitter tears. Smokey was equally touched, and proud too; proud of the action of a faithful dog who had given his life to protect the body of a friend.

Smokey secured Soupbone's body on the travois, placing the rigid body of Lobo beside him. Working as a team they started back for the ranch, dragging the bodies of two dear friends behind them.

With sadness in their hearts, those who were present watched as the frozen bodies of the cook and the dog were placed in an empty grain bin, there to rest until the frost left the ground in the spring.

✱ ✱ ✱ CHAPTER 13 ✱ ✱ ✱

In due time a friendly sun returned to the territories, the snowdrifts finally began to shrink in size and the cold north winds had been chased away by a warm westerly breeze. Announcing their arrival with an exuberant fanfare, the migratory birds of the region were returning from their annual flight to the southern lands.

The spring of 1887 was a time of discovery, welcomed by most folks, dreaded by others, who like Smokey Harrison had been completely wiped out. He no longer had a thriving ranch in Milk River country, stocked with a herd of longhorns and a crew of fighting cowboys to ride herd on them.

His camp cook had died battling the deepness of the snow, his faithful dog Lobo, had died fighting a pack of hungry wolves, and his father-in-law, old Angus McGregor had gave up the ghost as well, fighting to save his herd of starving sheep. All of the above had fought a gallant battle against a hard winter that would go down in history as one of the worst of the century.

As he was the oldest son, Billy McGregor was chosen as the top gun in the Clan of McGregor—an honored position passed down from father to son. A bit reluctant at first to accept such a responsibility, he soon became a highly regarded leader; respected by all. One of his first official functions was the burial of old Angus and Soupbone.

The Lobo dog was buried as well, along side the cook, two good friends resting together.

Several weeks following the burial ceremonies, Billy had to preside over yet another highly regarded function of the Clans, the marriage ceremony of Smokey and Aspen. He knew they were close friends, always had been.

And after Sage had died leaving two young babes with no Mom, Aspen had willingly filled in the void of someone who was missing. He also knew that little Willow and Rose loved Aspen as if she had been their real Mom.

To have taken Aspen as his third wife was a big boost in the sagging self esteem of Smokey Harrison. She could never replace his love for Dove and Sage, yet offered him a special love of her own. An attractive wild flower found only in Lobo Canyon, had now blossomed and found the mate of her choosing.

They lived out the winter at the sheep ranch, doing their share of the work to help pay for their keep. Often, as the season turned toward spring, they would ride out through the forest searching for any sign of cattle. Could be, Smokey reckoned, some might have survived the savagery of the blizzards, and be holed up in a sheltered nook somewhere in the vastness of the eastern front of the mountains.

One day, they stumbled on to cattle tracks in the snow—fresh ones too! To add flavoring to the exciting find, Aspen said she was sure she had heard the lowing of a cow off in the distance.

The tracks were simple to follow, cloven-hoofed impressions in the snow sprinkled at random with a well known trademark of the bovine beasts; freshly dropped cow manure. It was nearing dusk before they found what they had been looking for, five hunger-ravaged longhorns scavenging for food—one of them was a bull.

Though spooked some at the arrival of two humans riding horses, their gaunt condition canceled out any running they might have had in mind. "Reckon the critters would have soon fell victim to the wolves," Smokey said.

"The condition they're in, they wouldn't stand a chance," Aspen replied. "The only reason they've survived this long is the wolves in these parts have been feasting on dead Harrison cattle carcasses all winter long."

After surviving a make-shift night camp, a bankrupt rancher and his wife arose early and prepared a scanty breakfast. The cattle were not far away, and appeared eager to follow the trail in the snow left by the two riders from the night before—all they had to do was trail along behind.

Arriving back at the ranch late the next night, four longhorn cows and a bull were pushed into the sheep corrals and given a good feed of mountain meadow hay. Here they made themselves at home with what was left of the decimated McGregor sheep flock.

Though plenty of frozen snowdrifts were left in the forest, the meadows were turning green from a warming sun, a mixed herd of black-faced sheep and longhorn cattle grazed together on the mountain grass at the mouth of Lobo Canyon.

As spring turned into summer, Smoky Harrison became restless, down right irritable in fact. Surely, he reckoned, there must be more to life than this. Though he loved Aspen and his daughters, a tugging from inside his inner self could not be ignored. He knew then he must move on—and find an answer to this mysterious call of the wild.

One night as they lay in their bed, Smokey told Aspen of his problem. He told her it was something he had no control over, that he just had to go to he knew not where, but to go he must!

Aspen sensed what was happening to her husband, and had prepared herself to face the problem when it arrived. And now here it was laid out in three simple words—I must go!

"I agree with you Smokey," she said, an answer that left Smokey slightly puzzled, expecting her to object with much vigor.

"But, on one condition!

"That you take me with you—which is my final answer!"

A silence followed, both deep in thought, and it was Aspen who was the first to speak. She told him their two daughters would be fine, that she had already talked to Billy about such a thing occurring, who agreed to care for them as if they were his own.

Smokey still had not spoken, measuring in his mind both the pros and the cons, he had figured on a lonely ride with no trail partner to back his play.

Aspen spoke one more time, brushing tears from her eyes as she did so, "Don't you want your new wife to be with you?"

Then, with an infectious grin that spread from one ear to the other—and a cowboy whoop for good measure—Smokey almost smothered a delicate wild flower of the canyons with a bear hug that would reap long lasting rewards.

"Of course I do!" he replied, and right then and there received a taste of the sweet nectar available to those who rode together, partners in all things as they faced the mystery of an unexplored trail—the trail of life!

* * * CHAPTER 14 * * *

Smokey Harrison and his wife Aspen rode away from the McGregor place, a pack mule loaded with supplies trailing behind them. Their destination was still a mystery, yet they both felt they must go, an itching in their souls that just couldn't be brushed aside.

Traveling east for one last look at the river ranch, they were shocked at the condition of a once flourishing spread. There was nothing left of the home cabin and bunkhouse but a pile of ashes, burnt to the ground by they knew not who. The corrals had fallen into ruin and a two-hole privy was in decrepit condition, ready to collapse from the savagery of the howling north blizzards.

A lonely south-east wind moaned through the ranch site, disturbing the ashes from the fire, adding to the desolation and decay of the old Harrison place. On up the mile-long coulee it swept, spooking a covey of prairie chicken from their hideout in the berry brush, who in turn startled an antelope Mom and her newborn set of twins.

"Reckon my old ranch has gone plumb to hell," Smokey said, brushing a tear from an eye.

"I lost everything I owned here, except the clothes I'm a wearin' and these hosses were a ridin'"

"Let's go!" Aspen said. Your old ranch is down right spooky now—gives me the shivers to sit here and look at those ashes over yonder.

"I can never forget the time Sage and I came down here picking berries, and the kindness you showed us by insisting that we sleep in your bed; while you Smokey, slept outside under the stars!"

"Shucks Aspen, it is the code of the west to treat visitors that way, I was happy to do it."

Without a backward glance, the Harrisons rode down the Milk River to a parting of two Indian trails, one continued on following the river, the other turned into the west and became known as the popular Whiskey Gap trail.

Smokey planned on stopping at the Gap to bid farewell to the old trader, only to find his aged building deserted with no sign of life. All too plain to see was an open door swinging on a rusty hinge, and mud swallows flying in and out of the broken windows.

"Reckon the hard times have busted-up my old friend's as well," Smoky commented.

"Was he honest? Aspen asked. "Billy and Boot told us they were sly as a fox checking out a farmer's chicken coop, waiting for a chance to steal a fat hen."

"Well," Smokey replied, "after allowing his trading post to be used as a cover for a smuggling venture, his honesty is sure enough questionable.

"But he was friendly enough if you hand cash in hand, and looked him in the eye!"

Leaving the old structure behind the two riders continued on, following the trail into the vastness of the northwest. It was nothing more than a well-traveled set of ruts used by the smugglers—the Whiskey Gap Trail—that took their loaded wagons into the land of the Blackfoot, Blood and Piegan camps. It was here they swapped their illicit booze for anything of value, including on occasion the wives of the gullible, intoxicated natives.

183

Later that day the Harrisons arrived at a new settlement taking shape known as Lee's Creek. They made camp in a grove of cottonwood trees, ancient giants which grew along both banks of a lively mountain-fed stream.

On the far side of the stream were parked several canvas-topped wagons, arranged in a unique manner resembling a horseshoe. As twilight moved into the valley, blazing camp fires were lit, music began to play and the people began to dance and sing.

They were a jolly enough lot, bursts of happy laughter could be heard above the chatter of Lee's Creek, only to cease as the strains of a fiddle began to play music that was foreign to the ears of the Harrison duo.

The two riders had a fire of their own, a cooking fire that was much smaller than the big ones of the Mormons, and they were Mormon pioneers, who had recently arrived from the great Salt Lake country, as verified by a young rider who crossed the creek and invited Smokey and Aspen to join them for an evening of song and dance.

"Reckon we should go Aspen?" Smokey asked. "That bunch over yonder sure look friendly like.

"Besides, the smell from that food they must be cooking sure smells good".

Aspen readily agreed, her mouth was also watering from the tantalizing aroma of freshly baked bread, roast beef; perhaps even baked potatoes and gravy—that was drifting across the stream.

Once in the Mormon camp, they were treated as neighbors should be treated, food was offered them, and it was everything that Aspen had envisioned it to be. After the meal they were sitting cross-legged by one of the fires, watching the dancers and enjoying every minute of it, when the young rider who was the reason they were here in the first place invited Aspen to be his partner in a Virginia Reel.

Being shy around strangers, Aspen was not sure if she should accept the invitation or not, and looked at her husband for his approval. With a trace of a smile showing on his whiskered face, he gave her a wink of an eye, then settled back to watch.

"Aspen, be sure he brings you back to me, when this reel business is over!"

"It is a gentleman's way to do this—it is also the cowboy way!"

She smiled her consent and turned to face her dance partner.

The Mormon boy took her hand and led her out to join a group of dancers who were waiting for them to join in the fun. In no time at all Aspen was whisked away in the momentum of the dance, being passed from one partner to another as the wild and wooly action of a Virginia Reel took center stage at the Mormon outdoor ball.

Smoky was keeping close track of his wife, amazed at her agility in keeping step with the varied partners, when he felt a tap on his shoulder. Looking down at him was an older lady, wearing an ankle length dress and a sun bonnet hanging below her graying hair.

With a smile that reminded him of his mother, she asked, "Do you mind if I sit beside you? It has been such a long time since I've been around a real cowboy."

Though slightly embarrassed, Smokey stood up, Stetson in hand and stood tall beside her. She gazed in awe at the cowboy, who wore his usual range attire consisting of tanned buckskin chaps and spurred boots. A six-gun fit nicely on his hip and a faded bandana was knotted around his neck.

She was smiling as she settled down on the ground, waiting for him to do the same. "Saints alive," she said. "It is kind of you to allow me to bother you like this—you are a pleasant sight for my old eyes.

"You see, my husband was a cowboy, a real one just like you—he was taken from me as we crossed the plains. He was a scout who rode ahead of the wagon train, checking on Indian sign, and marking a trail for the wagons to follow. An Arapaho war arrow killed him, he was shot from ambush; never knew what hit him!

"His body is buried in an unmarked grave along side the Platte River. He never had the chance to travel on to the valley with me; the valley of the Great Salt Lake."

Aspen had now been returned to Smokey, and was sitting beside her husband. She had listened with interest to most of the good widow's story, and joined in with her in weeping bitter tears. As most ladies do, when one of them weep, the rest are sure to follow; and Aspen was no exception!

"I must go now," the widow said, struggling to rise to her feet. Smokey immediately stood up and assisted her to do so. "You have made me so happy," she said, looking up into his eyes.

"You have brought back memories of my husband that I will cherish forever—thank you so much!"

With that said she gave him a warm hug and turning to face the crowd, was soon lost from view by a flock of swirling dancers.

An early-morning dew lay heavy on the grass in the Lee's Creek valley. A rooster crowed from his cage beneath a canvas-topped wagon, and a dog barked a warning at a movement in the eerie mist rising from the surface of the nearby stream.

One by one the cooking fires were kindled, the Mormon pioneers were preparing themselves for another day in the northern territories, and Smokey and Aspen were already on the move; reining their saddle horses into the unknown of the vast northwest territories of an English colony known as Canada.

"Sure a right friendly bunch," Smokey remarked to the little lady who rode by his side.

"And good cooks too," Aspen said. "The best prepared food I've ate since my Great Aunt Avon went back to Scotland, she told us kids that she wanted to die in the land of her birth—the highlands of Kirkcaldy it was—where she was reared as a child.

"She was the best I reckon—her roast beef dinners complete with all the trimmings—and fresh-baked apple pie was like ambrosia fit for the Gods; even old Wallace the Bruce himself."

"Avon you say!" Smokey said. "A down right purty name if ask me."

"Is it a Scottish name?"

"Far as I know," Aspen answered. "it is an English name closely associated with Stratford—the birthplace of old Shakespeare himself."

"The name was brought to Scotland with the English, who conquered our Clans a long time ago."

"Well thanks for the history lesson Aspen, I'm sure happy you are my ridin' pard today—sure beats going to school any old time!"

* * * CHAPTER 15 * * *

Far back in a virgin forest where the Porcupine Hills evolve from out of the the Rockies, Smokey and Aspen rode with caution up a seldom used game trail. A pack mule was plodding behind, loaded to the hilt with camp gear and grub of the adventure seeking Harrisons.

Though faint it was, the pathway was taking them to a junction with the Kutenai Pass trail that Smokey Harrison was looking for.

The Kutenai was the same trail he had traveled when crossing the Rockies many years ago, the same trail where Dove That Sings had found him and saved his life from a slow but agonizing death in the rock slide.

Not realizing why, a dim spark tucked in a far corner of his mind had been influencing Smokey to be here at this time. Ever since they had ridden away from the prairie and entered the timbered hills, this mysterious tugging at his heart strings had been leading him on.

A mystery of some kind must be hidden here, a mystery that only he and Aspen could unravel!

The sound of approaching thunder broke the silence of the darkening forest, causing the riders to rein in their horses and look up at a storm-tossed sky. "We must find shelter right pronto Aspen," Smokey shouted, "by the sound of things we could be in for a bad one!"

A raucous cannonade of thunder was now high above them, accompanied by vicious streaks of fire streaking to the ground. An eerie wind swept through the forest, moaning a fearful tune.

"Over there!" Aspen screamed, pointing to a stand of ancient spruce. Sometime in the distant past, one of the big giants had toppled over creating a wilderness shelter of twisted spruce boughs. On the lee side of the tangled mess, was yet another sheltered opening near its splintered base, large enough for the horses to enter and wait out the storm in relative safety.

A torrential rain battered the ancient derelict, sweeping across the forest by the force of a howling wind. Then came the roar of icy hail, drowning out all else save the explosive blasts of thunder.

Smokey and a terrified Aspen sat huddled together, a slicker from Smokey's saddle draped over their heads, a protection from the stinging pellets of ice that were penetrating the spruce boughs.

"Reckon we're downright lucky to have found this shelter," Smokey told his wife who was frantic with fear, an uncontrollable spasm of shattered nerves was taking control of her body.

He wrapped her inside his coat next to the warmth of his strong body, holding her close until her tiny frame showed signs of returning to its normal self.

The ice-laden fire storm moved on, leaving a swath of frozen white far out onto the open prairie. Taking a peek out of their wilderness shelter, the Harrisons decided to make night camp right here where they were at—a sea of white is all they could see in the twilight shadows of a storm-tossed night.

After a scanty supper of coffee and jerky, followed by the same for breakfast, they were heading up the trail before sunrise. A half-mile up the trail they rode on to bare ground, leaving the hail litter behind. The sun had now risen in the eastern sky, chasing away the gloom and doom of a night spent in the bowels of a long dead spruce tree.

After the passing of the terrifying fire storm from the previous night, the day grew warm and pleasant, rejuvenating both the riders and the denizens of the forest. A chattering mountain-bred stream crossed the climbing trail, offering the riders a reason to stop and refresh themselves with a cold drink of water, and refill their canteens.

Aspen had wandered back in the forest, stretching her legs and caring for other needs, when she froze in her tracks, listening for something amiss out there in the silence of the vast forest.

Her wilderness-honed ears had picked up a strange sound, so out of place in a wilderness such as this. She could have sworn that she had heard the crying of a child; it was a mournful heart-wrenching sound that had caught her attention!

"I know it wasn't an animal!" words that were spoken as she hurried back to tell Smokey.

He was equally interested, and together they entered the forest to see what they could find. Both were excited and anxious to solve this unexpected mystery, especially so was Smokey, whose inner self was urging him to go with Aspen; not giving him a minutes peace until he did so.

The forest was dense and thick with undergrowth, forcing Aspen to walk apart from Smokey, yet close enough to signal back and forth if needed. This gave them a better chance of locating the source of the strange cry that had upset her so. They both had a six gun strapped on their hip, Aspen was packing a saddle carbine as well.

Then the sound could be heard once again. It was much closer now, a young in years voice almost begging someone to come. Both of them had heard it, both of them froze—zeroing in on the source.

They were walking together when they found her, a small girl perhaps five or six years old lay huddled at the base of a tree. She wore no coat, nothing more than an ankle-length night gown. Her long blond hair was tousled and dirty, her face was smeared from incessant weeping, and she was suffering from an intense life-threatening case of the chills.

The little one was moaning, her eyes were closed, only to open again as she attempted to utter another cry for help.

"Oh! Oh my goodness," Aspen shouted, who knelt beside the little one and quickly wrapped the child in her own coat. "I reckon we should hustle back to the trail and get her thawed out," Smokey said, who then picked up the small bundle and followed Aspen back through the forest.

Once back with the horses, Smokey turned the little one over to his wife, then built a roaring fire on the edge of the trail. "Clean her up as best as you can," he told her, "while I heat some water and brew up a batch of good old jerky tea."

"Be sure you take off them wet duds she's a wearin', and keep her warm!" Aspen who was one step ahead of her husband, had already dug out a wool blanket from off the packhorse and was doing just that.

To be warm and dry was good medicine for the small child that Aspen held in her arms. And after a few swigs of Smokey's jerky tea, she began to recover from her ordeal of an inevitable death in the big forest.

Though she had made no sound, her blue eyes were finally open staring long at Aspen Harrison. She knew this kind person had saved her from the terrors of the forest, and that she would protect her from the evil ones.

"How's our little guest doing?" Smokey asked, and walked over to stand beside Aspen. He pulled back the blanket that had been tucked around her face, looking long at her now clean face.

A puzzled look appeared on his whiskered face, causing him to back away in wonder. "Why she's a right pretty little thing—the long blond hair—and her blue eyes that drill right through a person, looks plumb familiar.

"She reminds me of a right feisty little gal, one that I once knew!"

Smokey's whiskered face was all it took to bring tears to the little one's eyes. who shrank away in terror, fear once again consuming the child's mind. "Mommy!" she sobbed.

"I want my mommy!"

Cooing a comforting tune, Aspen was holding her close when she spoke. "Where is your mommy?"

Not receiving an answer, Aspen tried a different approach. "My name is Aspen, what is yours?"

"Ellie," came the reply. "Ellie Lou Tucker.

"My mommy's name is Laura Tucker!"

Smokey came unwound on hearing the girl say her mother's name, "Why I know a Laura Tucker, she is Kelly's wife, my old pard from the Wild Horse country—yonder across the Rockies."

* * * CHAPTER 16 * * *

At his wilderness home north of the Wild Horse gold diggings, Kelly Tucker often thought of his old partner Smokey Harrison. He missed Smokey whose optimistic outlook on life had been like a breath of fresh air to his younger partner. And they had been partners in all things, from riding the range as cowboys to mucking for gold along the Wild Horse country they had shared in the good times and the bad.

And then they had split, Kelly settling down with a new wife, Smokey riding across the Rocky Mountains to seek his destiny.

Starting a new life as a horse breeder was not in the cards for Kelly Tucker. He had given it a good try, but the setbacks were always there to hinder his progress. Indifferent bankers, his ranch too far from civilization to locate the right buyers, and the final slap in the face had been losing two of his prized brood mares to an onslaught of cougars.

It seemed he had waged an ongoing battle with the mountain lions right from the start. He had set baited snares to trap the hungry rascals, even brought in dogs to run them until they sought safety by climbing a tree. His success was fair to middling, but still they came. Kelly wandered the woods armed to the teeth, and by so doing had eliminated a few with his rifle. No matter how many he killed, there were always more waiting for a chance at the delicious, addictive horse meat.

Finally, the whole affair had became more than he could handle. He was flat busted and that is all there was to it. Confiding his feelings to a concerned Laura, he laid out his plans for a new start.

"Laura darlin'," he said. "I don't know how to tell you this, but I am a failure at running a horse ranch.

"We're broke! Hardly enough cash left to keep us in grub to eat—I do have a plan though," and it was then he shared with her his thoughts and desires for the future.

"Let's pack up our belongings, meager as they are, and ride across the Rockies and find Smokey Harrison. I sure miss my old pard, besides the son-of-a-gun just might be able to help us make a fresh start!"

Though tears were flooding her eyes, Laura remained quiet, listening to her husband's talk and not at all pleased with his decision to take her and little Ellie away from the homestead where they both were born.

"We're plain busted Laura!" Kelly said, sensing her displeasure over leaving the ranch. "I can't borrow a red cent from the bank over yonder at Wild Horse, all the greedy devils can think about anymore is gold, backing the big syndicates who are on the hunt for more gosh-darned gold!

"You see that coffee can sittin' on the shelf over yonder— it's nearly empty, and I don't have enough cash left to refill it!"

Laura remained silent for a long time before she broke the silence that had invaded her kitchen. She had silently weighed the pros and the cons, and though painful as it was, she knew that Kelly was right, they must move on and make a fresh start.

Looking at him through her tear-dimmed eyes, she finally spoke, "Ellie Lou and I will go where you go Kelly. We both love you very much and will stand beside you through this terrible time in our lives!"

Several days later they left the ranch, never to return. A small caravan consisting of three mounted riders, including Ellie Lou who was riding her Moms gentle old mare rode away from the homestead. Two loaded pack horses and a half dozen of Kelly's remaining herd trailed behind in single file. Laura, who had ridden the trail once before led them onward, not stopping until reaching the base of a giant rock slide that led up through the maze to the south pass of the Kutenai.

"No way that we can make it up through that mess of fractured rock," Kelly said, eyeing up the dangerous trail that wound its way skyward.

"Yes, Kelly there is!"

"Your partner Smokey, rode his horse right to the top. I know this to be true because I walked up there myself—in the dark; and found him and his saddle horse bedded down for the night."

"Very well then Laura, I reckon you're right; you always are! You and our daughter continue to lead these squirrelly broncs. I'll bring up the rear. keeping them strung out on this route you're using to take us up to the sky."

The ascent to the top of the Pass went off amazingly well. With Ellie Lou singing songs most of the way, the eleven-head string was calmed by the sound of her voice. A confidence had been created between a small girl and a group of her four-legged friends.

After spending the night on the Pass, Kelly Tucker's small caravan set their sights for Tornado Mountain and the trail leading out to the prairie. After descending yet another rock slide, they rode out onto an alpine meadow, allowing the horses to graze on the first grass they had found in the last two days. "Reckon we're in Indian country."

Kelly commented, spotting a small weathered shelter, woven from the slender branches of birch-willow brush.

"We'll stop over here for a day, let our hosses have a rest, and fill their hungry bellies.

"You two ladies," he said, a smile spreading across his face, "need a break from our long ride too."

Feeling much refreshed after a day of rest, the Tucker outfit headed into the east, following a trail used by the Indian, the wild animals of the mountains, and in the not so distant past; Smokey Harrison and his wife Dove!

They made good time that day, covering many miles, when suddenly out of no where it came. A wild and wooly thunder storm booming its way down from Tornado Mountain, complete with scary lightning bolts and torrential rain, turning into hail stones the size of marbles.

In no time at all the Tucker family were drenched to the hide. Their horse string became terrified of the unexpected fire storm and bolted into the dense forest. Kelly had his hands full keeping the two buck-jumping pack horses from doing the same.

The horse Laura was riding was a head strong beast, and taking the bit in his teeth, charged down the trail into the unknown of a swirling mist of hail and rain. Ellie Lou's old mare was equally alarmed and turned off into the shadow-infested depths of a storm-battered forest.

Kelly Tucker's wife and daughter had been swallowed up by the utter chaos of the storm, leaving him alone on the trail; cursing his stubborn bone-headed packhorses.

The storm soon moved on, leaving a sea of white, crunchy hail stones underfoot. Kelly Tucker was devastated. He had no clue as to where his wife and daughter were, his prize string of mares had been taken as well. All he knew was that all hell had broken loose on this high mountain trail.

Darkness swept across a lonely valley, a damp bone-chilling night made its presence known to Kelly Tucker, his wife Laura and a small child, who had been swept off the back of the old mare she was riding by the branch of a spruce tree.

It seemed like an eternity of time before Laura could regain control of her horse. That she was parted from her family, and taken far down the trail she was sure of. The horse had suddenly stopped at a fork in the trail, a small pathway led back into the woods to a wayside inn; nothing more than a long abandoned trading post that had been in the business of bartering for prime fur and beaver plew.

A dim light was visible from a grime-smeared window, and standing in an open doorway was a whiskered figure holding a double-barreled shotgun.

Laura was in rough shape from the wild ride, barely hanging on to the horn of her saddle when the horse took her down the path to the old inn. Once there it stopped by the doorway, at the same instant Laura lost her grip and tumbled to the muddy ground.

He looked long at the woman sprawled at his feet, shivering uncontrollably and plastered in mud. That she was unconscious he was sure of, and then with a grunt, sat his scattergun aside and picked up the body of Laura and took her inside.

"Look what I found—a layin' at our doorstep!" he boasted to the others, who were playing cards and drinking rum from a Hudson Bay labeled jug.

"She's in bad shape," he said, as he placed her on to an ancient bunk amidst the grime of seldom cleaned bedding.

"She's mine—'twas me who found her!

"Don't want you jaspers a foolin' with her either—leave her be—don't even know if the woman is going to make it or not, the shape she's in!"

The two never spoke, but had ceased with the cards, watching their old partner in crime fussing around this strange discovery.

One of them spoke, "We expect our fair share of the woman, remember our deal?"

"Nothin' doin', this is different—this time I'm in control!" and with that said he sat on the bunk beside Laura, his loaded double barrel in hand ready to wage war.

In a lonely land where the gentler sex are scarce as hen's teeth, to see a woman the likes of Laura Tucker was an unforgettable event in the lives of most mountain men. To be able to touch one, be close to one as was the case here, became a memorable day never to be forgotten.

Shortly before darkness had moved into the forest, Smokey Harrison's outfit camped within shouting distance of the Kutenai Pass trail. Aspen and Ellie Lou were exhausted, having just endured a twelve-hour ride, and so were the horses.

After a hearty meal, all three of them retired to their blankets, rejuvenating their weary bodies for what ever challenges might face them when the sun once again returned to the eastern front of the Rocky Mountains.

Smokey was restless, worried sick over what might have happened to Kelly Tucker and his wife Laura. Ellie Lou had mostly remained silent, her young mind still in a flutter over the loss of her parents, and the terror of wandering alone in the darkened forest.

Long into the night Smokey was awakened by the sound of muffled sobs coming from the child's blankets. Kicking aside his own blanket, he arose and went to the little one who was tossing and turning in wild abandon—weeping her heart out—reliving the terrible time of the previous night. He picked her up in his arms, and sat close by the waning embers of the camp fire, consoling Ellie Lou as best he could.

Aspen too was awakened, and sat up in her blanket to better see what was going on. To witness her husband caring

LOBO CANYON

for the little one like he was doing, made her very happy; and proud too. It was a reassurance of the character of the man she had married, knowing as she always had, he did have a tender spot in his heart for little innocent children. Especially the female ones, and their mothers.

It is the cowboy way!

Reaching the main trail that led into the eastern country, the tracks in the mud were plain to see. A lone horse had passed this way, traveling at a breakneck speed by the looks of it. Perhaps this was made by Ellie Lou, Smokey reasoned. Or even one of the Tuckers on the hunt for their daughter. Whoever it was and whatever their reason for doing so was of no matter now, Smokey swung his outfit on to the trail and followed.

Not far behind, hidden from view by a bend in the trail, came a nerve-wracked Kelly Tucker worried sick over the whereabouts of his wife and daughter. Pausing a moment to study the tracks of Smokey's outfit coming in off the game trail, he was heartened some, thinking that whoever it might be, could have seen one; or both of his missing family.

He stepped up the pace, his balky pack string no longer fighting to break free. Then after rounding another bend in the trail, he spotted riders in the distance, no more than several hundred yards in front of him.

He immediately drew his gun and fired three rounds, spaced at intervals, into the air. Why he did this he did not know.

Yet, from deep in his subconscious he did know! It was a signal that he and his old partner, Smokey Harrison had used, when young and full of it; a predetermined signal that had saved their hides on more than one occasion.

Smoky was startled when hearing the gunfire, and swung his bronc around to discover the incoming outfit streaking down the trail. "It is Kelly Tucker who fired those shots Aspen," he shouted. "I just know it is.

"No one else that I can think of knows of our signal, and the reason for using it! The son-of-a-gun has found us, he surely has."

It was a happy reunion when the two old partners met, arms wrapped around each other, stomping up a storm. To add icing to the cake happened when Kelly spotted Ellie Lou sitting on the back of Aspen's saddle, her tiny arms wrapped around the lady who had treated her with much kindness; squeezing her as tight as her small arms would allow.

"Daddy, daddy," she whimpered. "I want my mommy, we cannot find her." Though happy to see her daddy, who was now holding her in his arms, she was shedding bitter tears when she asked, "Find mommy for me, I am afraid something bad has happened to my mommy!"

By now all four of them were shedding tears, Kelly for being reunited with his lost daughter, Smokey and Aspen for witnessing a happy reunion between a small waif of a child and her big cowboy dad.

After a brief exchange of plans, it was decided to keep on following the tracks made by a running horse on the rain-soaked trail, perhaps a clue to a missing Laura Tucker. All was quiet except for the squishing noise of horse hooves in the mud, and the sucking sound made when the hooves were lifted up as they walked.

It happened much sooner than anyone could have expected. The tracks turned off on to a pathway leading down into the forest. There sat an old building with Laura's horse standing hip-shot, not far from a weathered plank door.

Leaving Aspen and Ellie Lou with the horses, Smokey and Kelly walked up to the door. Both pausing, listening to a ruckus inside. The roar of three angry men, the sound of a gun shot, and the scream of a woman who Kelly recognized as his wife, greeted the two cowboys.

Kelly Tucker was livid with rage, all set to bust through the door with guns blazing fire and brimstone. Smokey quieted him down, suggesting Laura might get caught in the melee, and become a victim herself.

It was near daylight when Laura aroused from the shock-induced coma she had fallen victim to. The first thing she was aware of was a dim light from the chimney of a coal oil lamp. At the same time she was sickened by the worst, foul odor that she had ever been exposed to in her life.

It was then she heard the snoring of a strange man sleeping at the foot of a bunk bed that she had found herself lying on. It wasn't hard for her to associate the snoring and the foul odor to the same source—a filthy old man who hadn't been around soap and water for months on end.

Stirring some, she noticed there were other men in the room, all of them appeared to be waiting for her to wake up, except one, who was perched nearby on an empty rum keg ready to pounce. Discovering that her eyes were now open, he approached the bed leering at a cringing Laura—a lecherous look spreading across his face.

"Leave me alone," she shrieked. "My husband will kill you if you touch me!"

And touch her he did, tearing at the tattered clothing of a fighting Laura. An agonizing scream escaped her chapped lips, cut short by a brutal back hand to her tear-stained cheek. Laura collapsed on the bunk, her mind once again slipping into a black void of nothing.

Laura's scream was the cue for action. Suddenly the door burst open, in came a roaring Kelly Tucker and his old friend

Smokey. The first one to die was Laura's attacker, the second one was the foul smelling one, who even though he had been trying to keep her for himself, fell to the floor; his double barrel shotgun still gripped in his hand.

The rest, and there were several, had been stunned by the suddenness of it all, and were clawing for their weapons. Blazing fire and brimstone reigned supreme in the old wayside inn, a haven for a group of murderers and thieves. When the smoke finally cleared there was only one left alive, the same one who had attacked Laura Tucker; and though he had been mistaken as being dead, he had survived.

A bullet from Kelly's smoking gun that should have killed him, had glanced off the rib cage of the swaggering bully; leaving him howling in pain.

Kelly carried his wife out to be with Aspen and Ellie Lou, asking Aspen to clean her up and find some clean clothes for her to wear. Laura was regaining her senses once again, spurred on by a sobbing Ellie Lou who was snuggled next to her Mommy's breast.

He then joined Smokey, who was dragging the howling woman molester out the door to a giant fir tree. It was here they fashioned a hangman's noose around his hairy neck, and watched him drop! It was a fitting punishment for a molester of the gentler sex.

It was the Code of the West to do so. Not to be outdone, it was the cowboy way as well!

✶ ✶ ✶ CHAPTER 17 ✶ ✶ ✶

Sundown in the forest is quick and sudden, giving way to a shadowed twilight, only to be consumed by the dark of night. Such was the case in a modest camp near the Kutenai Pass trail, where the two families had just finished eating their first cooked meal of the day. A cheery fire lit up a grass clearing in the pines, the reflection of the flames bouncing off a pair of tents pitched back away from the hazard of flying sparks.

Aspen and Laura were both skilled at the art of cooking over an open fire, and this meal had been no exception. They were both sitting on an old windfall tree, giggling and exchanging pleasantries as most good friends are prone to do. Nestled between them was little Ellie Lou, struggling to keep her eyes open after a long rough and tumble day. She was so happy to be reunited with her mommy once again, a joy that filled her young heart to the fullest.

She could never forget the love and kindness shown to her by Aspen Harrison, who had treated her as if she had been her own. From this time forward in Ellie Lou's young mind, Aspen would be considered as her second mom—after all, it had been Aspen and Smokey who had saved her life from the haunts in the scary forest.

Laura Tucker was equally thankful to be alive. As long as she lived she would never be able to forget the terrible storm, and the aftermath at the old wayside inn. Her young, healthy body was on the verge of being ravaged when Kelly and Smokey burst through the door, their guns blazing, shooting the bad men who were all set to ruin her.

After a long day of rounding up Kelly's scattered *remuda*, the two old partners of long ago were relaxing on yet another windfall, drinking coffee and smoking their pipes; and had remained mostly silent, soothed by the chatter of the women folks and the contented sound of their horses munching on the rich mountain grass. That Kelly's wife and daughter had been rescued in the nick of time was a great blessing, one that would never be forgotten!

Two cowboy partners from a time in the past were once again riding together. Smokey and Kelly had been comrades in the truest sense, sharing the good times and the bad, guarding each other's back, and willing to give their life for the other if that was how the cards had been dealt.

To be together once again was a great boost to the morale of them both, Once again life as they knew it had a purpose. And though they had both suffered through hard times and misfortunes, they still held their heads high, proud of their wives and families, and still proud to be known as cowboys.

Though Smokey never voiced his thoughts much, he knew that he could now forget the loss of his herd, an irritating pull at his inner self was no longer there. An intense fire inside himself that had kept him on the move, seeking he knew not what; had now been extinguished.

He reckoned it was fate that had urged him to ride into these mountains, at this time and this place, where he and Aspen were the means in saving Kelly and his family from an untimely death in the wilderness!

Having a happy, playful Ellie Lou in camp made Smokey and Aspen homesick for their own daughters. Later that night as they lay in their blankets, Aspen said "I sure miss them Smokey—it is time we returned to our own family."

"I've been thinking the same thing Aspen." Smokey answered. "we'll leave this place first thing in the mornin'— taking the Tuckers with us."

And this they did, vowing to one another that never again would they be parted from a blessing worth far more to them than a pot of gold; their own family, Willow and Rose Harrison!

✱ ✱ ✱ CHAPTER 18 ✱ ✱ ✱

Aspen and her brother Boot were the only members of the Clan of McGregor that were left at the old sheep ranch. Billy, seeking a better way of life, had returned to Scotland to find him a wife and seek his fortune.

Boot too was becoming restless, bored out of his mind with a humdrum way of life that had settled on to a once flourishing ranch. One day he saddled his bronc and rode away into the upper reaches of the Porcupines. It was while riding through the wooded hills, he found a job as manager of a large spread owned by a British syndicate of investors, in the new Colony known as Canada.

Aspen and Smokey made a deal to buy the Lobo Canyon property, payments to be made to her brothers on a yearly basis. It was here they settled down, converting the old sheep set up into a working cattle ranch. Slowly but surely, they were adding to the small herd of longhorns that had survived the hard winter,

Kelly Tucker took possession of the next canyon north of the Lobo. It was here, only five miles away from the Harrisons he and Laura settled in to make a new start in their rough and tumble lives.

A fine log cabin was built, and corrals for the brood mares they had salvaged from their bankrupt breeding venture across the mountains. It was here the growing herd was free to roam, far up a boxed in valley that became known as Horseshoe Canyon.

To bolster their meager finances, both of the old partners began trapping fur in the winter time. Smokey, who had received training from one of the best—Trapper Joe from Belly River country, in turn trained Kelly in the ways of a fur trapper.

Never before had a trapper set foot in the two valleys, resulting in an abundant harvest of prime furs, including beaver. Though a tough, bone-weary occupation, it was well worth it, allowing the two old cowboys the means to survive. To be able to keep food on the table, ammunition in their guns, winter feed for their growing herds and to be rid of the gut-wrenching worry of being a failure at their respective endeavors.

No longer did they spend sleepless nights, tossing and turning in their blankets, worried sick at the sight of an empty coffee tin, an empty flour sack, or the tattered clothing their wives and children had been forced to wear. Times had finally changed for the better, the answer to their hopes and dreams that had been beckoning on the horizon.

After partaking of one of Aspen's delicious suppers, the four of them had left the house to sit in the cooling comfort of an evening breeze. The shake-roofed porch was complete with several hand-hewn stools and an ornate bench, made from the trunk of a giant fir tree.

With his pipe tamped full and ready to put fire to, Smokey was relaxing after a long day in the saddle. He was enjoying the pleasant chatter of Aspen and his two daughters, only to have Willow interrupt his reverie. "Papa, look!" she cried, and gasped at what she could see plodding down the trail that followed the course of Lobo Creek.

Whatever it was that had startled her so was now hidden by a thicket of willow brush that grew in abundance along the creek. All four were standing now, including a concerned Smokey, who with his six-gun in hand was closely watching the willow thicket.

Seconds later, the Harrison family was shocked to see a large, grizzled-brown animal come out of the thicket. "My lord, it's a grizzly," Smokey said, "an old sow with two cubs trailing behind her."

The Lobo Canyon trail cut through the ranch yards, passing within mere yards of the horse corral. It was here the valuable animals spent each night in relative safety from the meat eaters on the prowl. On spotting the grizzly and getting a whiff of her rancid smell, all hell broke loose in the old pine-rail corral

On hearing Smokey speak the word grizzly, and knowing that he only had his six-gun with him, Aspen scurried back inside the house, returning to stand beside her husband, gripping her loaded and cocked rifle all ready for action. Together they watched the grizzly move in close to the corral. "Don't pull that trigger until you get a clear shot," Smokey told her.

"A hurried shot just might down one of our horses!"

The Harrison horse *remuda* consisted not only of their saddle horses, but several brood mares with young colts by their side were in the corral as well. The entire band was in a frenzied panic, crowding along the far side of the lodge pole structure until it was on the verge of collapse.

"Now is the time Aspen," Smokey whispered, watching the bear standing on her hind legs, tearing away the flimsy poles.

"Shoot! Shoot the old hell-raiser before it is too late!"

A rifle shot rang out in the Harrison's barn yard. A colt-hungry grizzly tipped over and fell to the ground; two large clawed paws feebly scratching the rocky trail. The sound of the rifle shot, echoing far back in the forest was followed by a deathly silence, broken by the whinny of a concerned mother locating her tiny foal, the whimper of two motherless grizzly cubs; and the sobbing of a nerve-ravaged Aspen.

Smokey held her close, comforting her as best he could. "You did great Aspen, downing that ol' girl with one shot, like you did."

"I reckon you're the best long gun shooter in these here mountains!"

"The cubs!" she sobbed. "I killed their mother—what will happen to them now?"

The horses, though still alarmed by the giant carcass lying outside the corral, were calming down some, watching Smokey as he repaired the damaged structure.

Later, with a prized skinning knife given to him by old Trapper Joe, Smokey removed the pelt from Aspen's bear and hung it spread-eagled between two aspen trees to dry out in the sun. The grizzled hide hung about ten-feet off the ground, appearing like a huge phantom from outer space dropping in for a landing. A grim reminder to other members of the bear family to stay away from the ranch, or else be gunned down by a sharp-shooting Aspen Harrison.

The two cubs never stayed around long, and though barely able to fend for themselves, were only too eager to leave. Urged on by Aspen's outraged Scotch collie, that was slowly but surely herding them far back into the forest—never to be seen again.

No respectable ranch is complete without a good dog or two around. They not only are faithful companions, they are as well guardians of the ranch and its inhabitants. Sacrificing their life if necessary, to protect their two-legged friends.

Early one morning Aspen saddled her favorite horse and rode away from the ranch. She was riding over to visit Laura Tucker, whom she hadn't seen in a coon's age. It wasn't far, five miles is all, an hours ride to the Tucker's horse ranch located at the mouth of Horseshoe Canyon.

She knew that her husband had left long before daylight, to put the finishing touches on a trapper cabin that he and Kelly Tucker had been building several miles up Lobo Canyon. Smokey had assisted Kelly in building his new log home, now Kelly in turn, was returning the favor to his old friend and neighbor.

Aspen was a bit concerned over leaving the girls home alone, but Rose had come down with a bad case of the sniffles, and Willow had volunteered to stay at the ranch with her, caring for her wants and needs. Besides, Smokey had told her that he would be coming home early, and for her not to worry.

It was the making of a perfect day here along the eastern edge of the forest, a cool pleasant start to a new day in the high country—a country that Aspen loved more than anything else in the world; excepting her husband and family. Her husband would always be first in her heart of hearts, followed next by her family. Nothing else, or no one else could influence her to be otherwise. It was a true, honest love that this mountain-bred girl had for her cowboy husband, and his two daughters!

The warmth of a rising sun was now creeping through the lodgepole forest. Birds of the deep woods greeted her with their mind-soothing songs, inducing the tree squirrels to follow suit with their tail-jerking signals, furry cheeks bulging with food for their hideaway in a hollow tree.

On her arrival at the Tucker place, she was greeted by the barking of a dog, a small spotted dog, who though put up a brave front at the sight of an approaching stranger, greeted her with a wagging tail and a friendly tongue-hanging smile when she dismounted.

Laura, who had been over by the corrals grooming her own saddle stock, spotted Aspen riding in off the trail and hurried over to greet her. Giggles and hugs and women's happy chatter, was in abundance at the meeting of two dear friends.

The hullabaloo outside the cabin had awakened Ellie Lou, who had still been fast asleep in her bed. She had stayed up late the night before with her Mom and Dad, listening to a pack of timber wolves that had recently moved into the canyon, voicing their eerie howls until long after midnight.

It became a relaxing and happy day for Aspen and Laura, who as good friends should, were enjoying each others company to the fullest. Though disappointed that Willow and Rose were unable to come and play with her, Ellie Lou too was happy, sharing her time between her Mom and Aspen. She loved her own Mom the best, but running a close second was Aspen. Who along with Smokey, had discovered her near deaths door in that rain-soaked forest and nursed her back to a speedy recovery.

The new cabin had now been finished, a sturdy log structure that would come in downright handy for the partners trapping venture. Complete with bunk beds, a table and several hand-crafted chairs to sit on. It also was equipped with a rock-lined fireplace and plenty of shelving for storing grub and other needed essentials.

It was late afternoon before Smokey and Kelly gathered up their tools, and stepped back to admire their wilderness handiwork. They both agreed, after long hours of plastering creek mud in the cracks between the logs, that it was now a mouse-free structure, including pack rats.

211

"I reckon I should high-tail it back to the ranch," Smokey said, "and see how my girls are making out—Rose has been under the weather lately—and Aspen might not yet be back from her visit with Laura."

"I'm ready to go myself," Kelly replied, and crawled aboard his bronc, rifle in hand, and reined the horse toward a dim game trail, a shortcut to his Horseshoe Canyon horse ranch.

Smokey did the same, only his route was back down the Lobo Canyon trail to the old McGregor sheep ranch, which was now home for his family, and the hub of his return to the life of a cattle rancher.

He arrived back at the ranch about the same time as Aspen, and found the girls in good shape and happy to see them. With the help of a recovering Rose, Willow had even started supper for her Dad and their second Mom, Aspen McGregor Harrison.

* * * CHAPTER 19 * * *

A succession of powerful winds howled down from the Rockies, littering the forest floor with a cover of crisp golden-hued leaves. Having been set free from the mother tree where they had been born, the leaves could do nothing but bow to the whims of this wilderness phenomenon of the southwest mountains.

A killing frost had swept across the land, bringing with it a drastic change to the forest. For days on end formations of noisy geese and trumpeter swan flew high in the clouds, their destination far to the south in warmer climes. A confused chatter of mallard and pintail ducks hovered far below their larger cousins, seeking open water, a sanctuary where they could rest their weary bodies in preparation for the final flight to the south.

A transition was happening to the fur bearers of the forest, both small and large it did not matter. The pelt of the weasel and snowshoe hare was now a snowy white, to blend in with the snow that would soon cover the land. The fur thickened on the lynx and the martin, the wolf and coyote too. Now in prime condition, the fur bearers became a highly sought after commodity, some worth far more than their weight in gold.

The horned animals and those with cloven hoof were answering the urging of one of Nature's most important events. The annual rut!

It was her way of ensuring the survival of a species.

The shrill mating whistle of an enraged bull elk echoed far in the distance, on the hunt for a mate, to be answered in a milder manner by an interested, coy female. Then, another blast of a different tune, suggesting to other bulls who might be loitering nearby to vamoose, else face a battle that just might be the end of their romance-seeking lives.

No one escaped this yearly transition of the seasons, including Smokey Harrison, who was busy preparing for the coming winter. Guns were oiled and cleaned, traps were sorted and made ready, and a rough hand-drawn map of Lobo Canyon was marked as to the location of the designated trap line.

It was early in December when Smokey rode up the Lobo trail to start laying out his trap line. Trailing behind was a pack horse, loaded to the hilt with the makings of a trapping venture, such as he had planned.

He set up a base camp at the new cabin, unloading the supplies and equipment that would be needed for the coming season. He knew from experience that it would take all of two weeks to set and bait the traps at pre-arranged locations,

He also knew, that this would be the last time he would be able to use the horses until the warming influence of spring returned to the mountains. Much sooner than one might expect, the deep snow of winter could make the Lobo Trail impossible for horse travel. Navigation then would be by two strong legs and a pair of snowshoes.

Smokey's plans were to have the trap line in place by Christmas Eve. Then he would return to the ranch and celebrate this joyous time with Aspen and the girls. This had always been a special time for Smokey, a sacred tradition that had been handed down through generations of his family.

However, this year would be a Christmas shared with good friends. The Tucker family had been invited over to spend a few days, and join in with the Harrison family in celebrating this special time of the year together.

Smokey, who had been schooled in the trapping profession by old Trapper Joe himself, had completed his task on the trap line and arrived back at the ranch barely in time for Christmas Eve. It was here he would spend several days with family and friends, before returning to the rigors of a Rocky Mountain trapper.

The three girls were thrilled with what Santa Clause had brought them, consisting of warm clothes and each one a pair of snowshoes.

The gifts received by the girl's parents were not of a material nature, but gifts they enjoyed just the same—mingling together as friends, happy children opening gifts from Santa Clause, and to have plenty of special food for the holidays; surely heaven sent gifts as far as they were concerned.

Food was plentiful, and with two good cooks to prepare it, a wild-turkey dinner with all the trimmings was like a feast sent down to them from the Gods. As a finale to the feast, a jug of cider was brought out, and a toast was made by all present to have a happy new year.

In the southern territories, a modest Indian reservation thrived along side a mighty river. It was here in the shadows of their colorful tepees, a Clan of the People would pay homage to the Great Spirit of all creation. They too revered this special time of the year, and in their aboriginal manner, were praying and dancing and singing their praise to a star in the heavens; home to their sacred creator.

They were a spiritual people, not only paying their respect to the Great Spirit at Christmas time, but after each month had passed; when the moon was large and bright in the sky, they would dance and pray and sing in this same manner. It was the way of the People.

Meanwhile, at a tepee not far from the large fire surrounded by the dancing circle, stood a saddened mother. Tears were streaming down her dusky cheeks as she watched her two half-breed sons ride away from the reservation where they had been raised, on a quest to find a father they had never known.

Knowing that she might never see them again, her tears were tears of sadness. At the same time becoming tears of joy, knowing that it was the right thing for them to do.

The brothers rode into the north, following a distant star. The sage words of their mother had urged them to do this, knowing that it would be good medicine for her sons to find their cowboy father—her husband of long ago—whom she still loved with all her heart.

In her heart of hearts she knew that he would be happy to see his sons, that he would welcome them into his lodge, and make them into strong, brave cowboys such as the one she remembered.

To Dove That Sings her teen-age boys were leaving on a vision quest, an age old tradition of the People, who if successful, would no longer be boys; but be changed into brave men like their father.

Clucking the chipmunk talk that she was noted for, she closed the flap of her tepee and joined the circle dancers, whose heads were raised high, offering their thanks to a Great Spirit who must surely be looking down on them with mercy and great pride.

Three moons passed before the boys crossed over the Medicine Line into the northern territories, an unseen boundary line that Dove had told them about. From there, she had counseled them, "Stay near the big forest—and the big mountains that reach to the sky—a sacred star in the northern sky will guide you to your father; who will be happy to see his two sons."

Spring had arrived at the Harrison ranch. A season of trapping prime fur was nearing an end, except for beaver, whose rich pelts were now ready for harvest. Smokey had been spending a few days with his family, enjoying a break from the tedious grind of walking the trap line.

Besides it was now calving time at the ranch, a most important time of the year at the Lobo Canyon ranch. The longhorns must be brought in to the calving corrals, and a twenty-four hour vigil kept on the herd. To the bear, the cougar, and the wolf that thrived in this mountainous region, the rich, tender meat of new-born calves was a temptation they could not pass up.

He was uncertain as how to trap beaver and calve out the longhorns at the same time. He knew that it was more than he could handle by himself, there was just not enough hours in the day for this to happen!

True, Aspen would be happy to help him if he asked her to, but it didn't seem fair for her to be away from the girls from sun-up to sun-down, only to find the daily tasks around the big McGregor house waiting when she returned. Finally, after much thought on the matter, his decision was to forget about the beaver and concentrate his efforts on the herd. After all, his chosen profession was to be a cowboy and a rancher, and that was all that mattered.

Life on a trap line was no picnic, day after dreary day of plodding through deep snow, only to return to the cabin and spend half the night skinning and stretching pelts, was tough, grueling work. To be with his family like this was a just reward for Smokey.

With his pipe in hand, freshly tamped and fired up, Smokey was relaxing after a long day of rounding up his longhorns. He was enjoying the pleasant chatter of Aspen and his two daughters, only to have Willow interrupt his reverie.

"Papa, look! Two riders are coming up the trail—riding spotted horses—and their hats even have a feather sticking in the air!

Rose, who was the timid one of the two sisters, expressed her own view on the matter, "I'll bet your boots they are scary Indians coming to carry away your two daughters—after scalping you and Mom!"

"Don't talk that way, Rose. They look peaceful enough to me. I can see no war paint smeared on their cheeks, or war whoops a puttin' chills to one's bones.

"You can hand me my six-gun a hangin' inside the door though, just in case."

Side by side the strangers entered the door yard, the older of the two with a hand raised in the peace sign of the tribes. Reining in a fine looking appaloosa pony, he began to talk. "Ho, my friends!

"My brother and I have come in peace, we are looking for a cowboy whose name is *Smok'ee* Harrison—could you tell us where we might find him?"

Smokey looked long and hard at the two young Indians, and that they were of mixed blood was not hard to tell. A puzzled look appeared on his face, and though he was unable to identify them, they looked vaguely familiar to him.

It was then a thrill of unknown origin surged through his body, one that he could not explain; closely followed by a chill that was racing up and down his spine. What is happening to me, he wondered, why is my body acting this way?

After a long pause he answered, "Who is looking for this Smokey? And why do you wish to find him?"

"My Indian name is *Little Smoke*, my white friends know me as Smok'ee. My brother's name is *Smokes a Lot*, because he is fond of tobacco—a sacred plant of our people. He will answer to the name of Toby.

"*Smok'ee* Harrison is our father—we wish to find him to fulfill our medicine dream—and bring him our Mother's best wishes for a long and happy life. She is *Dove That Sings*, a woman who honors the birds and chipmunks. She told us that *Smok'ee* called her his Dove!"

Smokey was stunned, plumb speechless over what Little Smoke had told him. He looked long at the young lad, and knew that this one was indeed his son. Though his hair and eyes were black as a dark night, his facial features were much like his own, a close resemblance to his white-eye father.

Then turning his attention to Smokes A Lot, who was a spitten image of his brother, he questioned in his mind the authenticity of the second boy as being his own.

How could it be so?

Dove had ridden away from him with a six-month old Little Smoke strapped on her back, and then it struck him. All he had to do was remember the facts of life, as given to Adam and Eve themselves. Dove had been expecting another child when she left her husband, and returned to her People.

He arose from the bench, a smile spreading across his face as he walked to his sons, who were now standing beside their horses uncertain of what might happen next. A cowboy whoop of joy gushed from his mouth that startled both of the boys, and with an arm around each of their shoulders, he gave them a warm hug.

Aspen and his daughters were shell shocked as well.

"I am Smokey, your father," he told them.

"You are the sons of my first wife Dove, who has kept you away from me all this long time."

A happy father then introduced them to the women folks, who were wide-eyed with wonder over this unexpected addition to the family. The girls, who had always wanted a big brother, were overjoyed by the arrival of the two boys, and they too walked over and gave them a big hug.

"Wow!" Willow said. "We've always wanted a brother—and now we have two."

Little Smoke turned to his father when he spoke, "*Dove That Sings* asked that you show us how to be cowboys, it will make us very happy if you will do this."

Life along the Lobo was now changed. Toby was a natural born trapper, and was given the job of harvesting the abundant beaver population. He was thrilled to be here with his father, and equally so, to be given charge of the trapper cabin with all of its trappings and tools of the trade.

Smok'ee showed great interest in the horse *remuda*, the longhorn herd and the vast wilderness of this mountain ranch. He knew at first sight they had found their father, and as the days swiftly passed, his respect for their cowboy Dad did nothing but grow. He was smitten with the riggings of this sort of life—the spurs, the chaps, the lassos and the big hats. And to be able to pack a six-gun on his hip, was an answer to his vision quest as far as he was concerned.

And Smokey was equally impressed with his sons. They were ardent students in learning there respective positions, quick learners and eager to begin their new life. They showed much respect to Aspen and the girls, and they worshipped their Dad as if he had been the Great Spirit himself.

From the time back at the Milk River ranch, when a saddened cowboy had told two lovely sisters about his former wife and son, Aspen and Sage had fallen for him. Sage was thrilled to become his wife, giving her husband two lovely daughters, and now Aspen had filled her dead sister's shoes—raising Willow and Rose.

Aspen was happy to have her husband's two sons here at the ranch. She knew that life would now be much easier for Smokey, and that he would be able to spend more time with his wife and daughters. Beside, she liked the boys who were always giving her a hand. Packing in firewood for her cook stove, keeping the water pails filled from the deep stone-lined well out back; and on occasion assisting her with the household chores. Life would now be much easier for Aspen as well.

The girls were thrilled with their two half-brothers, whose presence at the ranch brightened up an otherwise dull routine of daily life immensely. The boys would take them horseback riding, trout fishing in Lobo Creek and even up to the trapper cabin they would go, a first time for Willow and Rose.

The annual trapping season ended with an abundant harvest of prime beaver pelts. After a few days of cleaning out the cabin, packing the fur down to the ranch, and such, Toby Harrison was able to enjoy a few days of leisure time. Toby was pleased with his new job on the trap line, and so was Smokey, who praised his son highly for the efficient manner in which he had trapped beaver.

With the trap line shut down until late in the coming autumn, Toby was now free to learn the ways of a cowboy. Smokey outfitted both his sons with the riggings of a range rider: boots and spurs, cow-hide chaps and lassos, and each with a six-gun strapped on their hip. He also gave them a cowboy hat, to wear at all times except in their beds, which made them the proudest pair of cow-pokes in these southwest mountains.

The two brothers now rode together as Lobo Canyon cowboys. In fact they were the only ones, except their cowboy father and Kelly Tucker.

The calving bunch was kept in the corral, safe from the meat eaters of this mountainous region, and as each one dropped her calf, the mother cow and her baby would be turned out into a maternity holding area. It was here they were kept for a few days under the cowboy's care, until the little ones were suckling their longhorn mothers with much vigor.

Milk is what the little ones needed to stay alive at this fragile time of their young lives, lots of rich mother's milk! Only then would a proud Mom and her baby be given their freedom. The sly old longhorn matrons would then high-tail it for parts unknown, some never to be seen again for weeks on end.

An all important assignment was given to Smok'ee and Toby at this time, and it was to keep track of the longhorns with young calves by their side. And more important than all the rest, was to keep them from wandering south of the border into Blackfoot country.

The new cowboys never questioned the orders that were given them each morning by the big boss of the ranch. In some uncanny way, they sensed their Dad was testing their ability to handle the tasks that were given them. And thus it was the boys sharpened their skills at roping, riding the rough string, outguessing the crafty longhorns; and adhering to the code of the west.

The release of the final longhorn cow and her baby into the high mountain grazing country, marked the end to another calving season. It was here the sly old mossy-horns would band together with three or four of their friends. Together they would make a stand against the predators on the hunt for baby calves.

As told by the cowboys, it was an awesome sight to see and hear. A fearsome chorus of enraged bellows could be heard echoing throughout the forest. Riding in close, the hair rippled on the back of their necks as they watched the wild scene unfold.

Glistening spear-shaped horns were swinging this way and that, guarding the little ones that were huddled behind them. Their slobbering mouths were open wide, tongues hanging low as they roared a blood-chilling defiance at the baby killers.

More often than not, a feisty group of feral mothers would put the fear into the cougar, the wolf, and even the bear; many of whom had felt the searing pain of those deadly horns before; many of them had died trying.

With the jingle of a belled pack mule echoing behind them, the two brothers rode deep into the forest, having been assigned to ride up into the southwest extremities of the range. It was here they were to check on how the new grass was doing. And above all else, be aware of the condition of the herd and their new calves. Also, after three nights of camping out in the mountains, they were to return to the ranch and report their findings.

The higher up they rode, the narrower became the trail, forcing them to ride single file. "I reckon there's a spring up ahead," Smok'ee said, turning in the saddle to talk to his brother. "Be a good place to stop and eat lunch—it's been a long ride since we last ate any grub."

"I reckon you're right," came the reply. "Ol' Toby's hungry enough to eat the skunk that's heading for that spring over yonder," signing to the fresh tracks in the dampness of the trail. Both boys were picking up the slang and humor-laced expressions spoken by their Dad, and were enjoying every word of it.

Hearing the ruckus of the incoming horses, the skunk circled wide of the spring and disappeared in a thick tangle of brush. "I reckon that ol' polecat took one look at us Injuns and vamoosed," Smok'ee said, "afraid we might take his scalp."

After eating their lunch, the Harrison boys continued on up the trail. Not that far above the spring, they discovered fresh sign of where a small bunch of cattle had been driven towards the border. One look is all it took to know that it was Indians riding barefoot ponies.

Smiling with pride over their knowledge of such things, another thought entered their minds that chased away the smiles. Only this very morning Smokey had cautioned them about this very thing. "Seldom do the high-strung critters bunch up, unless being driven," he told them.

"Be sure and keep a sharp eye out for this sort of thing, could be rustlers helping themselves to our cattle!"

Both of the half-breed brothers were excellent trackers, having been exposed to the ancient art when just mere boys. They knew right off this was the work of Indians, militants they reckoned. In their way of thinking it was downright thievery.

The rustlers appeared to be indifferent of their rustling ways, making no effort to conceal what they were doing. The tracks continued into the south, crossing the Medicine Line into Blackfoot country.

The mere mention of the word Blackfoot, sent scary chills rippling through the boy's youthful bodies. Back in the camps of their People, when they were just young lads, many were the gruesome stories they had listened to around the night fires; tales told by the Elders of the cruelty of this savage war-loving tribe.

Rising above the tempo of the tom-toms, could be heard the chant of an old medicine man chiding the ways of this militant tribe, the words matching the beat of the drums.

On and on it would go, long after Dove's two sons had returned to their tepee and found sleep in their blankets.

Knowing they were entering forbidden territory was of no matter, the Lobo cowboys crossed over into a foreign land, following the orders of Smokey Harrison, who had entrusted them with keeping the herd safe and sound on the north side of the border.

They rode with caution, staying in the thick brush that bordered on the beaten path left by the cattle. Using the stealth and savvy of their ancient relatives, the gap was rapidly narrowing between the longhorns and the cowboys.

Having been kept concealed in their saddlebags, a well-crafted sling now dangled from the horn of each of their saddles, complete with a satchel full of missiles for the same; round polished stones.

It is a weapon dating back to the early aboriginal people, consisting of a piece of leather tied to cords that are whirled by hand for releasing a missile. As small boys they had been trained in the use of a sling, and it wasn't long until they could outshoot all the others in their camp. After long days of endless practise, they were keeping Dove's cooking fire supplied with an unlimited supply of grouse and prairie hens.

But now, when the chips were in the fire, the sling could be used for a different more deadly purpose, especially so when the sound of a gunshot might reveal one's hidden presence. It then proved to be a weapon far more valuable than a satchel full of gold dust. Not even Smokey himself knew of their secret weapon. However they planned on showing it to him some time.

Suddenly, Toby reined his spotted pony to a halt. Looking back at his brother, he signed him to stop, look and listen. Not really that far away, could be heard the familiar sound of enraged longhorns. Something or someone must be messing around with their calves.

Vaulting from their saddles, they secured the horses, and like a pair of shadows disappeared into the unknown of the lodgepoles. Gliding this way and that, they approached unseen to a small clearing where all hell had broken loose.

A small group of Harrison longhorns had declared war on four native rustlers, who had been playing cowboys, one of which had managed to put a braided strip of deer hide around a little one's neck. In reality, they had plans to satisfy their craving for fresh roast beef. A cooking fire had already been prepared, and soon the tiny calf would be dangling on a spit waiting for them to eat; or so they thought.

The calf was fighting the noose like crazy, crying in terror, pleading for his Mom to come and save his life

An old mossy-horn did just that, and with one swing of her massive horns, upended the roper and his horse. Bellowing a spine-chilling roar, she began to utterly destroy the unfortunate pair. The actions of the old cow chilled the blood of three more mounted riders, who had strung their bows in an attempt to down her with their flint-tipped arrows.

Two of them were bucked off, finding themselves in the middle of the raging battle, as by now the remaining cows had joined in the fight. It was a fight between the longhorns and the Indians, with the Indians not faring so well.

One of the braves had backed away, and with his bow string pulled to the limit, was aiming at the cow that had started the fight in the first place. A split second before he released the deadly shaft, an unseen missile whirred across the battle ground; striking him along side his left ear.

Down he went, never to know what had hit him!

The smell of fresh blood had spurred the cows into the battle, and finding no more humans standing in the clearing, became homesick and headed back to their home range. Trailing behind, followed a small calf with a braided strand of deer hide dangling from his neck.

The Lobo Canyon cowboys took one last look at the carnage scattered across the clearing, thanking the sun, and the moon, and the stars that it hadn't been their bodies scattered in bits and pieces across this wilderness clearing. After returning to their horses, they swung into the saddles, and with much discretion followed the cows back across the border; leaving the land of the black moccasin people behind them.

On their return to the ranch, the boys were seated at the supper table, enjoying the first home-cooked meal since leaving for the high country. As they were eating, they casually mentioned the longhorn incident to the family.

Smokey, who was having a hard time believing their story, remained silent as he listened to his son's tell of their strange experience.

Then, with a puzzled look on his face, he spoke. "You mean to tell me our longhorns killed all four of them rustlin' devils?"

"I reckon so," came the reply. "We never fired a shot from our guns!" And Smok'ee was telling the truth.

Back across the 49th parallel, shortly after the departure of the two cowboys, one of Mother Nature's laws of the wild began unfolding that very few humans have ever witnessed— meat-hungry scavengers of the forest had picked up the scent of fresh-spilled blood.

Perched secure in the pines, a gathering of ravens and magpies had a ringside seat to the whole affair, and were the first to arrive at the scene of mayhem and death. With much greed they gorged themselves on the rich findings, only to be spooked away by a family of coyotes.

Much sooner than the coyotes might have liked, a timber wolf slunk out of the surrounding brush, and then two more appeared, attracted by the scent of freshly torn flesh. A vicious battle ensued, with the smaller coyotes receiving a sound trouncing.

With no prior warning a mature cougar appeared on the scene, directing a series of spine-chilling squalls at the startled wolves; with much discretion they too left the scene of destruction and death.

And if that wasn't enough, a grizzly bear plodded into the outdoor arena. The cougar held his ground, not about to give way to this monster of the animal kingdom, when the bear suddenly attacked. Roaring a frightful tune, the grizzly reared on to his hind legs, swatting his huge paws at the mature cougar, making contact too. The strength of the grizzly was no match for the much smaller cat, who fled from the scene of battle as best he could, nursing a badly lacerated shoulder and lucky to be alive.

All of the carnivores had feasted on the leavings of the battle, before being driven away by another who was their superior in size and cunning. A law of the wild had been enacted; survival of the fittest!

The birds became the winners, outwitting even the grizzly bear. They had been the first on the scene, only to be driven away by a much larger nemesis. Perched in the nearby pines watching it all, they would swoop down on the battle ground, stealing a morsel of the leavings, then return to the safety of the trees. It wasn't long until these scavengers of the sky became so stuffed with meat they could hardly fly, and wisely stayed in the trees—there would always be another day.

Twenty-four hours is all it took, twenty four hours for the minions of the old Mother to clean up the clearing. Nothing was left but small scraps of fractured hide and bone.

Hidden from view in a maze of buck brush, lay a skull stripped clean of hide and hair. For years to come it lay concealed, becoming a snug home for field mice and their vole cousins.

* * * CHAPTER 20 * * *

The inherited genes in Toby Harrison's half-breed blood must have been the reason he loved to wander and explore. He was unable to control this call of the wild, it was the way of his ancestors. Every chance he got, he would saddle up his spotted horse and slip away into the forest, not to be seen again for hours on end.

Late one night he returned to the ranch with some exciting news. Smokey was waiting up for him, concerned that his young adventurous son might have got into more trouble than he could handle.

Toby was happy that Smokey was there to greet him at the horse corrals, his heart full of pride that his Dad cared enough to do this for him. The lad could hardly wait to tell of what he had discovered—a discovery that not only shook the boots of Toby, but was now doing the same for his cowboy Dad.

Dating back to the time when buffalo still roamed the range, an old hide-hunters camp had been situated not far to the east of Lobo and Horseshoe canyons. Not much was left of the camp but several fire pits, a decaying log cabin and a small coulee crammed full of bones and massive horned skulls.

News traveled fast in this isolated region, the foothills grapevine it came to be known as, and this time it was Toby who was the carrier of an all important finding; not only to his Dad's ranch, but to Kelly Tucker's horse outfit as well. Both ranches only a few short miles from the old cabin.

Toby could hardly wait to unload the news to his Dad, who had to slow down the boy's talk so he could understand his lingo—pigeon-English mixed in with the talk of his mother's tribal language.

Slowly but surely Smokey was able to understand what Toby was telling him. And along with sign language and a lot of patience, the following story unfolded.

Toby had been riding in the aspens along the eastern fringe of the forest, enjoying the singing of the birds and the chatter of squirrels and chipmunks, reminding him of Dove's talk back in the Snake River country where he had been born and raised.

The familiar clicking talk of the chipmunks brought on a case of home sickness, the first since he and his brother had left the *palouse*.

Suddenly he shook himself, knowing that to reminisce like this was a dangerous thing to do. Could get him killed by some unseen enemy, could destroy the medicine that Dove had given her boys when they rode away from the Snake River.

It was only then he reined in his horse, his nose twitching, his ears straining to hear, his keen eyes searching every shadow—and even every quacking leaf that fluttered all around him.

And then it happened, Toby's keen sense of smell brought to him the odor of wood smoke. Ground tying his horse, and with his trusty sling in hand, he followed his nose with much caution—blending in with the shadowed woods, creeping steadily toward the source of the smoke.

He could now hear coarse laughter mixed in with obscene talk. The kind that Dove had told her boys was bad medicine to hear. The odor of smoke grew stronger. He crouched low in a thick copse of berry brush, his sling in one hand, a round polished killing stone in the other; watching the camp.

That they were bad men, he was sure of—listening to their vile talk, watching them guzzle the dreaded fire water and even fighting with one another. He knew all right, he knew in his heart they were a bunch of hard cases up to no good.

He reckoned he should go back to his pony, and ride back and tell his Dad what he had discovered when he heard a scream. That it was the scream of a young girl, he was sure of, the sound coming from behind him, not that far from where his pony should be waiting for him to return.

Toby was crouched low, silently flitting from one shadow to another, on the hunt for the source of the mysterious scream. He could now hear the sound of yet another scream, and the sobbing of a terrified girl. He knew that he was close, and then he stopped, making like a shadow himself, peering intently into a small clearing.

There, a young girl dressed in buckskin, was being mauled by one of the filthy hard cases from the bad man's camp. She was putting up a tremendous struggle to escape from this hairy one who was attacking her, only to be knocked back to the ground by a huge hairy fist.

"Take that you red-skin heathen," he roared, pulling a small razor-sharp knife from his beefy arm, where she had managed to stab him.

The girl lay still, dazed by the vicious blow to her face, knowing that she had lost the fight for her chastity, that the hairy one would now have his way with her.

Toby was enraged at what he was seeing, and knowing the plight of this young maiden, who appeared to be about the same age as he; a stop must be made to this evil man before he destroyed her innocence.

Loading his sling, he waited for the right moment, only then did he unleash the deadly missile. Down went the girl's attacker, never to rise again—he would never know what had hit him.

Toby knelt beside her, and found she was an Indian like himself. He raised her head into his arm, and cooed the song of a mourning dove that his mother had sang to her two sons, when they were both just wee toddlers.

The pleasant cooing of a dove cleared the girl's mind, who was in wonder at the calming influence of this strange bird. Her eyes opened, looking into the eyes of Toby Harrison, knowing in a minute that he would not harm her.

She was soon able to stand, smoothing her rumpled clothing and doing the same with her long black hair that was a tangled mess; and only then with an embarrassed look showing on her face, did she look once more into his dark brown eyes.

He was smiling when she thanked him in a language that he did not understand. Though he wouldn't know for sometime to come, she belonged to the Blood tribe, a distant cousin of the mighty Blackfoot people. Her given name was Fairy Bell, in honor of the delicate flowers that grew on this woodland plant—a comparison made of a delicate young maiden was the reason. Her family and friends knew her as their Fairy.

While gathering wild flowers at her father's summer lodge in the mountains, she had been stolen away and brought to this place of fire water and evil men.

Though neither understood the language of the other, Toby and a young maiden known only as Fairy, got along just fine by the use of sign language. With the girl riding behind the saddle hugging a young cowboy in a tight embrace, Toby took her home with him to Lobo Canyon.

"I have something to show my big Chief," the boy told his Dad, and signing into the shadows on the far side of the pinto pony, both father and son watched as out stepped a shy native girl and stood timidly by the boy who had rescued her.

"This is Fairy Bell," he told his Dad. "She has come to live with my sisters!"

Fairy Bell was welcomed into the Harrison family, and though she was several years older than Willow and Rose, became an instant hit with the two sisters. After hearing Toby's story of finding her like he did, the rest of the family treated her with much kindness and respect.

The news of the hide-hunter's cabin and a questionable bunch of hard cases taking possession of the site, was reason enough for Smokey's peace of mind being shattered. He was highly concerned over the safety of his family, and Fairy Bell as well, who until they could return her to her parents camp, was treated as if she was one of their own.

"Reckon some squatters down yonder are in a bunch of trouble!" he told Aspen, who was equally as concerned as her husband. "I'm a ridin' over and have a medicine talk with Kelly—who is in the line of fire, the same as we are."

"I'm coming with you," she replied, and Smokey knew there would be no use in trying to leave her behind. Besides there was no other he would rather have riding with him than Aspen.

"The boys are at the ranch today, and will keep our three girls safe from any trouble." she told him

Smokey and Aspen rode away from the Lobo, well armed and ready for war if need be. Their good friends at the Horseshoe must be told of this threat to the safety of the two ranches.

Kelly Tucker was outraged at the news and so was Laura, who much like Fairy Bell's experience, had been mauled and mistreated by the same type of evil cowards.

"Hell's fire," Smokey said, "we'll have to watch our possessions night and day—including our wives and kids!"

Kelly exploded with anger. "Be the devil to pay if I catch them showing up around here! Laura is a better than average shooter, even little Ellie Lou knows how to use a gun! Between the three of us we can stand off a small army if need be.

"I tell you what ol' pard, why don't we ride down and push the son's o' rattle snakes back across the border from where they must have come from."

"My thinking is the same as yours Kelly, I too reckon they're whiskey smugglers, hiding back here from them new Fort Macleod police—spreading the word around to the Indians that the tail-gates of their wagons are now down; ready to open up their rot-gut likker store."

Aspen and Laura, along with Ellie Lou were sent back to the Lobo for the security of both the families, and once there, Aspen was to send Toby and Smok'ee back to take part in a soon to be declared war.

"And keep your guns handy and loaded," he told her. "Never know when one o' them snoopin' devils might be hangin' around the ranch!"

All went as planned, except the two half breed brothers never showed up. After a longer than expected wait, Smokey said, "I reckon we should head on down, them boys o' mine will find us—they are the best trackers I've ever seen."

"Let's do it!" Kelley shouted. "Let's put the spurs to our broncs and do some Injin' tracking of our own!"

Down into aspen and willow country they rode, with no problem in finding the bootlegger camp. An unholy racket greeted them from several hundred yards out, causing them to leave the horses and sneak in the rest of the way on foot. Hunkering down in some willow brush, they couldn't believe what they were seeing, and hearing.

A wild melee of drunken Indians, stoned out of their minds were milling around a tarp-covered wagon. Some were staggering, empty whiskey jugs in hand. Others were dancing, and all were shouting strange howls into the aspen trees that circled the clearing.

There were still others who were stretched out on the ground—passed out from swigging the poisonous fire water, perhaps knocked unconscious by a swinging war club, possibly shot down in anger by an over zealous bootlegger.

Many had died where they fell. And though still breathing, there were some who would never live to see another day. One of the corpses was Fairy Bell's father, old Sparrow Hawk himself, who from previous encounters with the whiskey wagons; had become addicted to the Yankee fire water.

Having bartered all of his possessions from the last visit of the white-eye wagons, he was bound to the beck and call of a devil-made addiction, and this time Fairy Bell had been brought to the camp; bartering his only daughter for a jug of whiskey.

The shrill keen of intoxicated natives was lessening, in reality very few were left standing.

Smokey and Kelly were shocked out of their minds, never had they witnessed anything like this before. "I would never have believed something like this could happen this close to the ranch," Smokey said.

"It's sure enough a sorry sight to see," Kelly agreed. "And this close to our home and families is just plumb mind-boggling, to think of what might happen to them!"

Their talk was cut short by a gun shot, and then there were two more, and there in the camp two of the smugglers were systematically shooting any of the downed Indians who might still be alive.

Two flying missiles whirred across the clearing, two assassins dropped as if they had been pole-axed; and two half-breed brothers by the name of Harrison reloaded their slings.

Only two of the bloody outfit remained alive, the ramrod of the gang and one other, who with six-guns in hand, hunkered down in the lee of the wagon attempting to figure out what had happened to their fallen comrades.

Smokey had spotted the two in hiding, and roared out a command, "Drop them guns and come out so's we can see you—hands reaching for the sky!"

The ramrod, who had watched the results of the flying missiles, reckoned maybe they should.

"Kelly! Rig us up a pair of hangman noose's, I'm going to bring that pair back here so we can stretch their hairy necks—the least we can do," still eyeing the scene of carnage in the clearing.

Turning back to the wagon another surprise was in store.

The two border-runners were standing, arms in the air, as they had been ordered to do, but were facing the aspens. There stood Smokey's two grinning sons, slings loaded with the round shiny ammunition; swinging in the air, all set to down the two remaining bad men.

This was great fun for the two brothers, who were favoring Lobo Canyon country more so all the time. To be able to use their slings against the bad men was good medicine for the two lads from the *palouse,* the land where their mother Dove, had trained them in the ancient art of survival.

And now their Dad had witnessed them in action, aware of the deadly sling his sons were using instead of their rifles. He now knew what had happened to the four outlaws, who had rustled the longhorns up along the forty ninth parallel.

And though proud as punch over the dexterity of his two sons, he also knew that the boys and their slings were a deadly combination—two young cow punchers not to be messed with.

The four riders were in their saddles ready to leave, and taking one last look at the scene of death and destruction, shuddered at what had happened here; resulting in a group of slaughtered Indians and five whiskey peddlers, including two hanging from the branch of a poplar tree.

The next day a small patrol of North West Mounted arrived on the scene, having been told by a concerned Blood Chief of the whereabouts of the loaded whiskey wagons. As told to the Chief by a prominent lady of the tribe, she was concerned over her wayward husband who had ridden away with a group of thirst-crazed tribal members; to whoop it up!

"By jove!" the Corporal exclaimed, almost shocked out of his fancy britches. "A bloody massacre has happened here!

"You there," he said, pointing to a newly conscripted rookie. "Dismount and chase away the bloody ravens—and the other ones—marked like a milk-maid's cow," referring to the black and white colored magpies, "They are desecrating the bodies of these poor wretches.

"And you!" he ordered to another trooper, "go over and cut down those poor blighters that are swinging from them quacking trees!"

Not finding a shovel to dig a hole in the ground with, he then ordered a disgusted troop of the North West Mounted to drag the corpses over to the coulee, and toss them in with the buffalo bones.

The four riders returned to the Lobo to be greeted by four exited young girls, and two very relieved wives—Aspen and Laura. Still shaken from the bloody experience at the bootlegger camp, they were unable to reply to the many questions that were asked them. Smokey and Kelly needed time. Lots of time to sort out all of the horrendous greed and blood-letting that had been enacted before their eyes.

Smok'ee and Toby were not affected this way, remaining as nonchalant as before, as if it had been an every day occurrence. Deep in their hearts though, they had been shook up as well— too proud to show their emotions.

Darkness had now moved into the canyons, resulting in Aspen insisting on the Tuckers staying for the night. She wouldn't hear of them riding five miles through the darkened forest back to their Horseshoe ranch. After a hearty supper, all that were there retired to there respective beds and called it a day.

Smokey was up at the crack of dawn, and after tending to the saddle stock, was returning to the big house when he heard an unexpected sound, an ear-pleasing chant rising above the chatter of nearby Lobo Creek.

It was at the creek he discovered Fairy Bell attending to her morning rituals, a custom of her long dead mother. It was plain to see that she had bathed herself in the cold mountain water, and was now sitting on the shore, a hand-carved wooden object in hand; combing her long tangled hair.

The girl was chanting a strange sounding tune, thanking the *great spirit* that she was still alive, offering herself to the sky, the trees and the grass, and all the birds and animals that lived here. It was a song of thanks and respect for this wilderness land that she loved so well.

Smokey stayed back, respecting her privacy. There were tears in his eyes, remembering that Dove That Sings would do this very same thing. Every morning of their marriage she could be found by the water, and just as Fairy Bell was doing, prepare herself for the coming day.

It was a song of the wild, sang by young maidens; a custom of the People!

Watching as the young girl returned to the house, he knew they would keep Fairy Bell as if she was one of their own. Besides, she had no father or mother, no place to go, and most likely be shunned back at the Blood camps.

On hearing the news, Willow and Rose were happy as larks in the spring time. They now had an older sister and two older brothers.

Aspen too was happy, knowing that if Smokey's daughters were happy, she would be happy too.

After their morning meal they all gathered around Smokey, anxious for him to tell them about the one-sided fight between the whiskey-runners and the intoxicated Bloods. That it was no contest, they would soon find out.

The whole clan gathered around Toby and Smok'ee, praising them for their stand against the bad men, and their ingrained talent with the handcrafted slings.

"It's time you rascals showed us your secret weapons," Smokey told his sons, his voice on the rise.

Sensing their Dad was plumb serious, his son's did just that, and after showing all that were there the makings of their simple weapons, they put on a show that left the onlookers in awe at what they were seeing.

Toby's missile brought down a saucy magpie from out of a nearby tree. It was no contest for Smok'ee and a startled ground squirrel, who suffered the same fate as the magpie.

He then offered the loaded sling to Fairy Bell, and signed to a dead branch of an aspen tree. A whirr of a flying missile, the snap of a broken branch, and both the branch and the polished stone fell to the ground together.

A pair of *yakima* boys and a *blood* maiden had put on a show for their family and friends, an ancient means of survival handed down over the centuries by word of mouth from the *shamans* of long ago.

Though concerned they might lose the medicine given to them by *Dove That Sings*, the boys allowed all that were there a turn at using their secret weapons, including little Ellie Lou, who did nothing more but giggle as she swung the sling over her head.

Kelly Tucker was the first to speak, "Reckon you boys can make me one of these here contraptions...?"

A grinning Aspen interrupted his talk, "...me first—I now will be able to serve grouse for supper—without shooting my gun!"

* * * CHAPTER 21 * * *

The dog days of late summer was a trying time for the women folk living in the canyons, an uncomfortable time of humid heat-induced days and nights. It was with much relief they welcomed the cooler temperatures, when the Dog Star was no longer keeping pace with the sun.

Aspen Harrison and her girls had been patiently waiting for this large bright Star to drift away from the sun, knowing that the dog days had come and gone for another year.

Already they were making plans for berry picking time. The annual harvest of the wild fruit of the mountain and prairie—mouths already watering at the thoughts of eating Saskatoon berry pie, choke cherry jelly and jam, and much more.

All were a special delicacy to grace the tables on this southwest frontier, and best of all, the makings were free for the taking.

More often than not, Aspen knew the berries would be scarce here in the mountains, the abundance of sugar-addicted bears were responsible for this. Even many of the birds and deer were fond of old Mother Nature's wild berries.

"Once again we must search elsewhere for our winter supply of fruit," Aspen told her daughters.

"Down country we must go, to the mile-long coulee at your father's old ranch along the river of Milk; there will surely be enough there for both our Harrison family, and the Tucker's as well."

She sent Smok'ee over to Horseshoe Canyon with an invitation for Laura and Ellie Lou to come with them. There will be plenty of berries for us all, she had written on a scrap of paper, and the more of us the better—besides it will be a fun time to be together for a few days.

Excitement reigned supreme the morning of their departure, revealing a scene of hustle and bustle, young girls squealing, and mothers issuing frenzied orders, and off to the side sat the two brothers, amazed at the utter confusion.

Packing the tarp-covered wagon to the hilt was a chore in itself, including camping gear, food and containers to hold the berries.

Not to be forgotten was oats for the horses, rain gear and their guns. Smoky would not let them leave without a pair of Marlin rifles, as well as two holstered six-guns for good measure. Fairy Bell, who now had her own sling, was prepared with a satchel full of shiny rocks.

Smokey, who was giving Aspen a cowboy bear-hug, asked, "How long are you ladies planning on staying down yonder?"

"As long as it takes," she replied, a tear or two showing on her face. "No longer than a week though!"

"You reckon you can last that long without us?" she asked, an impish grin spreading across her face.

"It will be a tough one to handle," he answered, knowing she was teasing. "I'll manage somehow."

Smokey's ingrained sense of compassion was still smarting from witnessing the slaughter of Fairy Bell's intoxicated tribesmen. "I'm sending Toby with you," he told Aspen, reluctant to see his family of females leave on such a journey without a male escort.

"He's right handy with a rifle—and that sling of his will put the fear into any o' them border-jumpin' devils that might show up."

"I'll ride down in a few days and escort you all back to the Lobo."

Aspen's reasoning of the matter was the same as her cowboy husband, and was thrilled to have Toby with them.

"Thank you," she murmured, she too had been concerned about the safety of her berry-picking bunch of females.

A caravan of happy berry pickers left Lobo Canyon, their destination the mile long coulee in Milk River country. Aspen and Laura rode in the wagon, accompanied by Ellie Lou, and Rose to keep her company. Their escorts, Toby, Willow and Fairy Bell, brought up the rear mounted on ranch ponies.

It was late afternoon of the next day before they arrived at the coulee, pitching a pair of tents and organizing their wilderness camp. The ladies were all exhausted after the long dusty journey, and after a hearty meal, were more than ready to retire to their blankets.

They must replenish their jaded energy for the coming days, when the harvest would begin in the coulee of dense berry brush, branches sagging to the ground with lush ripe berries gleaming black in the fading sun.

The three girls were exhausted and made their beds in one of the tents. Aspen and Laura, along with Ellie Lou would sleep in the other. Toby told them he would sleep under the stars, where his wilderness medicine would not be hindered by the canvas enclosures.

He was proud of the assignment his Dad had given him— proud to be guardian of the white-eye squaws. Toby knew, as did his Dad, that he would risk his life if need be to keep the six females safe and sound.

Long into the night a ghostly shadow moved in close to a spotted pony, cooing the wilderness music of a mourning dove. After assuring his good friend that all was well, Toby Harrison crawled into the blanket that lay on the ground close by his pony and drifted into a troubled sleep. A relaxed snuffle from the lips of the animal allowed him to find sleep once again, as well as his human friend.

Toby was a light sleeper, always had been, and this night was even more so. The slightest sound that seemed out of place would see the blanket flung aside, and a young *yakima* shadow with six-gun in hand closely scanning the dark shadows of the night; his attention then returning to check on his pony's ears.

The boy reckoned he would be in deep trouble without his horse. The appaloosa was part of the lad's medicine, whose alert searching ears would point out the source of any lurking danger.

There was no doubt in his mind that the reason his Dad had placed this burden on his shoulders was to test his ability to be a man, a mature, seasoned cowboy, capable of coping with any danger that might cross his path.

The ladies awoke to the smell of willow smoke and coffee, discovering Toby sitting by the fire, legs crossed in the manner of his kind; a steaming cup in his hand. By the wheel of the wagon sat two pails of fresh-drawn creek water and a brace of fat sage hens. Both birds were plucked and ready to be roasted for the coming breakfast.

Aspen and Laura were the first to leave their tent, giggling and happy after a good nights sleep. Pleased to see that Toby was on the job, caring for his charges as Smokey had known he would do.

At this early hour it was plumb chilly along the river. The women hurried over by Toby's fire to warm up, enjoying the warmth radiated by the nest of glowing embers. The sun was just now peeping above the distant horizon, and would very soon subdue the much cooler air of the night.

"Thank you Toby," Aspen said, noticing the bundle of dried willow branches placed near the fire, knowing that all of this had happened while they were still asleep.

"Oh, look Aspen, by the wagon wheel," there was wonder in Laura's voice as she spoke, and was in awe at what she was seeing.

"You are now in an Indian camp Laura, our Toby is one of the best woodsman on the frontier!

Toby stirred some at hearing Laura's words of praise, and he had been dozing. Though he was pleased over what she had said, he was also slightly embarrassed. He was standing now, and with his feather-adorned hat in hand, said, "I must go now," and signed up the long coulee.

Swinging aboard his spotted pony that had been grazing not far from the fire, he pointed the nose of his best friend into the sky, on a scout to check out the coulee of many berries.

Soon the girls were up and about, lured from their tent by the pleasant aroma of sage hen roasting on a spit, sourdough biscuits browning in a cast-iron pot, and the coffee pot singing a merry tune. Led by Fairy Bell, all were shooed to the river to attend to their morning rituals, there to learn the ways of the wilderness by a big sister who had known no other.

Back to the fire they straggled, a sorry looking bunch shivering their heads off after being inducted into one of the age-old customs of Fairy Bell's culture. Their clothes had been scrubbed, their hair washed and groomed, and young bodies bathed clean in the swift flowing water.

But they were happy and hungry, nothing like bathing in cold river water to rejuvenate their spirits, and fuel an intense hunger for food.

Aspen was in high spirits, finding the berries as abundant as when she and Sage had first came to her husband's ranch. High up the coulee sat a lone figure on a spotted horse, guarding Smokey Harrison's women picking berries below.

* * * CHAPTER 22 * * *

In the grass hills south of the Milk River, three canvas-topped wagons rolled through a gap in the rolling terrain. They were led by a lone scout who had ridden ahead, searching for a trail that would take them to a settlement along a mountain-fed stream known to them as Lee's Creek.

The lead wagon was pulled by a four-hitch of mules. Lagging behind came the other two, both with a yoke of oxen at the helm. It was a trail used by the ancient ones, including the buffalo and different tribes of the prairie.

The small caravan had been part of a group of Mormon pioneers, whose caravan had camped one night on the lee side of the Rockies near a boisterous settlement known as Last Chance Gulch, there to rest the teams and purchase much needed supplies.

Finding it was a rip-snorting boom town the caravan continued on, leaving the four families and their outfits behind, who had been exposed to a severe case of the dreaded fever; gold fever!

It didn't take long for them to discover that all available space along the streams had been claimed by others, and the wild rumors of finding gold anywhere you might care to look were just idle talk.

And so with no gold dust in their pokes, and fearing for the safety of their wives and children; they left the wild and wooly Gulch, following the trail of those who had gone before them. Having missed a fork in the old pioneer trail, they traveled on into the eastern prairie until meeting up with the Fort Benton-Whoop Up trail, used by the bull trains of the whiskey smugglin' Yankees.

It was here they once again reined their wagons into the north, crossing over an invisible border, searching for the mountain stream known to them as Lee's Creek. Though somewhat lost, they had spotted the Milk River, and thinking they were home free, were overjoyed believing they had finally reached the northern territories of Canada.

But they could see no settlement, only a lone wagon parked near the bottom of a brush-infested coulee. Several children were at play, frolicking back and forth between the wagon and the coulee.

Where is the rest of the company? There should be another dozen wagons, not just one.

Perched on the seat of the lead wagon, a long beard fluttering in the breeze, an old timer was scanning the lone wagon and the children with a well-used telescope. The long glass was a memento of the Civil War between the States of which he had been a part of. He spotted a lone sentinel high above the camp, the spotted pony, the eagle feather in the rider's hat and a long gun in hand.

"Look up yonder, Ma," he said, handing the glass to his wife who was sitting beside him. "Looks to be an Injun watching us—could be we might have trouble on our hands!" With that said he reached behind the seat for an old seldom-used musket, another memento of the Civil War.

"Don't you start a frettin' Joshua," she was quick to reply. "Remember President Card sent word down to the Valley that the Indians here are friendly—Bloods I think he called them."

Grumbling some, he spoke again, "Best we be ready just in case!" watching with interest the distant rider moving down through the brush coulee.

Toby Harrison had spotted the wagons the minute they showed on the southern horizon. Reasoning they could be the Missouri river bunch, of which his Dad had told him to watch out for, he reined his spotted pony down through the maze of ripe berries to be with his Dad's berry picking women.

Aspen and Laura were pleased, filling pail after pail full of berries in no time at all. Never had they seen anything like this before. The squealing playful girls helped out as well, making a game out of it all.

The women were chattering and giggling as they worked. Happy to be together as good friends should be when Aspen suddenly grew silent, her keen senses scoping the small valley.

"Laura!" she cautioned. "The children, I cannot hear a sound from them anymore. They have been so noisy all morning, something must be wrong!"

Silence lay heavy in the coulee, both women's nerves on edge, wilderness-honed savvy probing the surroundings for any sign of danger.

"I reckon you're right," Laura replied, her voice a bit shaky. "Let's go find our kids!"

Together they set aside their pails and headed back down to camp. There, standing in a huddle, Ellie Lou safely standing in the middle, stood their four daughters watching a lone rider and three wagons crossing over the river.

The scout led the wagons onward towards the Harrison camp, watching with caution the girls and their mothers standing together, a loaded rifle held in the hands of Aspen and Laura.

249

About fifty-yards out the scout signed the drivers to pull in their outfits, while he continued on towards the Harrison wagon, a gloved hand raised high in the peace sign of the prairie and mountain. Laura hustled the girls inside the wagon for safety, then returned to stand beside Aspen, both of their weapons were loaded and ready to shoot if need be; a slight pull from a dainty finger is all it would take!

Hidden back in the berry brush crouched Toby Harrison, a pair of dark eyes scanning the approaching rider. After being involved in the recent massacre at the old hide-hunter camp, he would not allow the same to happen here. In one hand hung a loaded sling, a long gun was tightly gripped in the other.

One false move from the advancing scout and the half-breed lad would start a war of reprisal!

"Ho!" shouted the scout, reining in his horse. "We mean you no harm. We noticed your wagon sitting here and were hoping you might help us out.

"We've come from a valley in the southern lands, the Mormon colonies in Utah. We plan on settling in the new settlement of Lee's Creek, and reckon we've taken the wrong trail and got ourselves lost."

He had pulled in his horse a respectable distance from the women, and doffing an old campaign hat, continued his talk. "Would you ladies mind if we camped here by the river tonight? Our women and children are plumb worn out, and in need of a much needed rest."

Neither Laura nor Aspen had spoken yet, still uncertain if the scout was telling the truth or not. But several things the scout had said quirked a reason for Laura to believe him.

It was four items in his talk that showed he had character and compassion. He had politely doffed his hat to them, and had addressed them as ladies. The scout then spoke of the women and children needing a rest from the long journey that was now behind them.

And last but not least, spoke with pride of the pioneering Mormons, who had given there all to settle in a new country.

"We too are peaceful folks," Aspen said, and after leaning their rifles against a wheel of the wagon, the two berry pickers turned to face the scout. "You are welcome to camp here as you asked.

"Would you mind if we walk over and meet your women and children?"

The old scout with his hat once again covering his long, graying hair, was beaming from ear to ear when he replied, "By all means do ladies, you will be most welcome in our camp."

With that said he signaled to the others that all was well, and watched the women and their children scramble from the wagons, giggling and chattering, happy to finally be able to stretch the stiffness out of their travel-worn bodies.

Aspen was thankful to know the Mormons were friendly people, and nodded her head to their own girls to come with them. Shyly, with Fairy Bell in the lead, they followed their mothers over to the Mormon wagons parked by the river.

In no time at all the Mormon children had made friends with the new arrivals, and all began romping and playing together, including little Ellie Lou.

"They must be Injun women," old Joshua mumbled, noticing all were clad in a buckskin dress, except Ellie Lou, who was wearing a tiny pair of bib overalls made from the tanned hide of a yearling mule deer.

"Oh, fiddle sticks!" his wife replied.

"Don't be such an old grouch. Crawl down out of the wagon and tend to your mules, then come on over with me and meet them."

To be around Indians brought back bitter memories to the old campaigner, and though it had happened many years before, Joshua had been involved in the Indian wars in southern Utah and Arizona, and it still riled him to be close to an Indian.

The Mormon women noticed the berry stains on the girl's lips and hands, and having spotted the abundance of the ripe shiny berries in the coulee, asked Aspen if she would mind if they picked some.

"Not at all," she said with a wide grin. "There will be plenty for all, and then some. "Come girls, we must go and finish filling our containers.

"We must leave for home soon. Tomorrow we must return to Lobo Canyon 'fore our berries start to spoil."

Several hours later, as the sun was going down, Aspen's girls had finished up the berry harvest; the Mormon girls, who had been picking with them, had sufficient for their needs as well.

A tantalizing aroma of home-cooked food filled the cool night air, teasing the taste buds of all that were there, including Aspen's camp who had been invited over for supper. It was a simple meal, yet downright tasty.

Never before had the children eaten grits and Mormon gravy, smoked ham with horse radish garnish; even strawberry jam spread on fresh-baked corn bread. Though simple Mormon fare, it was a feast for their berry-picking guests.

Soon a fiddle began to play accompanied by a mouth organ or two, and an old time dance was in full swing on the level ground by the river, A large fire blazed into the night allowing the girls from both camps to partner up, a first time for Aspen's growing daughters. Even little Ellie Lou was dancing with her mother, keeping in step to the music as if she had been doing it all her life.

Aspen was sitting in the shadows, watching Willow and Fairy Bell dancing up a storm, both had been snatched up by two Mormon boys, who were leading them in a wild and wooly dance known as the Missouri river stomp. Old Joshua and his wife appeared on the dancing grounds performing an amazing dance the Mormons referred to as the Nauvoo jig. Not to be outdone, Toby Harrison joined the lively bunch, showing his version of the *yakima* prairie chicken dance, which brought cheers of praise from the lively crowd.

Aspen was happy to be at the dance, but saddened that Smokey could not be with her. The melancholy music of an old time waltz was now drifting across the dancing ground. Tears of sadness were rolling down her cheeks knowing that she and her cowboy husband had never been given the opportunity to dance with each other.

Suddenly, as if out of no where, a thrill surged through her body, causing her to gasp as a familiar scent surrounded her like a fog in the night. Turning to scan the shadows, she discovered a grinning Smokey Harrison standing behind her. With a squeal of delight Aspen fell into her husband's arms.

"Care to dance with a trail-worn cowboy?" he asked. Not waiting for an answer, he took her hand and led her out in the crowd, where they quickly fell in step with the music of an old time pioneer waltz.

Aspen soon found out Smokey was a fine dancer, thrilled to the core as he led her through the dance without a misstep. She never had the opportunity to dance much, just the Scottish Highland fling that old Angus had insisted she and Sage learn to do.

Later that night, an exhausted group of dancers returned to their camp. Smokey and Aspen rolled out their blankets in the lee of the wagon. They were happy to be together again, happy to be in each other's arms.

To sleep under the stars this night was a special treat for Smokey and Aspen Harrison.

Leaving Aspen peacefully sleeping, Smokey was up and about before the arrival of the sun. As was his way when out on the trail he kindled a cheery fire, after which he positioned a time-worn coffee pot in the glowing embers. He smiled at the old two-gallon pot Aspen had brought with her, knowing darn well that Toby would drink most of it, if given the chance.

Returning from tending the horses, he relished the pleasant aroma that was drifting in the cool river-bottom air. There sitting cross-legged by the fire was his son, as he knew he would be, already sipping on his second cup.

In the Mormon camp over yonder by the river, old Joshua too was an early riser. He was fussing with his mules, preparing them for another long journey to find the Lee's Creek settlement.

Suddenly, his manner began to change. A shaggy beard was itching like crazy, a pair of wilderness-honed nostrils flared wide, inhaling the enticing scent of fresh brewed coffee drifting over from the Harrison camp. The old timer was smitten, couldn't help it none he reckoned.

And though his wife had given him strict orders not to drink it anymore, he couldn't help himself when getting a whiff of the addictive drink.

Most of his life coffee had been a mainstay to his diet, the elixir of the Gods as far as Joshua was concerned, even his wife had enjoyed her pot of tea now and then. But that all changed after the Prophet's manifestation—the word of wisdom he called it.

But like many of the old timers like himself, he was unable to give up what had been part of his life since a young boy, and drank it on the sly every chance he got. Even his pipe had been taken away!

Peering closely at the wagon to make sure his wife was still asleep, he couldn't stand it any more and walked over to the Harrison camp. Emerging out of the shadows, he could see Smokey and his son sitting by the fire, each with a cup of steaming coffee in their hand.

"A good mornin' neighbors," he greeted. "Mind if I sit a spell?"

"Why a good morning to you stranger," Smokey welcomed, a friendly smile on his face. "Come on over and sit, I'll pour you a cup of coffee and we'll visit awhile."

Joshua's hands were trembling as he accepted the cup, and took a wee sip. "Bin a long time since I had a cup of 'Joe,'" he said. "Sure have missed it too!"

"You folks run out of coffee?" Smoky asked. "I'm sure Aspen can spare some of ours, be our pleasure to help you out of a tight spot."

Joshua never answered right off, and finally began to talk. "No, no it is not that we have run out.

"It is a hard one to explain. You see our Mormon religion bans the use of tea and coffee, even tobacco and sippin' whiskey too.

"The Prophet Joseph Smith, who is the founder of our church, received what is called a manifestation from the Lord, telling us that he frowns upon the use of these things. He claims coffee and such are not good for our bodies!

"Sure bin a tryin' time for us older folks, a tryin' time indeed."

Offering the empty cup to Smokey, he said, "Mind if I have another cup of 'Joe', then I must get back to my wagon 'fore my wife skins me alive."

Smokey looked long at old Joshua, amazed over his coffee story!

"Tell me this," he asked. "Why do you call this coffee 'Joe'?"

After another long pause, and appearing slightly distressed, the old timer voiced a reply. "I reckon it's more of a slang word, brought about by the persecution of the Missouri mobs that drove us Mormons out of the State.

"They were a bunch of murderous heathens, poking fun at the Prophet, and his word of wisdom! It was that bunch of hell-raisers who delighted in calling coffee 'Joe', and referred to him as ol' Joe Smith the angel talker.

"Sure bin a tough one for us folks to handle, one of the reasons we have came to the northern territories—a seeking freedom of religion.

Turning to go, he spoke one more time, "I sure thank you Brother Harrison, for sharing your pot of 'Joe' with the likes of me!" 'Joe'! A word long used by old timers such as Joshua, one that was embedded in their very soul.

Returning to his camp he found his wife was up and about, scolding him for not kindling her cooking fire. Wasting no time, he stirred to life a few smoldering embers from the previous night. Surrounding the embers with long-dead willow twigs and viciously fanning his hat; her cooking fire was soon ready to use.

He was standing beside her when she asked, "Is that coffee I can smell on your breath?"

Joshua quickly moved away from her, beads of sweat appearing on his brow as he struggled to voice a reply. "Now Ma, you must know better than that.

"Your husband was just inhaling the mind-soothing scent a comin' from that cowboy's pot of 'Joe'!"

* * * CHAPTER 23 * * *

The old Harrison ranch and Milk River country were now just a memory. Riding side by side, Smokey and Aspen were leading the two outfits into the west, following the winding Whiskey Gap trail to an all important junction of several trails.

Here at this cross roads of the border country, four well-used trails came together at a wilderness intersection marked by only a weathered buffalo skull. One fork came from south of the border, the Immigrant Gap trail heavily used by the Mormon pioneers. The second fork they were now traveling on came from south of the border as well, pointing northeast through the Gap known as the Whiskey Gap trail. A favorite route heavily used by the Yankee bull trains.

The third fork pointed north to the new Mormon Colonies scattered at random up and down Lee's Creek, a goal for the dozens of wagon trains seeking a new start in the northern territories.

More important than all the rest to the Harrison outfit, the fourth fork continued on into the west, losing its identity to a rock-strewn trace at their Lobo Canyon ranch—and home.

The west fork, depending on what clan they belonged to, was known to the Indians of the region by several different names, Could be Boundary Creek, or Hogs Back, and last but not least, the wood-chopper trail. An all important trail now patrolled by the North West Mounted.

Nearing a modest prairie coulee, the four corners a mere stone-throw away, Smoky called a halt to the caravan. A slow moving stream struggled through the coulee, lined on both banks with a healthy stand of bull rushes and the chocolate brown tips of mature cat tails adding to the scenery.

Beautiful to see in the noon day sun, the thorny bush of the wild rose grew up and down the coulee, adorned with scores of blushing pink-hued flowers. The prairie rose offered an eye-pleasing welcome to the arriving visitors.

The men hustled about, unhooking the teams and after a long drink of the warm creek water, the animals were allowed to graze on the lush coulee grass. A cooking fire was crackling a merry tune, and soon the women folk were ringing the dinner bell to come and get it.

"I reckon this is where we part ways," Smokey told the Mormon leader, pointing out to him the north fork that would take them to Lee's Creek. "Be about a full day's journey for them oxen o' yours to make it that far."

"Our ranch is up yonder following the west fork, be tomorrow 'fore noon before we get that wagon load of berries back home."

The meal was enjoyed by all, watching with interest the quarreling red-wing blackbirds, who were jealously guarding their nests from the dreaded parasite of the prairie; the despised cow bird.

Little did anyone know that someday in the not so distant future, this four corners country would be settled by none other than a caravan of Mormon pioneers. A settlement would be organized, complete with a school and a church, a graveyard and a ball field too.

Dozens of homesteads would be filed in the four corner country, each quarter section with its own log cabin, a two-hole privy out back, a hand-dug well and a herd of milk cows.

Through out the summer months the settler's children might gather at the slow moving stream, watching with awe the annual battle between the cow birds and red winged blackbirds, the garter snakes and green-backed frogs.

* * * CHAPTER 24 * * *

Far west of the four corners, on the upper reaches of the wood-chopper trail, two cowboy partners had settled in and were content at last. Here at their respective Lobo and Horseshoe ranches, Smokey Harrison and Kelly Tucker were slowing down, the advancing years catching up to them.

No longer did they wander the mountain and prairie hunting for the ever elusive pot at the end of the rainbow. No longer did they yearn for a wife and family of their own. It was here in the canyons, Lobo and Horseshoe, the two cowboys had finally discovered a happiness of their own choosing.

Frigid north blizzards and heat-baked summers had not cracked the spirit of the two pioneer ranchers, nor had the militant Blackfoot or Yankee booze-runners; though not from the lack of trying.

But! dad-blast it all, they were growing old!!

Growing old is not for the weak of heart. It is welcomed by some, a peaceful time of meditation and forgiveness in their souls. For others a time of heartache and sorrow, depressed over a wasted life behind them, for mistakes that could have been prevented.

To accept old age with grace is a hard thing for some to do, a fear of the unknown gnawing at their souls is almost more than they can bear.

Smokey was having a hard time accepting old age, and the changes happening to his once invincible body. To look into a mirror was a hard thing for him to do. There staring him in the face was a stranger.

A dark beard and thinning hair now sprinkled with a snowy-white hue, and a wrinkled brow, deep worry lines that could not be erased.

His hearing was not up to par, as were his dimming eyes, resulting in a growing envy for those who were fortunate enough to wear the new fangled spectacles.

A gradual change was taking control of his body, a whole new outlook on life was staring him in the face, time to slow down and smell the roses; as Aspen had begged him to do.

"Hells fire and damnation," he expounded to Aspen one day, "this getting old is no fun—soon be a pushin' forty years."

Even his faithful Bandit was growing old. No longer did the big appaloosa have the get up and go of his youth. No longer was he a handful to saddle-up in the cool, misty mornings.

He had traded for a younger horse from out of Kelly Tucker's string, an appaloosa with the same markings as Bandit. "I reckon his name is *bandido*," Kelly told him, "The son of a gun's dam was a Spanish barb—full of get up and go."

"I reckon you can handle him all right, once he gets to know an old hombre like you." And he was teasing his old pard and Smokey knew it.

Aspen was giggling when Smokey told her of the incident. "That's not true Smokey Harrison, not true at all. You are a long ways from being old, and don't you forget it!"

He was smiling at her talk, knowing that she had out-foxed him once again, and decided to let the matter drop.

Mother Nature's plan could not be stopped, he finally conceded, must be a commandment from heaven carved in stone.

Civilization was slowly but surely gaining a foothold in this wilderness of hill and prairie, Smokey reckoned. No longer were the two ranches the only neighbors for unknown miles in all directions of the compass.

They were no longer alone!

Barb-wire fences were showing up all across the hill country, first ones to use it were the Mormon settlers, he told Aspen one day. "Even the Yankee border over yonder now has us plumb fenced out!

"From now on when we're a roundin' up strays, reckon we'll have to open and close a confounded wire gate!"

Creating a division between two countries, a border marking of three tightly stretched wires had been strung across the prairie, to meet up with a brush-cleared border slash, hewed through the wooded hills and mountain forests. A border fence consisting of barb wire and willow-hewed posts was strung across the prairie.

The North West Mounted had put the fear in the Yankee booze smugglers, the native Blood and Blackfoot were struggling with a new way of life on respective reservations. Hopefully, a more peaceful way of life must be waiting for these nomadic people in the not so distant future.

With serious intent, Smokey related an incident from the days when he was still living at his old home beside the big river.

"An old timer and his wife were living miles from nowhere," he told Aspen, who was listening with much interest. "One morning he returned to the cabin after rounding up his wandering milk herd.

'Pack up our belongings Ma,' he told her, 'we're a movin' on—it's a gettin' too crowded around these parts.

'I just found the sign of a human foot print out in the back forty!!!'

Aspen's eyes were round as saucers as she listened to his story. Then, struggling to control herself, exploded with an uncontrolled burst of laughter.

"You're just funnin' me Smokey Harrison," she managed to say, wiping the tears from her eyes.

Smokey, who had not meant the incident to be humorous, swore to the heavens above that it was the gospel truth.

Not counting their oldest son, Aspen and Smokey were now living alone at the big house built by old Angus McGregor It stood as a sentinel, a landmark near a rollicking mountain stream know as Lobo Creek.

Toby had returned to his old home in *palouse* country, taking with him a now mature Fairy Bell to meet his aging mother, Dove That Sings. His plans were to marry the girl whose life he had saved, but in the *yakima* way; not the ways of his white-eye father.

Not to be outdone, Willow was now happily married to the young Mormon who had danced with her at the berry-picking camp. They now had two lovely daughters, Amy and Rachel, the first grand children for Smoky and Aspen.

Rose, who had never been parted from her older sister for as long as they both could remember, followed her down to the settlement where she found employment at a newly built Mormon trading company.

It was here she lived with Willow, paying for her keep by assisting her only sister with a growing family of girls, of whom they both adored.

Due to a medical condition beyond her control, the ecstasy of child birth had not been the lot of Aspen Harrison. No greater blessing could she have received than raising her sister's two daughters and Fairy Bell.

The big house was empty now, the happy presence of her children now just a memory.

The love of her life was her husband Smokey. From their first meeting at the berry-picking coulee, she had fallen in love with him—a secret love that she was too shy to share with her family, including her sister Sage.

Sage too had been smitten, and being noted for her straight forward nature, soon became the wife of the big, lonesome cowboy.

Not burdened anymore with a house full of girls, Aspen and Smokey became much closer. Wherever Smokey went, Aspen was right there by his side. She loved to ride her buckskin pony, as long as she could be with her husband. From sun up in the morning until the sun set in the west, mattered naught to her.

Smokey was pleased to have her with him, sure took the loneliness out of riding alone, he reckoned. Besides, they were together and that was all that mattered. Often, when riding the summer range, high up where the forest bumped into the rocks, they would roll out their blankets under the stars; reveling in the beauty of nature's grandeur, and each other.

* * * CHAPTER 25 * * *

Finding the grass in good shape, and the longhorns lazing around with a contented look on their face, more than made up for the long two-day ride.

At the crack of dawn next morning, Aspen arose from her blankets and found Smoky sitting by the fire munching on jerky and sipping on a cup of black coffee. It was a trail breakfast in its truest form, simple to prepare, yet offering enough energy for the start of a new day in the saddle.

"The coffee's hot darlin'," Smokey said, noticing she was awake. "Come and join me 'fore this cowboy brew loses its get up and go!"

"Why, it tastes horrible Smoky," she said, after joining him at the fire. "Whatever have you done to it?"

"Nothin' much," he responded, a smile spreading across his whiskered face. "Cowboy coffee doesn't calm your nerves much unless it is strong enough to float a spoon."

"Yu-kk!" was her only reply.

After packing up their gear, they climbed aboard their frisky broncs and started back down through the forest for Lobo Canyon, and home. .

Following a game trail that wound down through a thick stand of lodgepole pine, *Bandido* and the buckskin mare began acting up. Rarely had they made such a fuss, fighting the tight rein in a stubborn manner—attempting to leave this lonely forest behind and race back to the safety of the home ranch.

265

Suddenly, and with no prior warning, the two animals stopped their foolishness, refusing to take another step. That both were spooked there could be left little doubt, alert ears pointing off the trail toward the marshy residue of a beaver dam. A thick infestation of willow brush concealed the marshy setting from the riders view.

Becoming a handful to control, the two normally well-mannered horses began jigging on the spot, sensing a hidden danger in the willows.

"Smokey!" Aspen screeched, the next best thing to a scream. "I can hear a strange noise coming from down there—like the kind a longhorn makes when it is angry, or in distress!"

"Keep a tight rein on your buckskin," Smoky cautioned his riding partner.

"Could be a bear down yonder, best we take care!"

Aspen was doing just that when a challenging roar erupted from within the willow thicket. The crackling of busted brush added to the discomfort of the horses, resulting in both animals squalling in terror and bucking up a storm.

Much sooner than the humans realized what was causing the ruckus, their horses knew, and wanted no part of the foul scent that was drifting out of the willows.

Exploding up through the brush charged an outraged grizzly sow. Her neck fur was standing straight in the air, she was roaring a deadly tune; driving the two saddle ponies plumb loco.

Aspen's mare took the bit in her teeth, and like an arrow shot from a loaded cross bow, went streaking through the forest as if the devil himself was after her.

The bear was now on the trail, blocking the escape of Smokey and a lunging *Bandido*. One hand held a tight grip on the bridal reins. With the other he pulled his Marlin from the saddle scabbard, prepared to fight a war.

The action that followed was a whirl-wind of pain and ear-splitting noise for the old cowboy, his mind in a confused daze, struggling to sort out what had happened to him. Was he still alive, or had been taken up to be with the angels, he couldn't tell which?

Lurking far back in a corner of his mind was another thought. Aspen! Has my Aspen made it to safety?

A drama of the wilderness had been enacted here by the beaver dam, mere seconds is all it took before the curtain was dropped. No longer was an enraged grizzly roaring a deadly tune, no longer were two horses squalling in terror, and no longer was a petite cowgirl screaming her head off.

A deathly silence returned to the lodgepole forest, broken only by the sobbing of a heart broken Aspen Harrison.

She was sitting near the trail, her blouse in tatters, her face and arms bleeding from cuts and scratches too numerous to count; and in her lap rested the head and shoulders of her unconscious husband.

She too was lucky to be alive, having been swept from the saddle by the branch of a long dead tree. There she lay in a daze, struggling to regain her senses when she heard the shot from Smokey's rifle; followed by two more in rapid succession.

Struggling to her feet, she found she could stand upright, and began to stagger back to the scene of the battle, three-hundred yards away.

As she found out later, Smokey's first shot slowed up the charging bear, who continued on towards the horse and the man, murder reeking from its very soul. *Bandido* went completely berserk, bucking off the old cowboy who fired two more shots as he fell.

It was an unheard of feat in itself for an old rancher like Smokey, as told by a proud family for many years to come. No doubt the gun slingers could do such things on a daily basis, but what about their Dad?

The dying beast managed to reach Smokey, inflicting a severe mauling before collapsing in the dust.

After brushing away the tears Aspen could see more clearly, there stood her grinning step-son holding the bridal reins of three horses. "My Dad brave warrior now," he said with great pride.

"He has sent this devil animal to the happy hunting ground.

"The Great Spirit will treat Smokey with much honor, happy this bear did not kill my Mom and Dad."

Though she had just survived one of the most nerve-wracking times of her life, a thrill raced through Aspen's mistreated body on hearing her step-son refer to her as his Mom!

Smok'ee knelt beside his parents, a small jar of a secret salve in hand, then applied a generous amount to both of their wounds. "Dove's salve—good medicine" he said, returning the jar to his saddle bag.

He spoke once more, "Smok'ee go now,…more bear down there…," and he was signing toward the willow thicket.

"By deep water—where flat tails make lodge."

Smok'ee Harrison, the oldest son of Smokey and Dove, could speak passable English if in the right mood. Other times a snatch of pigeon-English blended with a dash of *yakima* lingo was plenty good enough for him.

The familiar scent of Aspen and her tears falling on his face was reason enough for Smokey to stir, and then his eyes opened, still in a fog over what had happened. A groan of pain escaped his lips as he sat up, finding he was wrapped in Aspen's arms.

The stench of the grizzly carcass lying at his feet was more than he could handle, and with the help of a still weeping Aspen they both moved far back from the scene of battle.

"Oh, Smokey." she sobbed, "I thought the bear must have killed you. You have been hurt really bad!"

"I too reckoned this old cowboy had crossed over the divide," he said, his mind began recovering from the trauma of fighting the bear.

"A weeping angel was holding me in her arms—the scent of her body was the same as your's Aspen—I knew then that I was in heaven with Sage."

"I felt her presence too Smokey," giggling and sobbing at the same time. "She was here, I just know it—making sure that her younger sister was taking care of you!"

"I'm sure one lucky hombre," he managed to say, his head nodding once again. "With two loving wives a lookin' after me—I just might live to be forty years old!"

With caution Smok'ee entered the willows, the agonizing moan of a longhorn was stronger here, causing him to stop and wonder. He dropped to his knees, crawling through the maze of willows until he could see the beaver pond, and there witnessed a sight he hoped to never see again.

There, mired in the boggy mud lay a longhorn steer, too weak to move after struggling for unknown hours to free itself. The steer's head was turned watching two yearling grizzly cubs feeding on his body.

The ravenous beasts had eaten a huge portion of one hind-quarter, all the steer could do was watch, moaning an agonizing, mournful tune.

As hardened as the half-breed boy was to the ways of Mother Nature, this was the worst case of cruelty he had ever seen. Anger rippled through his body, an intense anger that dated back to his ancestors of old. He was standing, rifle in hand when he shot the two gluttons where they lay feeding.

After a pause, Smok'ee discovered the steer was watching him with open blood-shot eyes, as if pleading for a release from the agony he was suffering. His mouth was open, tongue hanging free, no longer able to utter a sound.

No longer could Smok'ee watch the animal suffer, and put him out of his misery with a shot that closed the longhorn's eyes for ever. Only then did he look up in the sky, and howl a *yakima* war cry to the sun.

"Now you free," he was talking to the dead steer. "Now you go to happy hunting ground.

"No more suffer from devil bears!"

He then left the scene of this wilderness drama, and returned to his concerned parents and told them of what had happened. He told it all. How one of his Dad's longhorns was mired in the bog unable to defend himself. How two feared predators of the forest were gorging themselves on the still alive animal, and that he had sent all three of them to the happy hunting ground.

Smokey was still struggling to get over the bear mauling that came mighty close to ending his life. A surge of pride rippled through his body as he listened to his son's talk. It was an honest to goodness pride that only a father can have for one of his own.

"I am proud of you Smok'ee," he told him. "You are now a man, a brave man who is willing to face down the perils of the frontier without giving it a second thought."

Though his two sons were half-breeds, steeped in the ways of their *yakima* culture, he loved them with the same love as if they had been delivered to this earth by a white mother.

"I knew you would handle it like you did Smok'ee, no white man could have done a better job."

"My Dad, great cowboy Chief—kill devil bear—cowboy way." Smok'ee said, a serious look was engraved on his tan-hued face as he spoke.

"Chief bring good medicine to all who live in Lobo Canyon!"

It took some doing to get Smokey back to his Lobo ranch site. He insisted on riding *Bandido* as was his way, refusing to be loaded on a *travois* and drug back to the ranch, as his wife and son insisted that he do.

He conceded one thing and allowed them to tie him in the saddle, safe and secure from falling off, which would have worsened the lot of his damaged body.

Two days later, after a nerve-wracking time of it, the small caravan arrived at the dooryard of the big house along the banks of Lobo Creek.

Later that night, after Aspen had cleaned him up and disinfected the numerous cuts and slashes, life-time mementos of the clawed paws of a fighting grizzly bear, he was able to start eating food; and ordered a pot of coffee, strong enough to eat the rowels off his silver spurs.

A month passed before Smokey was able to do much. He was now helping Aspen with some of her household chores, even riding his old Bandit once again, though short rides they were. Aspen knew that it was driving him crazy not to be able to cowboy up, yet she was happy to have him close by where they could be together.

After tossing and turning most of a sleepless night, Smokey arose in disgust. Why can I not find sleep, he wondered? What is wrong with me?

True, his old wounds from the grizzly episode were still bothering him, especially so a deep gash on his posterior, the part of him that sat in the saddle. On several occasions his inner self had relayed a message to stay out of the saddle. That his riding days were now over!

With head hanging low, he sat on the edge of the bed, a boot in one hand; a sock in the other. His mind was in turmoil, his cowboy pride about to take a licking. With great reluctance he now accepted the fact that he could no longer ride old Bandit; that he could no longer ride him into the forest checking on the herd.

The deep gash on his rump was not healing like it should, the irritating pain from the pressure of the wound meeting the saddle seat was becoming more than the old cowboy could handle.

With his boots now on and his Stetson on his head where it should be, he left the house and wandered over to the horse corral to give Bandit his daily ration of oats, then turn him out in the back pasture to romp and play with *Bandido*, as was his custom.

Bandit must be still asleep, he reckoned. He's not standing by the corral gate waiting for me to come.

In reality Smokey now had two Bandits, having retired his long time friend to a life of ease here at the home ranch. The other, of which he had been riding for several years, had been bartered from out of Kelly Tucker's string over at the Horseshoe.

Out of respect for his first Bandit, he named the younger one *Bandido* as well, knowing his old friend would not mind sharing the name.

The darkness of the early morning hour was changing, the shadows of the night fading away into nothing at the arrival of the sun. Mumbling to himself, he continued on to a slab horse shelter and found it empty of everything but Bandit's calling card, fresh droppings still warm in the cool morning air.

"Can't be more than an hour old," he said. "The old son-of-a-gun must be around here somewhere."

Smokey continued his search, and while investigating the far side of the small shelter was stopped in his tracks; a state of shock surging through his very soul. There lay Bandit stretched out on his side, unable to rise, but still sensing Smokey's presence. His ears were no longer firm and alert as they should be, the spark in his eyes was rapidly fading into a vacant stare. Yet somehow, somehow he managed a final greeting to his old friend, Smokey Harrison.

A saddened cowboy knelt by his horse, tears streaming down his face as he caressed the fevered body of a long-time friend. An empty void entered his soul as he watched Bandit take his last breath. It was the same devastating emotion that surged through his body the day Sage had left him so long ago, back at the Milk River ranch.

Smokey was sitting now, the head of his horse cradled in his lap. There to mourn the passing of a faithful companion that only death could have parted.

The two of them had ridden many trails together, they had faced danger in the face with no hesitation or doubt. And when the good times returned, they both kicked up their heels, happy to have prevailed—happy to still be alive!

Aspen had prepared their morning meal, the coffee pot was singing a merry tune and still no sign of her husband. This upset her, knowing that when Smoky was at home, he insisted they be together when sharing the first pot of the day. A long time custom that must not be broken, a time when a husband and his wife could reminisce of the past and plan for the days that lay ahead.

He often had told her that coffee was good medicine for the soul. That it perked up one's jangled nerves when the chips were down, and put back the get up and go in one's cowboy swagger.

Something must have happened to him, she reckoned, and left the house to find him. Discovering the corral gate open she continued on, finding neither horse nor man until she thought of Bandit's shelter, built to protect him from the heat of summer, and the frigid blizzards of winter.

Aspen discovered the shelter was empty and continued her quest, knowing there was only one more place the horse could possibly be—on the far side of the shelter! Silently she neared the blind corner of Bandits favorite loafing place, listening to a strange, muffled sound rising above the chatter of nearby Lobo Creek.

Cautiously she peeked around the corner and gasped in shock. There lay Bandit with his head lying across her husband's lap. The noise she had heard was the sobbing of a heart-broken cowboy.

She respected his privacy, knowing how much Smokey respected and loved this great horse. Tears filled her eyes as she watched, sensing the grief that her husband must be suffering. Then silent as a mouse, she backed away and returned to the big house.

It seemed like hours before Smokey returned to the house, there to sit by the big plank table carved by old Angus himself. Aspen had a fresh pot of his devil's brew prepared and waiting, of which she knew he would sure be in need of. He never spoke, but consumed several cups of the scalding liquid; his head hanging low.

Aspen still respected her husband's great sorrow, knowing he would talk to her in good time.

Finally, he raised his head and through blood-shot eyes looked at her. She returned the look with a faint smile, and spoke, "Welcome back Smokey—you're just in time for breakfast—I was thinking you must have left me."

The sun had now returned to Lobo Canyon, the welcome light shining through the window, the rays illuminating Aspen's kitchen with a cheery glow. "I reckon I've been through hell and back," he muttered, still not looking her in the eye.

"Oh! Smokey, what has happened?" she exclaimed and walked over beside him, her hand resting on his shoulder.

"Bandit's up and died on me," he managed to say, his throat all choked up till the words were hard to recognize.

"I'm so sorry Smokey, I really am!" and she truly meant every word she spoke.

Refilling his cup, and with a cup of her own, she sat beside him, a dainty hand gripping one of her husband's work-hardened ones. She knew he would talk to her when he was ready.

Tears were streaming down both there cheeks, sitting together hand in hand. Aspen's strong spirit was surging into her husband's weakened one, a subtle union of the two, the strong one keeping the sad and dejected one from faltering. Offering strength and comfort to Smokey Harrison.

"Sure thank you Aspen, for your loving concern, reckon I'll be fine after a bit, sure been a tough one to swallow!"

"I too loved Bandit," she told him

"But not as much as the cowboy who rode him!"

Smokey finally settled down, and after the first initial shock had passed he began to reason rationally as was his way.

The horse had died of old age, twenty some odd years and counting, a remarkable age for one of the horse kingdom. Bandit had lived a life full of excitement and danger, who along with his cowboy partner, had faced the unknown of the Rocky Mountains, the heat of the sun-baked prairie, and the deadly north blizzards that howled in from the land of the strange lights that lit up the northern sky.

Bandit had the privilege of being close to Smokey's three wives, who each in their own respective time had loved the horse the same as did the big cowboy. Dove That Sings, Sage McGregor and then her sister Aspen, all treated him with much kindness and respect, knowing the invincible bond between the horse and their husband.

"Reckon I've let my emotions get out of control," Smokey told Aspen, who was still holding his hand.

"Sure do thank you for standing beside me like you have—means a lot to have a caring lady like you—sharing my sorrow and grief!"

"I don't recall of weeping like this since I was a small boy. A faithful friend of mine was killed—a collie dog with a broken nose—leaving me a lonely broken-hearted lad!"

"You are not alone now Smokey, I am happy to be with you and share your grief. For me it is a great honor to do so!"

"And you have even wept with me," he said. "How will I ever repay you for your kindness?"

"You have repaid me many times over Smokey. By taking me as your wife, by allowing me to raise your daughters and now, allowing me to comfort you in this bad time in your life."

With the assistance of a team of horses, Bandit's remains were taken over to a far corner of the horse pasture and there pulled into a natural-carved break in the landscape. There to be covered over with the rich loam from this mountain meadow.

To prevent predator desecration of the body, the grave was then topped off with a cover of creek rock taken from the nearby stream. As a final tribute to a great mountain horse, Aspen Harrison placed a bouquet of Indian paintbrush on Bandit's grave.

From the big horse barn by the corrals came the inquisitive whinny of another *Bandido*. He too sensed that something was wrong, that never again would the two Bandits be able to romp and play together.

* * * CHAPTER 26 * * *

Resigning himself to the fact that he could no longer ride the range, Smokey Harrison took over the trap line that his son Toby had once managed. Besides he was finding it difficult to accept old age, the trap line would give him something to do besides sit around and twiddle his thumbs.

Aspen sure didn't mind. She too was showing her age, tiring of the endless tasks involved in keeping the big McGregor house clean and in a presentable condition. Together as they should be, she and her husband moved up Lobo Canyon to live out there remaining days in the trapper cabin.

Their daughter Willow and her Mormon husband moved away from Lee's Creek to settle in her parent's old home. It was here her husband Jacob would learn the ways of a cowboy from Smok'ee. Toby, who was now living with his *yakima* kin, might never return to his life in Lobo Canyon, leaving his brother to ride the range and wrangle the longhorns alone.

Another reason for Willow's decision to return to the house where she was born, was to make sure her family of girls were raised in the same environment as she and Rose had been.

A wilderness canyon where the mountain breezes pestered the tall pines, Lobo Creek chattering an endless mind-soothing tune, and the mourning doves cooing their melancholy strains at the crack of dawn; a call of the wild for those who might care to listen.

Since her marriage, and though she loved her husband very much, Willow had been homesick for her Dad and the only mother that she and Rose had ever known. Jacob didn't mind the move, a happy Willow, made for a happy Jacob.

When first hearing of her Dad's life threatening battle with an enraged grizzly bear, and the injuries he had received by doing so, was yet another reason for her to be closer to her big cowboy Dad. Buried deep in her soul, was an intense sorrow and pain that could not be shaken.

Many were the nights that Willow had tossed and turned in her blankets, wide awake—weeping and praying for the recovery of her beloved Dad. To the first of his two daughters, he was an honest to goodness cowboy that Willow would worship for the rest of her days.

And then there was her birth mother Sage, who had given her life to deliver baby Rose into the land of the living! Her Mom is not far away, Willow was sure of, and had sensed her presence on more than one occasion. Guarding her two daughters as all mothers do, hovering close by if needed.

The body of Sage had been interred in the Clan's grave site on the far side of the big house, a great blessing to Willow and her daughters. They could now visit her grave each and every day, kneeling in reverence and offering a prayer.

Leaving a fresh-picked mountain flower on Sage Harrison's grave along side Lobo Creek, the same creek where Sage and Aspen had played as children, so long ago.

The frost had been on the pumpkin for some time, the mood of old Mother Nature was changing, from a mild warm manner to one of numbing cold, wild blizzards and deep snow.

It was now the middle of December, the last of the wild geese were now on their way south, the elk were winding down a wild and wooly rut, and Smokey's trap line was in place for the annual fur harvest.

He and Aspen were hiking the rugged canyon several times a week, a tiring leg-cramping trek of five miles up and another five back to the cabin. In order to reap the rewards of this lucrative wilderness venture, the traps must be supplied with fresh bait at all times. A must in the routine of a trapper, a chore no trapper could ignore if he was to succeed in the fur harvest.

Smokey's health was improving for the shape he was in. His leg muscles were gradually returning to their natural tone, his breathing was improving—the fresh mountain air and daily exercise was good medicine for his soul.

To have Aspen with him was like icing on the cake as far as Smokey was concerned. She sure did not mind, helping out where she could, and enjoyed every minute of the day as long as they were together.

Back at the cabin is where she excelled, able to have three martin skins pulled over her hand-crafted stretching board, while her husband was still skinning his first.

"You're a natural born trapper," he told her one night, both working by the light of the big stone fireplace, preparing the pelts of their latest catch, of which included a lynx, an otter, several martins and a pair of red foxes.

Giggling, she replied, "My mother was a half-blood Indian, remember? She showed Sage and me how to trap when we were just small girls.

We loved to trap along Lobo Creek, catching mainly mink and otter and a few ermine."

Though slightly embarrassed, Smoky told her that she was the best trapper ever. Even better than Trapper Joe, who many long years in the past had trained him in the basics of trapping.

Still giggling, pleased with her husband's praise of her skills, she continued her chatter, "Mom showed us how to skin the animals, scrape the fat from the pelts and stretch them on a drying board; carved from the branch of a cottonwood tree."

Though it was hard work, a husband and wife team enjoyed what they were doing thanks to the expertise of Aspen Harrison.

The days grew shorter, the nights even longer, and much sooner than they could have realized, Christmas was just around the corner.

"I reckon we should shut it down come Christmas time," Aspen told Smokey one day. I reckon ten days would be about right, a time to celebrate the birth of the Holy one, and be with our family and friends."

"I couldn't agree more," Smokey said, a big grin spreading across his face.

"I'm sure a gettin' tuckered out, and I'm sure you are too. Both of us could use a break from this sun up in the mornin' routine, to can't see in the evening, when the sun leaves us in the dark!"

"Whoo-ee! he almost shouted—let's do it Aspen—let's go celebrate with our family."

✳ ✳ ✳ CHAPTER 27 ✳ ✳ ✳

Out of an eerie haze appeared a buckskin clad figure plodding down a winding trail out of Lobo Canyon. The shuffle of snowshoes in the snow and the jingle of traps slung over his shoulder startled a snowbird family, who flew up in panic and fluttered off into the pines. On his other shoulder rested a long gun protected from the elements by a wrap of tanned buckskin.

Stopping for a well deserved breather, Smokey Harrison was greeted by the arrival of a pair of ravens who had been following him for several hours. The impudent rascals were taking turns uttering their raucous croaks, expressing their disapproval of his presence here in their canyon home.

Cursing some, he berated the ravens for their cheeky ways, and muttered through his beard, "Them blasted critters have bin pestering me for as long as I can remember—sure hope they soon croak of old age."

The old trapper cursed again as he looked up at the sky, a troubled sky being consumed by angry looking clouds fresh in from the northern lands, threatening the front range of the Rockies, concealing the high peaks and invading the canyons below.

A once sunny sky was fast losing its identity. Driven by the arrival of a bone-chilling wind, large fluffy snow flakes fluttered in panic, their plight unseen by a dense fog that had moved in across the high country.

Smokey was forced to stop more often now, his aging body demanding that he do so. He knew the years were creeping up on him, he also knew this steep rock-cluttered trail was becoming more than he could handle.

Though he was well clad with a pair of hand-crafted snowshoes he had bartered from a Blackfoot trader, his old legs were begging him to slow down.

It grieved him to think of the hundreds of times he had walked up and back in the canyon, his younger body enjoying every step. But now his old legs were telling him that it was time to quit,

To give up this way of life before it was too late!

Glancing at the stormy heavens, he mouthed another silent curse. "Time I wus hanging up my traps and snowshoes," he muttered, pulling a beaver skin cap around his ears.

"Besides, the fur in these parts is becoming as scarce as the buffalo—I reckon my Lobo Canyon is all trapped out."

"Hardly worth the effort," he muttered one more time, wiping away the tears that were flooding his eyes. The tears were Nature's way of protecting the all important organs from the frigid air that was invading the valley.

Smokey was plumb tuckered out, every muscle heavy with fatigue from long hours of walking. His throat was dry, his stomach empty. His mind was sluggish because of the weariness of his body, and he felt short-tempered and irritable because of it.

"Reckon come spring this ol' hombre will gather up his traps and call it a day."

Normally, he was a quiet, tolerable man with a dry humor and a liking for people, but in his present mood he was wary of himself, knowing a temper that was sometimes hard to control.

He stayed put for several moments, stamping his chilled feet to keep the blood flowing. Then, after adjusting the beaver skin to protect his face from the icy north wind that was howling like a banshee, he continued on down the canyon.

The slight stop had refreshed him, doing away with the nagging leg cramps of the past miles. And feeling somewhat refreshed, his mind was now at ease, his stride returning to the normal ground-covering pace he was known for. Another half hour he reckoned, about another half hour and I'll be back at the cabin—shucks, should be no problem; it's all down hill from here.

It was then a pleasant thought popped into his mind, he remembered that tonight was Christmas Eve. He also knew that tomorrow he was invited down to his grand daughter's place. Along with their growing family of girls, Willow and Jacob were now living in the old McGregor place, down the canyon where the Lobo leaves the forest.

The thoughts of a Christmas dinner just would not leave Smokey's mind. Roast wild turkey with all the trimmings, he could hardly wait.

Smokey continued on, only to be greeted by another blast of ugly weather. Driven by a northern gale, the falling snow became a force to be reckoned with, battering the lone trapper without mercy.

His mind began to wander, blotting out the wind and the snow, taking him back to the distant past; a diversion tactic he had no control over. This strange phenomenon was happening to him often as of late. Sometimes it brought back events of the past that he just as soon not be confronted with, other times it brought back pleasant ones that soothed his troubled soul.

One of these events was his old dog Stubb, a big collie-cross pup that had been given to him by Sage McGregor, the oldest daughter of old Angus, a sheep rancher whose spread was situated at the mouth of Lobo Canyon. It was a forgone conclusion the pup would be given this name due to the fact that he had been born with a bob tail.

He sure missed old Stubb, a four-legged friend who had been a great comfort to him in that lonely time of his life.

There was another time that he could never forget! It was his loving wife Sage, the older sister of Aspen who been taken away from him much too soon. It was never clear in his mind of how she had died, or why. Only that she had died delivering him another daughter, a sister to three-year old Willow. The new baby had been given the name of Rose, after the prairie rose her mother had chosen before her death.

Old Stubb loved little Rose too. As she began to walk and leave the cabin to explore the great outdoors, the dog was her constant companion, guarding her from danger, willing to take on the devil himself if he should happen by.

Oft'times when the little one ventured too close to the swift-flowing water, Stubb could be seen quietly moving between the creek and little Rose, and with much patience herd her back towards the cabin.

Over supper one night Aspen, who was now married to Smokey, told her new husband of yet another incident that had happened between the toddler and the dog. Little Rose appeared determined to wade into the dangerous flow of Lobo Creek. Aspen was close by watching. Stubb was standing beside her, both the dog and the woman preparing to stop the little one if need be.

Suddenly a bob-tail dog could stand it no longer, and after brushing by Aspen, his strong teeth snatched a hold on the seat of the child's pants tugging her back to safety. Little Rose began to scream in terror over the way the dog was treating her, but in no time at all her small arms were wrapped around his shaggy neck, showing the love she had for the big collie.

The dog was happy too and gave the child a dog kiss, a long tongue flashing across a rosy cheek.

Smokey Harrison, an old trapper caught up in a wild blizzard, shook the snow from himself, his wandering mind returning to the present; for a short time is all. A tear, and yet another trickled down into his grizzled beard. A silent curse escaped his wind-chapped lips.

"Reckon my luck has left me!" his words were lost in the fury of the storm.

"I reckon the first two women I really cared for have been taken from me by the whims of fate. First there was Dove That Sings, followed by Sage, who sacrificed her life to give Willow a baby sister."

From what old Angus had told him, he reckoned it had been meant to be. 'It must be a gathering of the Clans up yonder,' he told his heart broken son-in-law. 'who have taken Sage to care for the little ones, those who are up there with no mothers!'

Smokey brushed more snow from his face, disgusted with his superstitious father-in-law, and mumbled once more, "To me it was fate, a destiny handed down by the Gods!"

He had known for a succession of years this would happen, but now as he continued on down the trail, memories began in earnest to tear him apart. He also knew that this terrible sorrow would remain with him for the rest of his days, a sorrow that just would not go away.

"Wow!" he muttered, "I sure don't know what is wrong with me tonight."

"I must be going crazy."

After hundreds of treks up and down the canyon, he reckoned he could find his way blind-folded. It was an ingrained trait of a wilderness man, Smokey Harrison was no exception.

Muttering to himself as he cautiously moved one foot after another, he uttered a silent prayer, knowing that he was nearly home.

Entering the clearing, he stopped for a moment, relaxing some knowing that his ordeal with the storm was now over, that he had conquered the Lobo trail one more time. Still partly blinded from the effects of the ice and snow caked on his face, he was unable to see the cabin but could sense that it was there on the far side of the clearing, another trait of a wilderness man.

The fury of the storm was lessened here in the pine-sheltered clearing. He knew that Aspen would be waiting for him, as was her custom. The door would be partly ajar, a warm blanket tucked around her body, so happy to see him return to her safe and sound.

How did she know that he had entered the clearing? Having been born and raised in a wilderness environment, she too could sense things such as this, the blood of her Blackfoot ancestors still strong in her veins.

Once inside Aspen would assist him out of his winter duds, and after snuggling a warm blanket around his shoulders, settle him into a chair by the open fire—his feet propped on a chunk of pine. Only then would she place more logs on the fire and bring him a mug of hot coffee.

"You must be half-frozen!" she would tell him, and move her rocker close in beside her husband.

"I'm sure happy you made it back to me, safe and sound!" one of her dainty hands would be squeezing his work-hardened one.

Smokey was now close to the cabin door, waiting for his wife to greet him, as was her way. The door never opened, Aspen must be sleeping, he reckoned. He removed his snowshoes and groped for the latch string, then walked into a darkened cabin. All was dark, no cheery flames dancing in the fireplace, no candle fluttering on the hand-hewed table.

A panic surged through the old trapper's heart—something must have happened to my Aspen!

"Aspen! Aspen darlin'" he shouted. "Are you here?

"I would have been here sooner but, but the blasted blizzard slowed me down."

Fumbling around in the dark was no problem for Smokey, who had been blinded by the storm, several miles back up the trail this had happened. After pulling off his cumbersome bear skin coat, he managed to light the candle.

He found the cabin to be empty. Aspen Harrison was not here, resulting in another panic attack and a volume of unrepeatable words. His eyes were now partially back to normal here out of the wind. He could see more clearly and noticed a scrap of paper beside the candle.

Paying it no mind, he soon had a fire roaring in the fire place, a pot of coffee brewing, and was munching on a slab of cold venison. He then settled into his chair, his feet propped on a pine log absorbing the warmth of the fire. Once again he noticed the paper beside the candle, a strange curiosity urging him to pick it up.

My dearest Smokey
I have gone to Willows as planned
must help her prepare Xmas dinner and
clean rooms for the Tucker family who will be
there for several days

*Cum down when you get back
be sure to bathe and shave!*
Love Aspen

Smokey was dumb founded, he just could not believe what a dunce he had become. He had known about the plans all along, they had discussed them together before he left on the previous day. Due to the severe blizzard and the unrelenting visions of the past that had been harassing his mind—he had just plumb forgot!!

* * * *

Up Lobo Canyon they came, two young girls following a faint trace through the pines. Though they were both wearing snowshoes, the youngest was breaking trail through the deepening snow. Her older sister was following with a bulky satchel strapped on her chest.

It was late afternoon before they left the big McGregor house along Lobo Creek. They reckoned they should have left much earlier, but had timed it this way knowing that for their surprise to be successful, they must arrive at Grandpa Harrison's cabin after dark.

Amy, who was the oldest of the two sisters was becoming worried, the clear sky of the once sunny day was darkening, strange scary clouds were moving in from the north. A weird moaning sound from far back in the forest could be heard, perhaps an omen of things to be.

And it was becoming louder!

Their Mom whose name was Willow, had been raised in this Rocky Mountain environment, and had lectured her two girls about the ways of these mountain storms. Amy knew that a blizzard must be heading their way, the wilderness-honed senses of her Mom were never wrong. And right here and now, were a comfort to Smokey's two grand daughters.

"Come, Rachel we must hurry," Amy shouted, her own inherited genes starting to kick in.

"I reckon we're going to be caught up in a snow storm, by the sounds of what's coming we're sure enough in for it."

"I'll try Amy, I'm sure getting tired though.

"You break trail for awhile. I'll carry Grandpa Harrison's Christmas surprise the rest of the way."

Large fluffy snow flakes began to fall. "Reckon we've got to keep going," Amy shouted back to her sister, "before we lose sight of the trail."

After some heavy going through the deepening snow, the girl's caught scent of wood smoke, knowing that to follow the welcome odor would bring them to their grandpa's cabin nestled inside a modest clearing in the forest.

Still panting from the arduous trek, they suppressed happy giggles as they closed in on the cabin. The full force of the storm was now battering the cabin. Though at the point of exhaustion, the two sisters made one final effort and found themselves at the cabin door.

After brushing the snow away from the old plank door, Rachel sat the ribbon-adorned bundle on the doorstep. Then after knocking on the door with mitten-clad fists, the girls plan was to head back down the Lobo Trail, only to have Rachel lose her balance while turning and tip over into the three feet of fresh snow.

All that could be seen of her above the drift was a bright red scarf and the tail end of her snowshoes. "Oh, drat it all," Amy cried, and turned to help her struggling sister stand up once again.

When she finally got Rachel untangled and free from her wreck, the sobbing girl said, "I'm sure sorry Amy, I've ruined our Christmas Eve surprise.

"I've twisted my ankle—I don't think I can walk anymore in this deep snow." There were tears in her eyes when she spoke again, "It hurts real bad when I step on it!"

By now the girl's surprise package was bouncing around on the door step, and to make matters worse, the door opened and their stood their grandpa with a lantern in one hand, his double-barrel shot gun in the other!

His eyes that were usually hidden behind bushy eyebrows were now plain to see, scanning the storm-swept clearing with a steely gaze, returning to settle on his two grand daughters,

"What in tarnation are you two a doin' out on a night like this?" he managed to say, a look of disbelief showing on his whiskered face.

"I reckoned there must be a bear a snoopin' around out here."

Both girls remained silent, shivering from the frigid cold, not really knowing how to best answer his question.

"Well now that you're here," he said, his voice softening, "take off them thar snowshoes and come on in out of the storm—you both look to be half frozen." While he was talking the sister's surprise package began to bounce around his booted feet.

"What in blue-blazes is in thar?" he said, his voice rising once again, stepping back in surprise, listening in awe to the strange sounds coming from the satchel.

"Must be a wild cat you got in that bag, what with all the caterwallin' and what not!"

Old grandpa Smokey Harrison stepped back in the cabin watching his grand daughters kick free from the snowshoes.

Amy followed him in, one arm supporting a limping Rachel, in the other she held a squirming, questionable satchel. Tears were trickling down both their frosted cheeks as they watched grandpa putting fresh logs on the fire. "Close the door!" he ordered. "Pull off them duds you're a wearin' and come on over by the fire, reckon I've got to get you both thawed out good and proper like."

Watching them both settle down on a bearskin rug, he spoke again, "I reckon a good hot mug of cocoa is what you girls are a needin'. But first you must show me what you got cooped up in that satchel o' yourn." his attention straying over by the door.

"Sure hope it isn't a wild critter you're a bringing into my cabin."

The girls were not really frightened of their grandpa, intimidated sometimes by his gruff manner, but deep in their hearts they knew that he loved them, and that he knew they loved him as well.

"Grandpa," Amy said, a slight quiver in her voice. "We have brought you a Christmas present. It was to be a surprise until the darn blizzard ruined our plans." She then walked over to the door and returned with the satchel, sitting down on the rug beside Rachel. Together they opened the surprise for Grandpa Harrison to see,

"Merry Christmas Grandpa," they both spoke in unison, and pushed the present over by his stocking-clad feet.

"Here they are Grandpa," they were both giggling as Rachel spoke. "They are a Christmas present from your loving grand daughters."

"There is no wild critter inside, have a look and see!"

Grandpa Smokey took one look and gasped in shock. "I'll be a dad-burned maverick steer," he expounded, a mile-long smile spreading across his whiskered face.

"If that doesn't beat all," he said, still smiling.

"Holy Smokes, there are two of them inside this bag of yours!"

Only then did the girls reach into the satchel and bring out two tiny bundles of fur. Amy held one, Rachel the other, they then sat them in their grandpa's lap, who was sitting by the rug in his rocking chair.

With happy smiles on their faces, tears as well, the two sisters replied, "We love you Grandpa."

The pups, one a Scotch collie, the other a blue heeler of questionable lineage, were overjoyed at being released from the dark place they had been confined in for so long a time. Tiny tales wagging in unison, they immediately began to lick grandpa's work-hardened hands.

"We have given each of them a name Grandpa," Rachel told him. "The black one is Midge, the blue one is Molly."

After recovering from the unexpected surprise found in the satchel, Smokey realized his girls must be starving after their arduous trek up the canyon. After stoking more logs on the fire, he put on the kettle and in no time at all had two steaming mugs of cocoa prepared for his grand daughters.

Along with the cocoa were two plump venison sandwiches, quickly devoured as if they hadn't eaten for a week. While eating grandpa's bachelor fare, they were struggling to keep their eyes open, and when the last crumb had been eaten, both girls tipped over into the comfort of the bear skin—fast asleep.

After tucking a Hudson Bay blanket around their rosy cheeks, he reckoned he should feed Midge and Molly, whose whining puppy talk was begging for a meal of their own.

Scrounging through Aspen's cupboard, he discovered a stash of canned milk and breathed a sigh of relief. "Good thing I found this milk," he said, and filled two bowels full of the life sustaining fluid. Then, lifting them out of their warm bed, he watched with interest as the two bowels of milk were lapped up with great haste

Two tiny tails were wagging in unison as the pups began snooping around hunting for another helping, their tiny stomachs already bulging from the first one. He then returned them to the hardtack tin, an improvised puppy bed using one of his old shirts as a mattress. Watching closely as they snuggled together, drifting into a sound sleep.

"I reckon the two little pot-lickers will be fine now," he said, and returned to his rocker, a cup of chicory-flavored coffee in one hand, his pipe in the other. A quiet time for his mind to settle down and sort out yet another adventure in his life, involving a wild blizzard, two grand daughters and a pair of weanling pups; he too then drifted into a sound sleep.

The blizzard was now on the move, leaving Lobo Canyon behind and heading south into Blackfoot country. The storm rolled across the scattered camps with a vengeance, ripping and tearing at the buffalo-skin tepees of the native people, who knew the reservation as their home.

With no let up to one of Nature's howling protégés, the People cowered in terror at the fierceness of an insane, devil wind. Several of the old ones left their tepees, and facing into the howling north blizzard, raised their arms high, praying to the Great Spirit to protect their women and children from this fearsome devil.

Except for the snores of Grandpa Harrison, it was now quiet in the trapper cabin. As a rule he was a light sleeper, awake at the snap of a twig, but this night utter exhaustion had taken over. The long trek down the Lobo trail battling the blizzard, and the excitement of his grand daughters and the pups showing up, had worn him plumb out.

Much later he was awakened by he knew not what, and after fumbling around for a match, he lit his lantern so he could see. "Is that you Aspen?" he inquired, his mind struggling to make sense.

"No Grandpa it is me, Rachel." and she was silently weeping.

Smokey whose mind had finally returned to the present, answered his grand daughter, "What is wrong child, anything I can do to help you?"

"Yes Grandpa, I am scared!"

"Scared!" he answered her. "Why, whatever of? You must know I am here close by, and will protect you and Amy from any harm."

"But it is so quiet now—I have heard a strange noise off in the distance!" It was then Smokey realized the cabin-shaking wind had left the Lobo.

"What did this noise sound like?" he asked.

"Bells," she replied. "Jingle bells!

"I think Santa Clause is coming, and I am still awake. He will not stop here if he knows I am not asleep!"

It was then Smokey remembered that it was indeed Christmas Eve, a special time in the life of a child, and here he was alone with his two grand daughters—and no gifts!

"Best go back to sleep now Rachel, if Santa does stop by I will tell him that you have been a good girl, deserving of a fine gift. "All right," she replied.

"Don't you forget to tell him that I am asleep, you hear?"

"I love you Grandpa!"

Tears were streaming down his cheeks when he replied, "Grandpa loves you too Rachel."

After throwing more logs on the fire, he placed another robe over the sleeping girls. Though Rachel's eyes were closed, he knew she was still awake, and would remain so for the rest of the night.

It was then he realized how much he loved them, and how dog-gone proud he was of them too. How they must have suffered, struggling through a howling blizzard to bring their old grandpa a Christmas gift, was a miracle in itself. Remembering back to the time when he was just a child, attending Sunday School and hearing—'Christmas is a time of miracles'!

He was proud of Willow too, his oldest daughter who had lived with her grand parents much of the time after Sage's passing, and in due time had married a Mormon lad from the settlements along Lee's Creek.

Willow has been blessed with two fine daughters, his grand daughters who at this very minute were right here in his cabin. Fast asleep on a bearskin rug, or so their grandpa had reckoned.

Yawning some, he realized that he was still tired and could sure use another hour or two in his blankets—but that would never be! His Christmas present was now awake, making a fuss, appearing as if it was time for them to answer to Nature's call, a summons that neither man nor beast should ignore.

With the pups in his arms, he was nearing the door clad only in his long Johns, when he stopped and listened. He was positive that he had heard the sound of bells. Danged if it didn't sound like jingle bells, he reckoned, and it was becoming much closer.

Smokey hadn't been exposed to this sort of thing since way back when. A young boy at a Christmas pageant sponsored by the old country school that he attended. Watching in awe as Santa burst through an open door, with a bag stuffed full of goodies for all the children.

Prancing around the stage chanting a merry Ho' Ho' Ho', and the mysterious jingle of bells hanging from his red suit and long elfin cap; an awe-inspiring time that he could never forget.

With the door opened a crack, Smokey cautiously peeked through, the bell music ringing loud, moving into the clearing accompanied by the barking of excited dogs. By now Rachel and Amy were awake and standing beside him, listening with awe to the jingle bells.

"I know it is Santa!" Rachel shrieked.

"He has found us after all—I just knew he would come!"

"I don't believe there is a Santa Clause," Amy said to Rachel, a superior know-it all tone in her voice. "Our parents like to make us believe there is one, knowing darn well it is just a myth."

"Hush you two," Smokey cautioned them. "I'm not so certain myself," watching a dog sled enter the clearing with a red-suited handler standing on the back runners, cracking a whip, shouting Ho' Ho' Ho'.

It became a wild melee of sound and action when the sled pulled up to the cabin door. Nine dogs were barking their heads off, sleigh bells were jingling at a furious pace and above all else, the merry greeting of Ho' Ho' Ho' echoing through out the clearing.

Rachel just had to get in on the action, and some how slipped past her grandpa to join in with the rowdy chorus, voicing happy shouts of her own.

With the crack of a whip, a signal that stopped the dogs, Santa turned to the cabin, his white beard a bit lop-sided. After adjusting this important part of his make up, he walked towards the open door and a waiting Smokey and his two grand-daughters. Ho' Ho' Ho' once again echoed across the clearing, as Santa pulled two fancy wrapped gifts from his bag.

"See, Amy I told you so!" an excited Rachel shouted, and she was bouncing about in the two feet of fresh snow.

"...and he has even brought us gifts...!"

"Judas Priest, girls," Smokey said, speaking to Amy and Rachel, a tone of impatience sounding in his voice. "This is old Santa Claus in person.

"I don't want to hear you two arguing any longer about if he is real, or if he isn't."

Smokey Harrison was a believer until the last Ho' Ho' Ho' when Santa entered the cabin, and gave his old pard a wink and spoke in a quiet voice, "Sure hope the coffee pot is a perkin' Smokey, I'm sure a needin' a cup or two!

"I'm about plumb froze to death!"

And it was a cold morning, the temperature twenty below at least.

It was then Smokey knew for sure. He could never forget the familiar drawl of Kelly Tucker's voice, an old friend and neighbor from many long years in the past—a partner too.

Smokey's mind had been whisked back in time, to when he was just a lad attending a Christmas Eve pageant in an old country school.

Amy and Rachel were the reason this memory still lingered in his mind. Santa Clause had been there that night, bouncing on to a makeshift stage, his jolly HO' Ho' Ho' winning over the hearts of the children.

Smokey's mind was struggling, somewhat embarrassed, yet proud of the fact that an old cowboy still had the faith of a little child, knowing in his heart there is a Santa Claus; who was standing right here beside him.

Smokey was smiling as he whispered a reply, "Great job Kelly, you almost had me a believer."

Rachel and Amy stood apart from their Grandpa and a jolly Santa, in a state of shock to be in the presence of old St. Nick himself. Eyes wide as saucers, watching the old whiskered gent drink cup after cup of coffee, Grandpa was doing the same.

Then after a hearty breakfast, grandpa and the two girls were bundled into the sled.

It was then Santa, complete with a pipe clenched between his teeth, cracked a long black whip, and shouted, "Mush! Mush my little darlin's, we're no longer in the land where strange lights are dancing in the midnight sky!"

Each sharp crack of the long hand-braided whip was a cue to pick up the pace, there annual mission was not yet over. Reason enough for two sisters to cower in fear, watching with hypnotized eyes at Santa who was standing on the back runners of the sled.

"Keep up the pace my four-legged friends," Kelly Tucker shouted one more time, "...we're a headin' down Lobo Canyon to a Christmas feast, a houseful of friends and loved ones are there waiting for Santa to show up."

The two fur balls. Midge and Molly, each tucked into a pocket on Smokey's bear skin coat, were comfortable and warm. Two inquisitive noses were peeping out of their respective dens, both watching a red-clad Santa Clause, the commander-in chief on this Christmas night. Each crack of his whip caused them to disappear in terror.

Far, far in the distance, faint talk could be heard echoing in the forest. "We must be on time, old Santa has more presents to deliver before sun rise."

The bark of a six-gun sounded loud and clear, then another. Perhaps it was a gun shot, perhaps it was the crack of Santa Claus's hand-braided persuader? Which ever it was, the heart-warming sound of jingle bells continued to ring a pleasant serenade to the birth of the Holy one.

An eerie silence returned to the clearing in the pines, no longer did a spiral of smoke drift skyward from the cabin chimney. The barking of dogs and Ho' Ho' Ho' of Santa Claus were no longer there, only a wilderness silence.

A silence that was broken by the sigh of the mountain breezes, and the croak of a frustrated raven, that could still hear the faintest of sound far down the Lobo Creek trail.

Jingle bells ringing Angel music in Lobo Canyon.

LaVergne, TN USA
11 February 2011
216088LV00001B/3/P